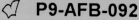

HOMETOWN HEARTS

SHIPMENT 1

Stranger in Town by Brenda Novak
Baby's First Homecoming by Cathy McDavid
Her Surprise Hero by Abby Gaines
A Mother's Homecoming by Tanya Michaels
A Firefighter in the Family by Trish Milburn
Tempted by a Texan by Mindy Neff

SHIPMENT 2

It Takes a Family by Victoria Pade
The Sheriff of Heartbreak County by Kathleen Creighton
A Hometown Boy by Janice Kay Johnson
The Renegade Cowboy Returns by Tina Leonard
Unexpected Bride by Lisa Childs
Accidental Hero by Loralee Lillibridge

SHIPMENT 3

An Unlikely Mommy by Tanya Michaels
Single Dad Sheriff by Lisa Childs
In Protective Custody by Beth Cornelison
Cowboy to the Rescue by Trish Milburn
The Ranch She Left Behind by Kathleen O'Brien
Most Wanted Woman by Maggie Price
A Weaver Wedding by Allison Leigh

SHIPMENT 4

A Better Man by Emilie Rose
Daddy Protector by Jacqueline Diamond
The Road to Bayou Bridge by Liz Talley
Fully Engaged by Catherine Mann
The Cowboy's Secret Son by Trish Milburn
A Husband's Watch by Karen Templeton

SHIPMENT 5

His Best Friend's Baby by Molly O'Keefe
Caleb's Bride by Wendy Warren
Her Sister's Secret Life by Pamela Toth
Lori's Little Secret by Christine Rimmer
High-Stakes Bride by Fiona Brand
Hometown Honey by Kara Lennox

SHIPMENT 6

Reining in the Rancher by Karen Templeton
A Man to Rely On by Cindi Myers
Your Ranch or Mine? by Cindy Kirk
Mother in Training by Marie Ferrarella
A Baby for the Bachelor by Victoria Pade
The One She Left Behind by Kristi Gold
Her Son's Hero by Vicki Essex

SHIPMENT 7

Once and Again by Brenda Harlen
Her Sister's Fiancé by Teresa Hill
Family at Stake by Molly O'Keefe
Adding Up to Marriage by Karen Templeton
Bachelor Dad by Roxann Delaney
It's That Time of Year by Christine Wenger

SHIPMENT 8

The Rancher's Christmas Princess by Christine Rimmer
Their Baby Miracle by Lillian Darcy
Mad About Max by Penny McCusker
No Ordinary Joe by Michelle Celmer
The Soldier's Baby Bargain by Beth Kery
The Maverick's Christmas Baby by Victoria Pade

HOMETOWN HEARTS

A Husband's Watch

KAREN TEMPLETON

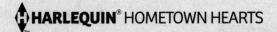

HARLEQUIN® HOMETOWN HEARTS

Recycling programs
for this product may
not exist in your area.

ISBN-13: 978-0-373-21475-4

A Husband's Watch

Printed in U.S.A.

www.Harlequin.com

Karen Templeton is an inductee into the Romance Writers of America Hall of Fame. A three-time RITA® Award–winning author, she has written more than thirty novels for Harlequin. She lives in New Mexico with two hideously spoiled cats. She has raised five sons and lived to tell the tale, and she could not live without dark chocolate, mascara and Netflix.

To Pat McLinn, who talked me down from the ledge
when jumping sounded much more pleasant than trying
to finish this book!

Acknowledgments

With many more thanks to Kasey Michaels for her input
on my hero's injuries; and to Loren Berger, who by three
already knew more about cars than his mother ever will.

Chapter One

At the moment, the only thing keeping Darryl Andrews from kicking the crap out of something was the fact that his foot was just about the only part of his body that didn't already hurt.

So instead he hung back close to the road, where there was nothing to kick except a few dried-up weeds, or a stray soda can, hoping maybe a little distance would make the scene easier to absorb. To accept. Slung low in a sky his oldest girl, Heather, called "forever" blue, the morning sun barely warmed his right temple through the thick wad of gauze, although the badass November wind drilled right on inside the old baseball jacket Faith'd dug out of the church's thrift shop donation box. So he wouldn't have to cut up the sleeve on one of his own coats, she'd said in that matter-of-fact way of hers, as if attending to that one little detail was the key to solving all the rest of it.

He kicked at one of the soda cans anyway, hurling it out onto the paved road to clatter mournfully for several feet before getting hooked up again in a small pile of trash across the way.

Darryl would've sucked in a breath, but his bruised ribs had other ideas. With his good hand, he scrubbed his eyes, only half kidding himself they were stinging because of all the wood smoke in the air. Oh, sure, he'd gotten choked up at his kids' births. And there'd been Griff Malone's ten-seconds-left-on-the-clock, state-title clinching touchdown his senior year, but, hell, everybody'd been blubbering at that one. Nothing wrong with a little display of emotion now and again, long as it was the right emotion, let loose at the appropriate time.

This wasn't it.

He swallowed, blinking until he could clearly see his father and the claims agent pick through the tangle of shingles, twisted metal siding and two-by-fours where not twenty-four hours before his auto shop and filling station had stood. Where he had as well, come to think of it.

Yep. The general consensus was that he was damn lucky to be alive.

He'd never even heard the tornado siren go off, not between his radio blaring and the earplugs he wore to muffle the sound of the air compressor. But then, who the hell expected a twister the day before Thanksgiving? Let alone *five*, if you counted the two that touched down between here and Claremore. Most of 'em had been puny little things, but even a puny tornado had few qualms about chewing up whatever got in its way. At least the one that'd visited this part of Haven had seen fit to bypass the gas tanks. If those lines had ruptured, especially so close to the downed power lines…

No doubt about it, coming that close to biting the big one definitely makes a man reassess his priorities. Still and all, Darryl's means of supporting his wife and five kids had been reduced to a pile of toothpicks. Maybe that business hadn't made him, or his daddy before him, rich, but Darryl'd been doing okay. Sure, they could have used a bigger house, even if Faith did insist there was a certain comfort in knowing she could go to the bathroom and still hear what every single kid was doing. But then, it wasn't in Faith's nature to complain, not about the house, or the ten-year-old Suburban Darryl kept jump-starting back to life, or even that she was still wearing the same dresses to church she had when they first got married. Those she could still get into, at any rate.

He looked over at her now, standing where the second bay used to be, eleven-month-old Nicky balanced on her round hip. Faith's blond curls, longer than they'd been in a while, danced around her face in the breeze; she was already dressed to go to her parents for Thanksgiving dinner later—no sense upsetting the kids any more than necessary, they'd both agreed—in her "good" jeans and a soft-looking sweater. And that puffy orange jacket she'd bought the first winter after they were married, the one that made her look like a pumpkin, although Darryl had the good sense to keep that particular opinion to himself.

It wasn't always easy to figure out what was going on inside Faith's head—although most every male he knew swore it was better that way—but the creases between her sandy brows, the flat set to her mouth, didn't leave much room for interpretation. Yeah, the insurance would cover rebuilding, but that would take months. Months in which he wouldn't be able to work, or even help with the reconstruction, not with an arm broken in three places.

As if she could hear his thoughts, Faith glanced over. It'd been real late by the time they got back from the hospital last night; she'd slept on the pullout couch in the living room, insisting he'd be more comfortable in their double bed without her crowding him, especially since he had to keep his cast elevated on pillows. Only, except for the times Faith had been in the hospital after the first three were born, they'd never spent a night apart. *More* comfortable? Hell, he might as well have been sleeping on a bed of nails for all the rest he got.

He started when his father's hand landed on his shoulder. "How're you feelin'?" the older man said, in a voice not unlike an idling lawnmower.

"You really want the truth?"

"Think of the alternative."

"Trust me, I have been."

L.B.—short for "Little" Bud, Darryl's granddaddy having been "Big" Bud—gently squeezed his shoulder, then folded his arms across a barrel chest. At six foot two, there hadn't been anything "little" about L.B. for years, although none of his three sons had inherited whatever genes had determined their father's height, Darryl being the tallest of the three at five foot ten.

"It's mostly structural damage," L.B. said. "Looks like a lot of the major equipment came through okay, the office just needs a new roof. And it's all covered. That was a stroke of genius, takin' pictures of everything, keepin' 'em in a binder with all the invoices."

Darryl managed a small smile. "I've got Faith to thank for that." As well as her insisting that the policy covered replacement value, not purchase price.

"Yeah, she's a smart gal, all right." L.B.'s gaze followed Darryl's, watching Faith talking to the adjuster. She hiked Nicky higher up on her hip, like he was getting heavy for her. Darryl sensed more than saw his father purse his lips, and he braced himself. Sure enough, L.B. said, "You thought about what you're gonna say if her folks offer to help? Financially, I mean?"

"I doubt they've got any more than we do, L.B.—"

"But if they do. You know how I've always felt about goin' outside the family. You need help, you come to us, you hear me?"

Never mind that Darryl had been part of Faith's family for more than twelve years now. But then, Darryl understood this wasn't about money near as much as it was about pride—the pride of a man who'd determined early on that nobody would ever call *his* sons trailer trash. A man who'd gone white as a ghost when Darryl'd told him he'd gotten the preacher's daughter pregnant. Hell, if Darryl hadn't stepped up to the plate to marry Faith on his own, it would have more likely been his father, not Faith's, standing at the altar with a shotgun in tow.

Darryl met his father's coffee-brown gaze, as penetrating as ever underneath heavy, dark brows, even if these days the occasional white hair jutted out like a stray broom bristle. "You know I've never taken a dime from Faith's parents, and I have no intention of starting now," he said, and some of the muscles in his father's face loosened a bit. But assuaging his father wasn't going to solve the problem, was it? God knew, Darryl wasn't any more keen than his father on accepting help from the Meyerhausers. But it hadn't only been Faith's absence from their bed, or even his injuries, that had kept him awake most of the night, but rather the incessant, nauseating tattoo of *Whatnowwhatnowwhat*now...?

Faith was really struggling with the baby by now—why she'd brought him when she'd left the other four with her folks, Darryl had no idea—so he excused himself and slowly headed in her direction. Every muscle screamed in protest; whatever hadn't been gouged or broken had been banged up pretty good. Par for the course, he supposed, when an entire roof falls in on top of you.

Nicky saw him and broke into a big dimpled grin, clapping his chubby hands. White-blond curls poked out from the edge of his red sweatshirt hood, his eyes a deeper brown, even, than Darryl's. "*Da!*" he squealed, his breath fogging around his reddened cheeks as he lunged forward, arms spread.

"No, no, Butterball," Faith said, straining to keep the kid from falling on his noggin. "Daddy can't hold you right now—"

"Sure I can." Darryl stretched out his good arm, even though his ribs clearly wondered what the hell he was doing. "Come here, Mr. Chunks."

But Faith pivoted, settling the baby more

securely up on her hip. "Darryl, for heaven's sake…you can't possibly hang on to a wiggly baby right now!"

"I'm perfectly capable of holding my own kid, Faith. Like everybody keeps reminding me, I'm not dead yet!"

Nicky's face crumpled up, his lower lip quivering. Wordlessly, Faith shoved the baby into Darryl's outstretched arm, then walked back to the Suburban and grabbed hold of the door handle, her head bent as if she was trying to pull herself together. Or maybe she was praying. Not all preachers' kids ended up being particularly religious, he knew that, but this was one case where the apple had definitely not fallen far from the tree. More often than not, Darryl found that comforting. Other times he found it a big pain in the butt. Especially when he got the definite feeling he was the one being prayed over.

At his elbow, the claims adjuster cleared his throat. His son clutched to his side, Darryl turned to the bland-faced little man, meeting a watery blue gaze behind slightly crooked rectangular glasses.

"Looks like I've got everything I need for now, so I'll just be on my way. The wife'll have five fits if I don't get home soon."

"Oh. Yeah, sure," Darryl said, trying not to flinch every time Nicky grabbed for the bandage covering the ten stitches marching over his temple. His broken arm throbbed—he needed to get it elevated, put ice on it like they'd told him to do. "We really appreciate you coming out on a holiday like this."

"No problem, I was in the area, anyway. Figured I may as well get a jump start on things. 'Specially as here and Ivy Gardner's were the only two places to sustain any significant damage. Can't say the same for Claremore, unfortunately—the outskirts got hit pretty bad. No loss of life, though, praise the Lord. Craziest darn thing, tornadoes this time of year—"

"I don't mean to pressure you, but any idea how long payout might take? I'm pretty anxious to get things set to rights again."

Behind the man's glasses, apology flashed. "Yes, yes, I'm sure you are, I'm sure you are. Might take a touch longer than usual, with the holidays and all, and they'll probably want to send somebody else out for a second look-see...." The man turned to set his briefcase on the hood of his runty little sedan, dropping his clipboard inside. "I'll be in touch shortly, but if you have any questions, don't hesitate to give me a call. Our aim is to make the process as painless as possible."

It did not escape Darryl's attention that the man never directly answered his question, but he probably had no idea when they'd fork over the money. So Darryl thanked him for his help, then watched him drive off to have his Thanksgiving dinner, during which Darryl doubted whether he, or his annihilated livelihood, would be given a second thought.

"I best be gettin' on, too," L.B. said behind him. "Unless you still need me to stick around...?"

Darryl shifted to face his father, who tickled Nicky's tummy. The baby gave one of his gurgly laughs, while Darryl thought his arm was about to fall off. Damn, this was one heavy little dude. How five-foot-three Faith lugged him around every day was beyond him. "No, you go ahead. I'm sure Mama's an inch away from crazy with SueEllen's folks joining you this year."

"You don't know the half of it," L.B. said, referring to Darryl's youngest brother's in-laws, who hadn't accepted *their* daughter's pregnancy at eighteen with nearly as much grace as Faith's had. Darryl glanced over at his own wife, who seemed to have given up praying for silently fuming. "Every year," L.B. added, "Renee threatens to skip Thanksgiving, but you and I both know she'd go nuts if she didn't have something to fret over…"

L.B.'s eyes followed Darryl's. "Go on, son," he said quietly. "I imagine she needs some re-assurin' right about now." He patted Darryl's back, then set off toward his truck, parked a few feet away. "And give your mother a call later," he called out as he climbed into the driver's seat, "let her know you're okay. You know how she worries."

"You know something, Mr. Chunks?" Darryl said to the baby as he made his way back to the car. "Being indispensable isn't all it's cracked up to be."

Faith reached for Nicky, who happily lunged back into his mama's arms. "You might be able to haul him around for a few minutes," she said with a grunt, "but you sure as heck aren't going to be able to get him in the car seat."

"Hell, I can barely manage it when I've got *both* arms in working order," Darryl said, surreptitiously working the kinks out of his shoulder while nostalgically gazing at his wife's bottom as she strapped the kid in. He was crazy about his kids, but their presence definitely wreaked havoc on the concept of spur of the moment.

Faith backed out of the car, her curls all messed up; ribs or no ribs, Darryl automatically lifted a hand to smooth her hair away from her face. But he knew damn well there was nothing he could do, not really, to ease the worry from those wide, blue eyes, the same "forever" blue as the sky. Still, habit prompted, "It's gonna be okay, baby. You know I'd never let you or the kids down."

The corners of her mouth curved up, sort of, before she nodded. Then she took the car keys out of his hand. "I'm drivin'."

"I got us over here—"

"Against my better judgment. Last thing I need is for you to pass out while you're behind the wheel, get us all killed…" Her mouth clamped shut. "Get in," she said, yanking open her door. "The kids'll be wonderin' what happened to us. And Mama is probably waiting on me to mash the potatoes."

He grabbed her hand. "Honey, I know things have been tense lately—"

Her eyes shot to his, shiny with unshed tears. "Not today, Darryl. Tomorrow, we can start figurin' out how to put the pieces back together. But today all I want is to go to my parents' house and eat turkey and pumpkin pie and act like everything's normal. Today I'm just gonna be grateful my babies aren't fatherless. Okay? Can you give me my one day?"

You know, it was kinda hard reassuring a woman who clearly didn't want to be reassured. Even harder when he had no idea what she *did* want.

And he never really had, not once in twelve years of marriage.

"Yeah, I can do that," he said, then tramped around the car to get in the passenger side, every step making his head feel like it was about to explode.

"I don't suppose there's much point in asking if you're comfortable?"

A towel-wrapped ice pack perched on the elevated cast, Darryl grimaced at his father-in-law from the plaid sofa in Faith's parents' den. Over in his playpen, a bouncing Nicky gnawed on the thickly padded edge, occasionally squealing at the overfed, overfurred cat cautiously regarding the far too noisy, temporarily caged human from where she lay sprawled across most of the coffee table.

"Actually, between the turkey and these

pills I'm taking, I'm not feeling much of anything at the moment."

With a soft laugh, Chuck Meyerhauser lowered himself into his navy-blue La-Z-Boy, the football game on TV flickering in his glasses. He must've gone outside for a minute—a leaf or two clung to his striped sweater, while several strands of graying red hair floated over his freckled, balding head as if they couldn't decide where to light. "Way my joints've been acting up lately, I wouldn't mind some of those pills myself."

"Oh, yeah, this is good stuff."

Chuck smiled, then focused on the game, as usual leaving a whole mess of unspoken thoughts shimmering between them. Faith's daddy was one of those rare preachers who spent more time living what he believed than yakking a person's ear off about it. Not once had either he or Didi made an issue of Darryl's getting their only daughter—their only child, for that matter—pregnant right out of high school. That didn't mean, however, that the situation hadn't thrown them for a loop. Probably more, in some ways, than it had Darryl, even though marriage and fatherhood at eighteen hadn't exactly been something he'd figured on. In any case, he'd been well aware of Faith's folks' concern about what might happen down the road, that the marriage might not make it.

A concern that still lingered like an odor you couldn't completely get rid of, no matter how hard you tried. Which was why, from the moment Faith eagerly accepted Darryl's weak-kneed proposal, he'd made a silent vow—to himself, to her, to her parents—that he'd never give them the slightest reason to think their daughter had married a loser.

A commercial came on; Chuck punched the mute button. "I suppose the town got off easy, considering," he said. "Not that that's any consolation to you, I don't suppose."

"Oh, believe me, I'm grateful nobody else got hurt." Darryl took a swig from his plastic glass of sparkling cider. He hated the stuff, frankly, but mixing beer with painkillers probably wasn't a real smart idea. "Never did buy into the whole misery-loves-company thing."

Nicky shrieked at the cat, who took that as her cue to get the hell out of Dodge. Chuck fondly regarded his youngest grandson for a moment, then said, "Faith says the insurance will probably cover most of the rebuilding, but I was wondering…you guys have supplemental insurance? To cover your loss of income while you're out of commission?"

Darryl nearly laughed out loud. They'd been doing well to make the insurance payments on the property as it was—Oklahoma had one of the highest rates in the nation. Not to mention health insurance premiums, which they could only afford with a huge co-pay. Still, having to say no hurt like all get-out.

"Listen," Chuck said, the sympathy in his voice nearly making Darryl cringe, "we've got a little put by, if you guys need any help...."

"No, we'll be okay," Darryl said automatically. "Need to have the pumps inspected, but it doesn't appear they were damaged, so I'll still have income from gas sales. And once the cast is off, I'll be back at work in no time. The wrecker wasn't touched, did Faith tell you?"

"Yes, she did. But three or four months can seem like forever when there's not enough money coming in. Believe me, I know. Let us help, son—"

"I'll admit, this is a setback I hadn't counted on," Darryl said through the painkiller fog, "but it won't keep me down for long. You'll see."

The pastor's gray eyes all but looked straight through him. "There's not a soul alive who'd think ill of you for accepting a little help to get you through this. And if you really have Faith's best interests at heart," he said over Darryl's next objection, "you won't let that pride of yours cloud your reason. Do I make myself clear?"

Heat crawling up his neck, Darryl focused on Nicky, who held out his arms, squealed, then promptly toppled onto his diapered butt in the playpen. "If we do have to borrow from you," he said at last, "I'll pay you back every penny, I swear."

"I know you will. But there's no hurry. Oh, for crying out loud, wipe that look off your face—sticking together is what families do." Chuck grabbed a tissue out of a nearby box and leaned forward to wipe drool off Nicky's chin, the recliner squawking when he settled back into it. "You know, it's easy to see where you get your dedication to your family. Your daddy was always talkin' up you boys, when you were little—'Guess what that Danny did today?' he'd say, or 'Hope you don't mind me braggin' on my oldest.' And the way L.B. dotes on your mother... I think he'd move heaven and earth for her, if she asked him to."

"Yeah, that's L.B." Darryl shifted, trying to get comfortable. No such luck. "From the time I was little, I remember him saying a man's most important duty is to make sure he never gives his wife a reason to regret marrying him."

"A code more men would do well to live by, I'm sure."

"Yes, sir."

Except, over the past dozen years, Darryl had come to realize good intentions weren't always enough to put theory into practice. Because way too often these days he'd catch this look in Faith's eyes as if she couldn't quite figure out how she'd gotten there. She never nagged, never complained, but still, it was enough to make a man wonder if his best was even remotely good enough.

Faith came into the den just then to announce that dessert was ready and did Darryl want her to bring his to him so he didn't have to get up? Before he could answer, though, their eldest son pushed around his mother and streaked across the room, fully intent on launching his solid six-year-old self right at Darryl's chest.

"Jake, no!" she yelled, as her father grabbed

the kid around the waist before he made contact.

"I just wanted to hug Daddy!"

"I know, sugar. But Daddy's kinda banged up right now. The last thing he needs is you using him for a trampoline...."

"Come here, Jakester," Darryl said, carefully lifting his arm. "I need a hug, too." He lowered his head as best he could to peer up underneath the boy's shaggy bangs. "Only, you need to be real gentle. I'm basically one big bruise."

Somber-faced, the boy walked into Darryl's one-armed embrace, gingerly wrapping his arms around his neck. Even so, it still hurt, a little. Okay, it hurt a lot—Darryl ached in places he never knew he had.

But what really hurt was the odd, unreadable look on Faith's face.

Faith slapped Cool Whip on top of the piece of Mrs. Smith's pumpkin pie so hard it splattered clear across her mother's countertop. Thank goodness whichever kids weren't in the den with Darryl and her father were outside playing tag. Yeah, she'd wanted her day, and she'd gotten it, but now that it was mostly over she was plumb worn out from leaning against the door to her thoughts in a lame attempt to keep the big, bad truth from shoving its way inside.

Her mother glanced over from where she was trying to lift a piece of apple pie out of the plate without leaving half its insides behind. "Well, well…look who just got back from the Land of Hunky-dory," Didi Meyerhauser said mildly, ripping a paper towel off the rack and handing it to Faith. "I wondered how long it was gonna take for this all to hit."

Faith snorted, wiping up her mess with more energy than was required. A frisky Dolly Parton oldie came on the radio, one Faith herself used to sing, once upon a time; she turned up the volume, thinking maybe the lively tune would bolster her sagging spirits. The silverware drawer jangled when she yanked it open to grab a handful of dessert forks, letting them clatter onto the counter. She grabbed one and attacked the piece of pie she'd just cut.

"Oh, believe me," she said, guillotining the bottom third of the pie and shoving it into her mouth, "it *hit* the second I got the call from Pete tellin' me the paramedics had just pulled Darryl out from what was left of the garage."

Just the memory of hearing the sheriff's, "Faith, honey, there's been an accident…."

was enough to send her heart right back up into her throat. Chewing, she finished wiping up her mess, then wadded up the dirty towel and tossed it into the garbage can under the sink, banging shut the cabinet door. It was definitely a day for taking out one's frustrations on inanimate objects. "I don't think I breathed normally until after we got back from the hospital."

Her mother tilted her head to regard her through the top part of her glasses. "So is this called you bein' in denial?"

"No, it's called me trying to keep it together for the kids' sake."

"Like I said."

Faith shoveled in another forkful of pie, wishing she could soak up at least some of the patience in those soft blue eyes, that she could lose herself in them the way she used to. "If anybody's having a dicey relationship with reality right now, it's that man I married. I swear, if he says 'everything's gonna be okay' one more time, I'm gonna lose it for sure."

Returning her focus to the apple pie, her mother chuckled, her silver-blond waves barely moving when she shook her head. "That's just who Darryl is, honey. Has been for as long as I can remember. And once those painkillers wear off, I imagine he's going to feel like a bug on its back. Which means he's gonna do a lot of kicking until he figures out how to right himself again." She opened the freezer door to get the vanilla ice cream. "Count your blessings, honey. He could've…"

"Died," Faith finished softly, pinging her fork on her plate. "Believe me, I've hardly thought of anything else for the past twenty-four hours."

The ice cream abandoned, her mother wrapped one arm around Faith's shoulders, enveloping her in a Windsong scent. "I'm not scolding you, baby. But it's real easy sometimes to let the bad stuff blind us to the good, you know? Now what do you suppose happened to all those napkins I put out this morning?"

Her mother hustled off to the pantry, leaving Faith to continue stuffing her face as she glared out the window, thinking about those words she'd happily lived by her entire life. Except more and more she found herself wondering if that seeing-the-good-in-everything business wasn't sometimes just an excuse to avoid facing the parts that weren't so good.

Like somehow, if you ignored them, they'd either fix themselves or self-destruct.

On the surface, she and Darryl had beaten the odds. They were still together after twelve years; he was devoted to the kids and the marriage; nobody was a harder worker than he was. But...

But.

There it was, that stinking three-letter word that had taken to making her feel lately like her skin was too tight. Then again, her skin feeling too tight might have something to do with the fact that for the past twenty-four hours she'd been eating everything that wasn't nailed down.

She ditched the fork: much more efficient to eat right out of her hand.

Granted, maybe her motives for wanting to marry Darryl weren't as solid as they should have been. She'd been barely out of high school, for pity's sake. But blind trust in her own determination to make things work had fueled her initial enthusiasm, kept things chugging along nicely for at least the first few years. Now, though, it was getting harder and harder to deny they'd been drifting apart almost from the beginning, slowly but inexorably, like the plates in the earth. Not so's anyone could tell, she didn't imagine—they rarely argued, they still had sex probably about as regularly as any couple with five young children, they treated each other with as much consideration as they always had. Yet, she wondered… If she hadn't've gotten pregnant, would they even still be together?

Her father stuck his head in the doorway the same moment her mother returned from the pantry with a bag of paper napkins. "Just wondering what the dessert holdup is," he said pleasantly.

"Wouldn't think you'd have room for pie," Didi said, "what with all that turkey and mashed potatoes you put away."

Grinning, her father sidled up to Didi and slipped his arms around her waist, making her giggle like a girl. "But there's always room for apple pie…"

Faith turned away, nearly overcome with annoyance that her life had turned into some sad-sack country song. She fixed Darryl a plate of pie—a slice each of apple and pumpkin, like always; the man was as predictable as the moon—then cut herself another piece of pumpkin, just to be sociable. But when she started out of the kitchen, she saw he'd hobbled back to the dining table instead of stay-

ing in the den. He glanced up at her, his smile
stopping short of those melted-chocolate eyes
that could still rattle her to her toes, nodding
and saying "Thank you" when she set his
plate in front of him. She grabbed Sierra as
the boisterous three-year-old flew past, plopping her back into her booster seat at right
angles to her daddy; Faith's heart ached at
Darryl's barely suppressed wince when the
child let out a shriek of protest.

"Sierra, no," she said firmly, which was
met with a tiny glower. Then, to Darryl: "If
you want, I can give the squirts their pie in
the kitchen—"

"I'm hardly so bad off I need to be quar-
antined from my own kids."

"That's not what I meant and you know
it," she said in a level voice, strapping Sierra
in. Not that it would do much good, since
her youngest daughter had figured out how
to spring herself a year ago. "I was only trying to make things easier for you, that's all."

He stiffened, not looking at her. "You know
I hate being coddled," he said, his voice even
deeper than usual.

Faith shoved her hair out of her eyes with
the back of her wrist, thinking it was a good
thing she had a hair appointment coming

up, only to remember she probably shouldn't spend the money on a haircut, considering. "Yes, I do. But you've been working your butt off since the day we got married, with nothin' even remotely resembling a real break in twelve years. So, since nothing *I* say seems to get through, maybe that tornado was God's way of tellin' you to ease up for a minute."

A bite of apple pie halfway to his mouth, Darryl gaped at her from underneath his long, dark lashes. "My business is a pile of rubble— a business that supports you and the kids, in case you've forgotten—and I can't even pick up any freelance work long as I've got this dumb cast on my arm, and you're tellin' me you think that's *God's* work?"

They'd never exactly seen eye to eye on spiritual matters, and her bringing up the subject now probably hadn't been the smartest move she could have made. However, his reaction jolted something inside her brain.

Duty. The word stuck to the roof of her mouth like stale peanut butter. A word that more than defined the man sitting in front of her. Not for a second had Darryl hesitated asking her to marry him when she'd told him she was pregnant, or even considered shirking the first of what would become a hundred obligations. Now he struggled under their accumulated weight like that Greek dude with the world on his shoulders.

She crossed her arms. "You telling me everything *isn't* going to be okay?"

Everything in his posture told her she'd just stepped over a line she hadn't fully realized was there until this moment.

"Of course not," he said, his voice controlled, even as the veins stood out on the back of the hand clutching his fork. "I'll get us out of this, somehow…."

He started when she leaned over and laid a hand on his arm; when he looked up at her his eyes were loaded with suspicion. "We're in this together, Darryl. We'll work it out together."

After a glance at Sierra, happily smushing her pumpkin pie with her baby fork, he looked back at Faith, every muscle in his face sharper, harder. "And I don't want you worrying about this, you hear?"

Lord help her, for a long time she'd found his macho protectiveness endearing. Comforting. And heaven knows, a major turn-on. That quality, perhaps more than any other, was why she was here. But a dozen years, five kids and a close, personal relationship with reality had a way of changing a person's perspective. Especially when that person's husband had a head harder than granite.

Still, she snorted a laugh. "Short of giving me a lobotomy, ain't gonna happen. So deal with it."

They stared each other down for several seconds, then she turned to call the rest of the children to the table, running smack into her father's questioning gaze.

"Faith? Everything okay?"

As she'd done for the past twelve years, she tacked on a bright smile and said, "Nothing I can't handle," because she'd put out her right eye before admitting a few ancient concerns had come back to take a big old chunk out of her rapidly expanding butt.

Chapter Two

In his pajama bottoms, Darryl stood in his and Faith's tiny master bathroom, glowering at his banged-up reflection in the medicine chest mirror. At his side, Dot, a young brindle boxer some fool had abandoned at the station a year or so ago, stood with her front paws on the sink, regarding him with bug-eyed apology—her standard expression—as if his injuries were somehow her fault. Faith was of the opinion that the dog suffered from low self-esteem, although whether brought on or exacerbated by her abandonment, she couldn't say.

He glowered some more—how the hell was

he supposed to change this bandage? Discovery Number Twenty-Two about having one hand out of commission: he could get the old bandage off, but no way could he get the clean one *on.* While he was contemplating this new aggravation, Jake shoved his way into the little room—already crowded with Darryl and the dog—and banged up the toilet seat to pee like he'd been at a keg party.

"Heather's in the other bathroom," the gap-toothed boy said by way of explanation, knocking the seat back down and flushing, but only after Darryl glared at him. "A body could 'splode waitin' on her to get out."

"Yeah, I know how that goes. Put the lid down, too, buddy."

That earned Darryl a pained look. "What for? Whoever uses it next only has to lift it again."

"I know, but your mother has a hissy whenever she finds the seat up. You really want to deal with that?"

Jake slammed down the lid, the effect muffled by the fluffy, dark-green toilet seat cover. One thing about Faith—she'd always kept the house looking nice without resorting to lots of flowers and ruffles and crap like a lot of other women. The kid plopped his skinny behind on the seat and leaned his elbows on the edge of the sink, frowning up at Darryl's stitches. Dot got down, wriggling her head onto the boy's lap to get her floppy ears scratched, groaning in what Darryl assumed was ecstasy. "You look like Frankenstein or somethin'. Does it hurt?"

Only when he moved. Or breathed.

"Let's just say—" Darryl raised the one arm that was working and gingerly lifted his hair away from the wound "—it's an experience I'd've been more than happy to have lived without."

The boy seemed to think on this for a second, then said, "You know what would be really cool? If you could come to school for show-and-tell—"

"Jake Michael Andrews!" Faith said from the bathroom doorway. "Didn't I put you to bed ten minutes ago?"

"I had to pee an' Heather was in the other bathroom. 'Sides, it's only ten o'clock."

"Which is *only* an hour past your bedtime. And yes, I know you're on vacation, but I'm not. So you need to get back in bed. Go on, scoot. And take the dog with you." She swatted the boy lightly on the backside as he zipped past.

"Night!" he hollered, thumping from one side of the narrow hallway to the other on the way back to his room, prompting Faith to say with a sigh, "Well, the others *were* asleep."

"You know," Darryl said, "one of these days we seriously need to think about letting the dog sleep outside."

His wife gave him one of her don't-talk-crazy looks, then crossed her arms over her wrinkled satin pajamas and open fuzzy robe, both in some light color that might have been either blue or green, at one time. She frowned at him in the mirror. "You plannin' on standing there all night staring at your boo-boo, or do you need help?"

"I can't use my other arm to change the dressing."

"I can see that. Sit down."

"It's pretty gross."

"I can see that, too. *Sit*. And get that cast elevated."

Darryl lowered himself onto the toilet seat, his arm on the sink, which put him eye level with his wife's breasts. Something resembling interest stirred. At least in his head. Other places seemed to be having a little trouble getting with the program, probably on account of these damn pills. Although there was something to be said for the who-gives-a-rat's-behind? buzz they produced.

Faith ripped open a clean gauze pad and soaked it in hydrogen peroxide. Darryl carefully shook his head. "Already did that."

"Could've fooled me. Quit squirming," she said when he flinched before she even made contact. "Honestly," she said, grabbing his chin, her breath wicking away the dampness on his forehead as she gently dabbed at the stitches. "You're worse than the kids." She'd already put on the lotion she wore to bed every night; she smelled so good his mouth watered. Hers pulled tight as she wet the other end of the gauze. "That E.R. doc did a good job. Looks to me like you might not even have a scar."

"Too bad. A scar might add a certain bubba appeal, don'tcha think?"

She almost smiled.

He lowered his eyes and watched her nipples shifting restlessly against the satin, like kittens playing underneath a sheet. "Sorry about earlier. At your folks, I mean."

She glanced down at him for a second, then went back to her dabbing. "'Sokay. We're both pretty stressed out, I guess. You take your pain pills?"

So much for talking things over. Not that Darryl really wanted to talk, especially not tonight. Half the time, talking only made him confused. Or mad. If not both. But he wasn't so clueless as to not know that Faith's not wanting to talk was a bad sign. "Just one, a couple minutes ago. Gonna try to go without tomorrow, though. Last thing I need is to get addicted to the things."

"Yeah, like that's gonna happen. What are you staring at so hard?"

"Give you one guess."

She shook her head; Darryl went back to staring. "Heard your father say Olive Pritchard's askin' after you again, wondering when you're coming back."

"And if I told her once, I told her a million times... Sorry," she said softly when the wince popped out. "Long as the kids are still little, there's no sense me bein' in the choir. Shoot, I'm doing well to get us to church on time as it is, let alone early for practice... Darryl, for heaven's sake!" she yelped when he reached underneath her pajama top to cup one breast. "What on earth do you think you're doing?" she said in a frenzied whisper.

"I think it's called living in the moment." An odd sense of well-being came over him, as all his troubles seemed to fade...away... He rubbed her nipple with his thumb, grinning when it snapped to attention. Grinning even harder when other things did. "When was the last time we lived in the moment, Faithie?"

"At least four kids ago," she said with kind of a sad look on her face. "But this is not the night to rekindle those memories."

"Why not? Seems to me we could both use the tension release, don't you think?"

"That's the meds talking, Darryl, not you. Besides, Heather's still awake. Honestly!" Faith said in a gasp when he pinched her nipple between his thumb and forefinger. "Cut it out! I'm tryin' to get you dressed!"

"And I'm tryin' to get you undressed. And yeah, you can grit your teeth all you want, but those little dots of color in your cheeks give you away every time." He leaned close enough to tongue her nipple through the satin, and she made that gurgly noise in her throat that still got him, even after more than a dozen years.

"Mama? Daddy?"

Darryl yanked his hand down so fast he smacked his own knee, a move his banged-up ribs had definite issues with, even with the pain meds. Fortunately, since Faith's back had been to the bathroom door, Heather hadn't gotten an eyeful. But that didn't stop a blush from racing up Faith's neck and across her cheeks like a brushfire. It was kind of cute, actually. Like they were teenagers again, fooling around in the storeroom in old man Prickett's pharmacy that summer Faith had worked the soda fountain.

Except she'd never looked mad when they'd fooled around in Prickett's.

She yanked her robe closed, nearly strangling her waist with the belt as Darryl said to his daughter, "We'll be out in a minute, sugar. Soon as Mama finishes patching me up, okay?"

"'Kay. C'n I wait on your bed?"

"Sure, honey," Faith said, finishing up the bandage with a stone-faced expression that gave no clue to how turned on she'd been not thirty seconds before. "There," she said, tucking everything neatly back into the first aid kit, which she set on the shelf over the toilet. "Let me go check on the little ones and I'll be back in a minute—"

He grabbed her hand. "Later?"

"Oh, right." Her expression was wry. "With a doped up man held together with tape, plaster and...whatever the heck they use for stitches these days. Darryl, for goodness' sake—be real."

After she left, Darryl stood, checking out his reflection. The new bandage was half the size of the one they'd put on in the hospital, he noted. Neat and efficient, just like everything Faith did.

She hadn't always been so efficient. So predictable. When they'd first gotten married, she never went to the grocery store that she didn't have to turn right back around and go get the five things she'd forgotten. She'd put in a load of laundry and not get around to drying it for two days, or start a pan of eggs to boil and not give them another thought. But if their first years of married life had been filled with the occasional blackened pan or slightly mildewed clothes or not being able to make a sandwich because they'd run out of bread, Darryl also fondly remembered unplanned camping trips and parties for no particular reason and—his personal favorite—surprise intimate encounters in the shower or the kitchen or the laundry room.

He missed that. Even more to the point, he missed the Faith who used to do those things. And if he could only shake the feeling that her changing was somehow his fault…

"Daddy? You okay?"

Leaning heavily on the sink, Darryl carefully turned to look at his oldest girl. The reason they'd gotten married in the first place, he obliquely thought. An excuse to get married he'd welcomed with everything he had in him.

"I'm fine," he said with a rush of air, then ushered her out of the bathroom.

"You don't *look* fine."

"Appearances can be deceiving."

Swallowed up in one of those baggy, too-long sleep tees, she flopped onto her tummy on their bed. Pushing twelve, the girl straddled that fine line between innocence and wisdom that sometimes scared Darryl half to death, especially since most days he wasn't all that sure which side of it he was on himself. "We're in serious trouble, aren't we?" she said, her narrow chin propped in her hands, those wide blue eyes fixed on his. "Because of the tornado destroyin' the shop?" When he hesitated, her pale brows crashed over her nose. "You can tell me the truth, Daddy. I'm not gonna freak on you or anything."

Faith returned just in time to hear this last line; now they exchanged a glance that ended in Faith's giving him a go-ahead nod. So he lowered himself to the bed and said, "Let's just say things are gonna be kind of tight for a while."

"Will we have to move?"

"No," he said, even though he hadn't thought that part of things through. They'd refinanced last year and lowered their payments, but without his income… "I promise we won't end up camping out in somebody's pasture."

She looked mildly relieved. For a moment or two. "But we don't have money for extras, right?"

Faith sat beside Heather, wearing her "Oh, dear" face as she rubbed the girl's bony back. "Honey, this probably isn't a real good time to bring this up…"

The girl twisted around to look up at her mother. "But it's gonna eat me alive until I know—"

"What's going on?" Darryl asked.

Gently sifting Heather's slippery blond hair through her fingers, Faith said, "You know how Heather and I were taking dance classes over at Carly Stewart's?"

Yeah, he knew. Carly'd recently moved to Haven, had started up a dance school in an old barn next to Sam Frasier's farm. Faith had been real excited about the exercise class she'd started, hoping to work off some of the weight she'd put on from the pregnancies. And Heather had started taking ballet classes, too.

"What about it?"

Faith stroked Heather's hair some more. "Turns out Carly thinks Heather has real potential. To be a ballet dancer, I mean. But because she's starting so late—most little girls begin lessons when they're five or six—she'd need private lessons to catch up. We'd only found out yesterday, so I was planning on talking it over with you last night...." Her sentence ended in a one-sided shrug.

"I see," he said, although he didn't really. Not that he didn't want his kids to do whatever made them happy, but... Heather becoming a ballet dancer? *Anybody* becoming a ballet dancer? Besides, kids changed their minds all the time. Look at his older brother, Dave, who'd begged their father for oboe lessons, only to lose interest after six months.

"Carly already offered me a partial scholarship," Heather said, the hopefulness in her eyes searing straight through him. "So maybe it wouldn't cost all that much."

Darryl pushed out a sigh, then faced the

mirror over the dresser. Both females watched him, waiting for an answer he couldn't give.

"You know how I hate sayin' no to any of you kids," he finally said to his daughter's reflection, "but I honestly don't see how we can swing it right now. Maybe next year."

"It'll be too late by next year!" Heather's eyes filled. "You don't have to get me anything for Christmas. And I'll contribute my whole allowance. Please, Daddy? I want to do this more than anything in the world!"

Out of deference to his ribs, Darryl carefully turned, his heart squeezing in his chest at the earnestness in her expression. "How can you be so sure of something you only just started doing?"

"I don't know. Except…maybe I think it must be like how you feel about fixing cars. It just feels really, really right."

He caught Faith's gaze, saw how much the whole thing was tearing her up inside, too. And unlike him, Faith didn't tend to indulge the kids. Saying no came a lot easier to her than it did him. Which meant this must be really serious. And real important. But that didn't change the facts of the situation.

"I'm sorry, baby, I really am. But I honestly don't see any way of pulling it off right now."

Her lower lip caught between her teeth, Heather traced the quilted spread with one finger for a second. Then her head popped back up, hope making her face shine. "Maybe... maybe she'd teach me for free?"

"Oh, sweetie..." Faith wrapped herself around Heather's shoulders, pressing her cheek to her temple. "That wouldn't be fair to Carly, would it? She has to make a living, too. It was already generous, her offering that partial scholarship. I know this is horrible, horrible timing, but—"

"It's okay, I understand." Heather scrambled off the bed, not looking at either of them as she scurried through the door. Faith shot Darryl an indecipherable look, then followed, leaving him feeling several notches below snail slime.

"She okay?" he asked when Faith returned a few minutes later.

Instead of replying, she wordlessly motioned for him to get up so she could remove the peach-colored, tailored bedspread she'd bought maybe a month ago. Not that he'd thought there was anything wrong with the old one, but Faith insisted the room needed "freshening up," or something. Darryl pushed himself to his feet, helping her fold the spread back as best he could with one hand. Anything to keep from feeling helpless. Useless.

"What else could I have said, Faith?" he said in a hushed voice, standing to one side so she could set the folded spread on the chair in the corner, like she did every night. "You know what the bank balance looks like as well as I do."

"Yes, I do. But do you have any idea what a big deal this is for her?"

"Oh, come on...lots of little girls want to dance. Not that I don't feel bad that I can't let her have her fun, but it would probably run its course anyway, right?"

"We don't know that. Maybe this is an incredible opportunity for her to work with a real professional dancer, maybe become one herself and not end up stuck in this town for the rest of her life!"

Her eyes widened slightly, as if she hadn't expected that to come out of her mouth. Darryl got a bad feeling in the pit of his stomach, but he replied, "Or she could get a bum leg like Carly and end up back here, anyway."

"It's not about how she'll end up, it's about what she has the chance to do in between. It's about giving her opportunities that—"

Faith stopped, then grabbed her pillows off the bed.

"That what?" Darryl said quietly, catching out of the corner of his mental eye the stirrings of an elephant he'd thought had moved on a long time ago. "That you never had?"

"I didn't say that."

"You don't have to." He grasped her arm, probing her gaze with his own. "Is that what's going on here? That you feel stuck? In this marriage? With *me*?"

For several moments, he saw his own frustration mirrored in her eyes. "It's not that simple," she said at last, and the bad feeling got a whole lot worse.

"Care to explain that?"

"Believe me," she said with a harsh sigh, "if I could, I would. But anyway, this isn't about me. It's about Heather. And how we're going to solve this. At some point. Not tonight. I'm way too tired to figure any of it out right now." Clutching the pillows to her chest, she headed toward the door.

"You're spending the night on the sofa again?"

"You have to sleep on your back. And nowhere in our marriage vows does it say I have to sleep in the same room with a snoring man—"

"Do you love me?"

Already in the doorway, she spun around. "What?"

"You heard me."

"Darryl, we're both exhausted, and stressed—"

"Simple question, yes or no. *Do you love me?*"

Their gazes warred for several seconds before she reached behind her to quietly shut the door. When she faced him again, she looked…worn-out. "We're part of each other by now, aren't we? All braided together like a pair of saplings planted side by side. After all this time, I wouldn't know how *not* to love you. But let me ask you something…." Her mouth quirked, and she leaned against the door, strangling the pillows. "Would you have married *me* if I hadn't been pregnant?"

Her words slammed into him like fists. "For God's sake, Faith—after everything we've been through together, after everything I've done for you and the kids…how can you even ask that?"

"Because," she said, her eyes hooked in his, "there's a difference between love and…and *obligation.* There's doing what's right, and doing what's *right*."

Darryl's brows pulled together. "You think I married you because I *had* to?"

"Didn't you?"

He looked at her as if she were speaking another language. "Have you forgotten how we couldn't keep our hands off each other? Hell, there's still times I want you so bad I can hardly think straight!"

"That's hormones, Darryl. And proximity. But what I'm wondering now is…was it ever more than that? Really?"

He dropped onto the edge of the bed, swallowing hard before saying, "Dammit, I'm doing my best here."

"I know you are," Faith whispered. "And you always have. God knows there's plenty of men in your situation who would've headed straight for the hills, rather than faced their responsibilities the way you did. And I love you for that."

He smirked. "For doing the right thing?"

"Is that so terrible?" She sat beside him, laying her hand on his uncasted arm. "But in any case, this isn't about you. It's true," she said when he snorted. "Which is exactly what makes this so…so weird. I wanted to marry

you, too. To be with you. So I don't understand this craziness any more than you do."

While he sat there, hoping to hell it was
the meds causing her words to make so little
sense, she got up, hugging the pillows to her
chest. "You need anything before I leave?"

"No." Then his gaze slashed to hers. "How
is it we can say all the right things, and yet
the answers still feel all wrong?"

"I don't know," she whispered, then left
the room, the elephant lumbering along after
her...leaving behind a not-so-little reminder
of its visit.

Wasn't a painkiller in the world strong
enough to dull this pain.

The sky was just beginning to pink up the
next morning when Faith heard Darryl shuf-
fle down the hall, yawning loudly. He paused
at the door to the kitchen, frowning at her and
Nicky, prompting Faith's heart to start beat-
ing loudly enough to echo inside her head.

"You had pumpkin pie for breakfast?" he
said in his morning-roughened voice, nodding toward the empty foil pie plate on the
table in front of her.

"It was the last piece. I figured it wouldn't
be any good by lunchtime."

He shook his head, one side of his mouth tilted up. "I didn't know you were still nursing the baby."

The plastic clock over the sink sounded like an old woman clucking her tongue at her as she sat at the kitchen table, Nicky at her breast. "Just once a day, in the morning," she said, smoothing down the baby's curls so she wouldn't have to look at her husband. "After you're gone, usually."

"Don't recall you keeping the others on the breast so long."

"I know. Seems harder to wean him, I guess because he's the last one...."

Her words faded into a silence that positively screamed between them.

"Didn't expect you awake this early," she said, as much to shatter that silence as anything else. "Sun's not even up yet. Neither are the rest of the kids, thank goodness."

She sensed him inching toward the refrigerator, barefoot as usual even though it was none too warm this early in the morning. Usually Darryl propelled himself through space like he could never get where he was going fast enough; today, however, he moved cautiously, as if he was trying to sneak past the pain. Sympathy twanged inside her—this was a man who rarely got sick, even when everybody else in the house was like to die from some crud or other. And everybody knows pain's all the worse when you're not used to it.

One hip propping open the door, he pulled out a carton of orange juice—he never had been a coffee-first-thing-in-the-morning kind of person. In the glow from the open fridge, she could see he hadn't bothered combing his thick hair, that he looked to be wearing the same T-shirt he'd had on yesterday. That the waistband snap to his jeans was still undone.

"You need help doing up your pants?"

He stilled for a second, then twisted off the cap to the carton one-handed, poured the juice into a glass. "No."

She swallowed. "Soon as I finish with Nicky, I can fix you some breakfast—"

"I'm not hungry."

Faith took in a deep breath, trying to break the bands constricting her chest. "You get any sleep?"

"Not a whole lot, no. But thanks for asking."

"Darryl, I—"

"There's nothing to say, Faith," he said, not looking at her. "Like you said, I was the one who brought up the subject." He set the juice back in the fridge and let the door slam shut, making Nicky jump. The baby stopped nursing for a second, then latched back on, his blue eyes wide and trusting. Now standing at the window, Darryl sipped the juice, then made a face. "This our regular stuff?"

"No, they got a new brand in, I thought I'd try it—"

"Is there somebody else?" he said quietly.

"What?"

He turned, his expression flat. "I said, is there somebody else?"

She caught the laugh a split second before it escaped. "Of course not! What on earth put that idea into your head?"

"I'd be a fool not to ask, wouldn't I?"

The baby done with his feed, Faith shifted him to sit up, fingering his fluffy curls as he let out a trucker-size belch, then gleefully slapped the table in front of them. "No, Darryl, there's nobody else." A rueful smile pulled at her mouth. "When on earth would I have had time?"

He smirked. "Still. I don't know as I much like being thought of as a habit you can't break."

"It's not like that—"

"Isn't it? Oh, you said it prettier, all that

stuff about us being like a pair of trees that have grown together, but the upshot's the same. So." He downed the rest of the juice. "You want out?"

"No!"

"Why?" He banged the glass onto the counter, the sound reverberating through the semidarkness. "Why would you want to stay if you're not sure what you feel for me anymore?"

"Stop twisting my words!" she said in a low voice. "I said I loved you, what more do you want?"

"Oh, I don't know. Maybe a little honesty?"

"I am being honest! As honest as I know how, at least. For heaven's sake, if I didn't feel anything for you, do you think I'd still be sharing your bed?"

She was throwing him scraps, and she knew it. Just like the hard set to his mouth told her he knew it, too. "Thought that was just the hormones talking."

"Maybe it is," she retorted, exhausted and scared and frustrated, with him, with herself, with everything that was going on. "And maybe habit and hormones is the best most people can hope for after twelve years, I don't know."

"And that's enough for you?" he said, the bitterness in his voice lancing through her. "'Cause I'm here to tell you, it sure as hell isn't enough for me."

Faith got up to set the baby in his play yard, hanging on to the side and watching him pick up what she knew was the first of many toys to be jettisoned onto the kitchen floor. "I know this is going to sound lame," she said, blinking back tears, "but this isn't any picnic for me, either. Especially knowing how much distress this is causing you."

"Is that supposed to make me feel better?"

"I may be messed up, Darryl," she said quietly, "but I'm not stupid."

The sun peeked over the horizon, flooding the kitchen with softly pearled light. "So... what now?" he said. "We just pretend everything's okay, is that it?"

Faith looked over at him, her heart cracking at the confusion swimming in his eyes. "What choice do we have? For one thing, we've got five kids who for sure don't need another crisis to deal with on top of everything else. And for another, you really want our parents to know about this?"

After a moment, Darryl snagged that old jacket she'd ripped up to accommodate his cast off the pegboard by the back door, awkwardly shrugging into it. She couldn't tell if the pain contorting his features was due more to his bruised body or their conversation. "I'm going down to the garage," he said, turning toward the back door.

"What? Why? There's hardly anything left!"

His eyes touched hers, his voice like steel. "Oh, I'm pretty sure underneath the wreckage, there's more left than you might think. Sooner I can get it cleared away, sooner I can start rebuilding."

Chapter Three

Somebody or other was cheerfully belting out "Jingle Bell Rock" as Faith pushed her cart alongside the meat bins in the Homeland, keeping an eye peeled for the Reduced for Quick Sale stickers. There was something almost anesthetizing about the upbeat music, the swags of silver and red tinsel draped between the aisles, the rows of tightly plastic-wrapped chicken parts and pork chops and steaks, the quiet purposefulness of the other Monday morning shoppers. With the three oldest in school, she only had Sierra and Nicky in the cart. Which was more than enough. To keep them quiet, she'd snatched a bag of animal crackers off the shelf and practically thrown it at them, not even caring—too much—that they'd ruin their lunch. Not even caring—too much—that she'd just bought herself a one-way ticket to Bad Mama Hell.

Soon as she got out of the one for Bad Wives, where basically she'd lived for the past three days. Cramming a small handful of the crackers down her own gullet (Lord, she felt like she had this gaping hole inside of her that just would *not* get filled up) she pounced on a chuck roast—one of the few things she could actually cook—marked down forty percent, wedging it into the cart someplace where hopefully Sierra wouldn't grind her Barbie sneaker into it.

Now that the Truth had moved in—and theirs was far too small a house for something that big and ugly and stinky—every conversation between her and Darryl had become so guarded and polite Faith was ready to tear her hair out. Given a choice, habit and hormones wasn't looking so bad. And heaven knew this was no time for her to be going off the deep end. Even if Darryl seemed hell-bent on driving her there himself.

Honestly! Why was all this stuff coming to the surface now?

Because, chickie, it was bound to eventually, wasn't it?

She shoved more animal crackers into her mouth, thinking at this rate she was going to have to retrieve her maternity clothes from the church giveaway box just to have something she could get into.

A scream from the cart brought her back to attention. Nicky had twisted around and grabbed his sister's hair, a move Sierra wasn't taking too well.

"Nicky, sugar…" Faith leaned across the cart to untangle the baby's sticky fingers from his sister's fine hair, half of which remained in the chubby fist when Faith finally separated the two. By this time, Sierra was howling, not good for the nerves of someone who'd been on the breaking point for several days already.

"Nicky, no! It's not funny!" Faith peeled a half-dozen silky blond hairs out of his clenched fist. "You hurt your sister! You can't do that!"

At her stern tone, the baby's sunshiny smile vanished, to be replaced by a quivering pout that rapidly gave way to a full-out wail.

Faith shut her eyes and prayed for patience. And that she wouldn't break down into sobs along with her children, right here in front of God and everybody.

"Faith! Yoo-hoo, *Faith!*"

Not today, Lord, she thought, her eyes still closed. *Please?*

Too late.

Plastering a smile to her face, she turned in time to see Luralene Hastings huffing and puffing up the aisle, her white, crepe-soled slip-ons squeaking like mice against the beige-and-white-tiled floor. "What's the big idea, missy, canceling your hair appointment!" said the skinny redhead, oblivious to the cacophonic bellowing coming from the cart. "I tried callin' you, but I guess you were already gone. Darryl answered the phone. How's he gettin' on, anyway? 'Cause, frankly, between you and me? He didn't sound so good. That was a real shame, the service station gettin' hit by the twister like that. A *real* shame. Any idea how long it's gonna take before it's up and runnin' again, 'cause Coop says he's in no mood to go lookin' for another mechanic this late in the game."

Faith suddenly realized both babies had gone stark still, staring wide-eyed at Luralene, who was clutching a plastic-wrapped deli sandwich to her heaving chest. Not that

Faith blamed them—a tornado had nothing on the far-side-of-fifty owner of the Hair We Are when she was in full sail. Faith took advantage of the momentary lull to stick Nicky's pacifier in his mouth, only it popped right back out. She fumbled for it, catching it a foot before it hit the floor and a split second before the wails once more reached eardrum-splitting level. She plugged him up again, trying to decide which question to answer first. Not that she was inclined to answer any of them, but sidestepping Luralene was like trying to pass an eighteen-wheeler on a two-line highway.

"We don't know yet when Darryl'll be back in business," she finally said. "It depends on, well, a lot of things. And sorry about the hair appointment, but… I decided to let it grow out for a bit. It's been ages since I've had it long."

Luralene squinted at her, stopping just short of tangling up her false eyelashes. Her lids were all done up in a medley of purples and lavenders today, not one of which even came close to matching her violet smock. "And you know full well that any longer than shoulder length and your head looks like a tumbleweed. And that was your description, not mine, before you go getting your panties in a twist." Then she laid one hand on Faith's wrist, her frosted-rose acrylics shimmering in the glow from the freezer case. "Going through hard times is nothing to be ashamed of, honey," she said in an uncharacteristically low voice. "There's not a soul in this town who hasn't, at one point or another. So come on over, let me give you a trim, on the house. Won't take but twenty minutes—"

"No, I couldn't, really. I mean, I've got the babies. And frozen food—"

"It's thirty degrees outside, nothing's gonna happen to the food. And the babies can play in the kiddy corner, I'll put you in the chair right beside it so you can keep an eye on 'em. Beatrice Moody canceled her eleven o'clock, so I can fit you in, no problem. Honey," she added when Faith started to protest again, "all this is is one woman lookin' out for another. 'Cause nothin' bolsters a woman's ability to cope with a crisis better than knowin' she looks good."

Faith supposed there was more than a little truth in the older woman's words. She'd always found life's challenges much less formidable when armed with the right shade of lipstick and a good haircut, although she'd never quite been able to decide if this made her shallow or simply adaptable.

"And besides," Luralene said, leaning so close Faith nearly choked on the Aqua Net, "I imagine it wouldn't hurt to give Darryl a little pick-me-up as well, if you get my drift."

Faith let out a sigh, surrendering as gracefully as she knew how.

Darryl slouched in one of the plastic chairs in Ryan Logan's home office waiting room, tapping his heel against the dark, scuffed wooden floor. Except for the chairs, nothing much had changed since this'd been old Doc Patterson's office, even down to the worn set of wooden blocks stacked in one corner. Magazines were a trifle newer, though that wasn't saying a whole lot. But the same wooden blinds covered the mullioned windows, the walls were painted the same manila-folder color, the rug taking up most of the bowed floor was the same multicolored patterned number he remembered from when his mama used to bring him and his brothers here for his shots, except it was more faded now. And now, as then, he couldn't sit in this office without a sense of trepidation, a suspicion he wasn't going to feel *better* for having been here.

"Darryl! Didn't know you were here already!" Ryan, who'd taken over for the old doc after his retirement, stood in his office doorway, looking more like a cowboy than a doctor in his jeans and denim shirt. Lines fanned out around bright blue eyes as the doctor's dark-blond mustache curved up at the corners. Clearly, marriage and fatherhood—Ryan had married a young widow with three little kids a couple years back, then added one of their own to the brood—agreed with the former recluse. "Come on in, come on in!"

Darryl pushed himself to his feet. "I really appreciate you seeing me. I know I should've gone out to the clinic and not bothered you on your day off—"

"Forget it," Ryan said, leading Darryl into his office. "Those your records from the hospital?"

Nodding, Darryl handed them over.

"Can you get up on the exam table on your own speed, or you need some help?"

"No, no, I'm good," he said, although it was no mean feat getting his butt up on the paper-covered vinyl with only one hand to steady himself.

"So," Ryan said, "all things considered, how're you feeling?"

"So-so. The ribs still ache, but not as bad. And the stitches are itching like hell…."

"Yeah, let's just take a peek at that." The doctor carefully removed the dressing, nodding in approval before tossing the bandage in a metal can. "That's healing up real nice. You don't need to keep it covered anymore if you don't want to. We'll yank those stitches out in a couple days, and that'll be that. No headaches, I take it?"

"Not from the accident," Darryl muttered, which drew a curious look from the doctor. "No," Darryl said, more clearly. "No headaches."

"You still taking the Vicodin?"

"Not since the first day. They made me… I don't know. I didn't feel like myself on 'em."

"Your arm's not paining you, then?"

"Actually…that's why I'm here. I remember breaking my other arm when I was a kid, and it hurt like hell for a couple days, till the bone started to set. What I don't remember, though, is losing the feeling in my fingers."

The doctor's brows crashed together. "Some of the feeling, or all of it?"

"It comes and goes. There's times when

it feels like my hand isn't even there. Other times it tingles like it's on fire."

Ryan walked back to his desk and picked up Darryl's folder. For several seconds, he read silently, flipping a couple of the pages back and forth, the seriousness of his expression making a cold, hard knot form in the pit of Darryl's stomach.

"Doc? What is it?"

"The good news is it's not as bad as you might think."

"And…what's the bad news?"

Ryan's sympathetic blue gaze met his and Darryl came real close to blacking out.

Muttering under her breath, Faith hesitated before squeezing her car into one of the angled parking spaces in front of the Hair We Are between Dawn Logan's Explorer and Maddie Logan's ancient Impala. Running into her friends right now provoked some real mixed feelings, that was for sure. Especially Dawn, who'd been Faith's best friend in high school. On the up side, even though Dawn had spent ten years in New York City becoming a lawyer, at heart she wasn't any different after her return to Haven last year than she had been before. Actually, she and

Faith had resurrected their old relationship with hardly a missed beat, and Faith knew she could always count on Dawn to be a true and honest friend. Still and all, not only was the woman extremely successful by Haven standards, a fact that had led to Faith's praying to be delivered from envious thoughts on more than one occasion, but she was also technically a newlywed. All that unbridled bliss grew downright tedious after a while.

However, there was nothing to be done for it now, Faith thought as she hauled her children out of the car and herded them inside. It was face Dawn now, or Luralene later. No contest.

And yet the moment Faith set foot inside and five people greeted her as though her arrival had made their day, at least half her troubles sloughed off her shoulders. As usual, the shop smelled of freshly brewed coffee and hair spray and nail polish, the exuberant pastel decor a radical declaration of femininity, a sanctuary from all that was ugly and depressing outside its doors. Faith had had her first haircut here when she was ten and her mother finally gave up on her daughter's unruly hair. And now, more than twenty years later, she realized being here settled her frazzled nerves far more than a drink in some bar could ever do.

She couldn't say the same for her children, however. Although Nicky had conked out in his car seat on the way over, poor Sierra was not at all sure about the shrieking ladies swooping down on her. The child ducked behind Faith's legs, burying her face in the folds of Faith's jeans at the knees, which God knew was the only place clothing was likely to bag on her body these days.

"Back off, y'all," Luralene barked to her staff—Stacey, who everybody still called the "new girl" even though she'd been there for two years already; Evelina, the manicurist; and Vyanna, whose beehives (both hers and her customers') had more than once been compared to a perfect meringue. "Can't you see you're scarin' the poor baby half to death? Hey, sugar," she said, her knees cracking like gunshots when she squatted. "Your mama's gonna have a seat in that big chair over there right beside that big old toy chest and get her hair cut. And I bet there's some doll babies inside just waitin' for you to love 'em, what do you think about that?"

Faith smiled down into Sierra's questioning gray-green eyes, thinking she wouldn't mind a little loving herself, a thought she immediately replaced with a stern *Don't go there*.

"Come on, sweetie," she said, Nicky's baby seat banging against her leg as she led Sierra over to the play area. She lowered the seat to the floor where she could still see him, then knelt in front of the three-year-old, pointing to the empty chair. "See? I'm right here. So you go on ahead and play, okay?"

Sierra peered around her at Luralene, then whispered, "The lady's scary."

"You'll get used to it," Faith said, giving her a kiss on the forehead, then climbing into the chair. After a couple of very skeptical seconds, Sierra began to systematically haul each toy out of the open wooden box by the wall, inspect it, then toss it over her shoulder, rejected.

"Tough customer," Dawn shouted over the roar of a hair dryer from the next chair.

"Don't I know it," Faith said, the incongruity of her friend's being here finally hitting her. As long as she'd known her, the brunette had always worn her hair natural and nearly to her waist. "Oh my God—you got your hair cut!"

"Don't she look *great*?" Stacey said from behind Dawn's chair, grinning underneath two inches of spiked black hair. "Like some actress or something, huh?"

"Oh, Lordy, *Lordy*," Luralene said. "Where's my camera?" She abandoned Faith to scurry back to the reception table, banging drawers open and shut for several seconds until she finally unearthed an old thirty-five millimeter. "Here it is, here it is…." She scurried back, the camera already up to her eye. "We have got to put this up in the front window! Stacey, you have outdone yourself this time, gal…for pity's sake, Dawn—smile! Think of Cal or something!"

"Yeah, that'd sure do it," Evelina said from over at her table, where she was doing Hazel Dinwiddy's nails, and more than one woman there squelched a sigh at the thought of those smoky green eyes and that smile a woman only had to see once to remember the rest of her life.

Anyway. Like everybody else, Faith joined in the oohing and ahhing over Dawn's hair, which was still past her shoulders, but now a mass of wavy layers with wispy, sexy bangs that made her brown eyes look positively enormous.

"You know," Maddie Logan rasped from three chairs over, "you already had an unfair advantage over the rest of us, having the best boobs in town. This is just plain out-and-out overkill."

"No, I think Faith's got me beat in that department," Dawn said, glancing over. "Pardon me for saying this, but that is one impressive rack, lady."

"Five kids'll do that to you."

"Yeah, right," Maddie said, fluffing her fingers through her just-trimmed, golden-brown shag. "It took me four to work up to a full A. At that rate I'd have to have twenty-two to get anywhere near you guys."

"Honey," Luralene said, "the bigger they are, the harder they fall. Long as Ryan isn't complaining, you've got nothing to worry about." She turned Faith's chair around so she could tilt her back to wash her hair in the sink. "He's not, is he? Complaining?"

A comb flying across the salon was the last thing Faith saw before she closed her eyes, savoring the warm water streaming over her head. "So why'd you do it?" she asked Dawn. "I thought you loved your hair long."

"I did. Until I went to check my makeup in the mirror yesterday and my mother looked back out at me."

Faith chuckled—with her eccentric clothes

and long gray hair, Ivy Gardner, Dawn's mom and the midwife who'd delivered two of Faith's babies, was a definite holdover from the hippie era. That she was going to be the new mayor come January was a testament to Haven's being on the cutting edge of something, Faith supposed.

"How's she doing, by the way?" she asked, eyes closed.

"Still bummed about losing her refrigerator," Dawn said, referring to Ivy's own close encounter with Mother Nature the week before. In Ivy's case, the wind had uprooted a fifty-foot mulberry from her backyard and smashed it into her roof, right on top of her kitchen. Fortunately, Ivy hadn't been in the house at the time; unfortunately, the house was currently uninhabitable, which meant Ivy was staying with Dawn and Cal at his horse farm outside town, which Faith guessed had something to do with Dawn's precipitous decision to change her hairstyle.

The old rotary phone on the front desk jangled as if it'd been goosed. Luralene went to answer it, then shouted over, "Faith, honey? I need to pop over to Coop's for a sec, I'll be back in two shakes, okay?"

Faith heard the redhead scoot through the

door to her husband's barbershop next door, startling the little silver bell over it into a tingling tizzy. She opened her eyes to find herself the object of a pair of worried gazes.

"So how are you and Darryl doing?" Dawn whispered, dark eyes huge underneath her newly cut bangs.

Faith smiled brightly. "Oh, you know us, we'll muddle through."

"Hey," Maddie said, poking her. "This is us you're talking to."

"That's right." Dawn waited until Olive passed, then took Faith's hand in hers. "I know things weren't exactly copacetic between you two before—"

Faith's gaze shot to Dawn's. "What are you talking about? I never said—"

"It's not what you said, it's what you didn't. And I doubt losing the garage is making things any easier between you two."

And the sympathy in Dawn's eyes was nothing compared with the empathy in Maddie's. Having landed in Haven two years before with no money, two small children and another on the way, Maddie more than understood the concept of "financially embarrassed." Faith tamped down a sigh that was equal parts annoyance at their nosiness and gratitude for their friendship. One of the ironies of life in a small town.

Sierra brought Faith a dolly, begging to get in her lap; Faith gestured to Maddie to hand her a towel, which she wrapped around her dripping hair. With her munchkin ensconced, singing softly to her new "baby," she checked to be sure no one else was eavesdropping, although people around here tended to have highly developed listening skills.

"Frankly, I'm not sure what's going to happen," she admitted, explaining about how long it would take to get back on their feet, as well as Darryl's refusal to accept help from her parents. "And Christmas is coming, and Heather wants to take dance lessons, and…" She shrugged. "I know how it looks, that we didn't have a contingency plan in case something like this happened, but when you're barely getting by as it is…"

"Shoot, honey," Maddie said, "you don't have to explain that to me."

"Me, either," Dawn said, then frowned. "Maybe you could get a job, at least for the time being."

Faith's eyebrows flew up, even as a tingle of possibility sparked over her skin. "A job? With five kids still needing me at home?"

Dawn frowned. "It's not inconceivable that Darryl could hold the fort while you're gone, at least with the older kids. It's amazing how much a person can do with only one arm," she said over Faith's protest. "Besides, you've already got Nicky and Sierra in day care a couple mornings a week, right?"

"Well, that's true. But what on earth would I do?"

That got a chuckle from the brunette. "Oh, come on…after twelve years of marriage and motherhood, you must have *some* marketable skills."

Faith snorted. "None I could exactly exploit, if you get my drift."

Dawn said something about that being a shame as Maddie tentatively said, "Well, I s'pose you could come help me make pies. I've got three restaurants in Tulsa that's takin' 'em now. I could use the extra help."

Faith burst out laughing. "This is the woman who burns fish sticks, remember? Thanks, honey, but you've worked long and hard for your success. The last thing you need is me in your kitchen."

The younger woman looked extremely relieved. Then Dawn remembered her secretary was going out of town for a couple weeks, but they all decided by the time Faith learned the computer program for the billing and such, Marybeth would be back.

"Working at the day-care center with your mother?" Maddie said, but Faith shook her head.

"No openings. And the church can't afford to hire me out of pity."

"Cleaning houses?" Dawn gently suggested.

"Around here?" she said, and both ladies agreed she had a point. Then Maddie hit herself on the side of the head.

"I am slow today, boy," she said, her eyes bright. "There's going to be an opening at the Homeland, starting next week. Melva Rice told me she's quittin', that she just can't take standin' on her feet all day anymore. It's not a bad job, and there's benefits once you've been there for a while. Melva said she was giving notice yesterday, so you'd better go get your application in, like now."

"Now, wait a minute, I never said—"

"She's not goin' anywhere until I get that hair under control," Luralene announced over the tinkling bell as she returned, marching across the floor like an army sergeant.

"Geez, Luralene," Maddie said, "you got this place bugged or what?"

The older woman shooed the others out of her way, smiled for Sierra—who flinched—then set the girl on the floor with instructions to go play for a little longer, Mama needed to get all prettied up now. Then she spun Faith around, shoving her back toward the sink so hard she bounced. "She's already missed one appointment, she's mine now. However, to save time…" She took the hose to Faith's hair again, working shampoo into her scalp hard enough to deep-clean her brain. "Why don't one of you gals go over to the Homeland and pick up an application for her?"

There was no point in arguing.

Chapter Four

With his good arm, Darryl yanked open the
doors to the freestanding garage out behind the
house, his nostrils flaring at the blended scents
of motor oil, paste wax, gasoline. With a rever-
ence usually reserved for undressing his wife,
he slowly peeled back the tarp he kept over
the restored '59 Big Bird. His breath caught,
as it did every time, at how beautiful she was.
It was probably stupid, hanging on to the car
when he couldn't even afford the insurance to
drive it—it'd probably been a good three, four
years since he'd last taken her for a spin—but
to this day, he remembered the kick to his gut
when he caught sight of her in Coop Hastings's

garage. More rust than paint, her white vinyl roof ripped and cracked, her chrome trim dull as a dead man's eyes…and Darryl knew, with all the intensity of a sixteen-year-old in love, that it was up to him to save her. And if saving her meant months of agony and grossness by working his ass off on old man Yaeger's farm to earn the three hundred dollars to buy her… well, let's just say he'd yet to regret it.

He skimmed his hand along the gleaming, icy fender, restored as near as he could manage to the factory-finish Cherry Red, her new roof as pristine and unmarked as fresh snow. Underneath the hood sat a completely rebuilt V-8, packed with three hundred horses itching to be given their heads. He'd even managed to track down a decent set of white leather seats to replace the trashed originals. Oh, yeah, she was seventeen feet of sex on wheels, his Marilyn, with her lush curves and velvet purr. And she was all his, a thought that, for whatever reason, somewhat dulled the pain of the news he'd just been given.

"Darryl?"

He hadn't heard Faith's approach, despite the thin layer of ice covering the ground. She was standing in the doorway to the garage, her hair blowing every which way, Nicky in her arms. Behind her, Sierra chased Dot around the yard, giggling her head off. Or the dog was chasing her, it was hard to tell.

Darryl's gaze veered back to Faith, who looked like she'd been lit up from inside. Her hair was shorter, too, he noticed. Frankly, he liked it long, but he damn sight knew better than to come between a woman and her hair. "I thought you said you canceled your appointment with Luralene?"

"I did, but I ran into Luralene in the Homeland. She took one look at my head and did everything short of dragging me bodily back to the shop. It was a freebie," she said, as if she was trying to cover her butt. "Well, sort of. I traded for some of those blackberry preserves your mother gave us, since we'd be in our nineties before they got used up. Anyway... I've got news! I got a job!"

Darryl frowned. "Come again?"

"A job, at the Homeland." She swiped Nicky's curls off his forehead. "As a cashier, startin' next week. Now I know this is going to take some adjustment, especially since you'll have to supervise the older kids with their homework and on weekends. I know—the weekend part is the pits, but it's the only job in town. That I can do, anyway. The pay's not great, but it'll help fill the gap, at least. And there's benefits, if I end up staying on for a while...." Her brows pushed together. "Why aren't you saying anything?"

Because he felt like that roof had caved in on him all over again? "How on earth did this happen?"

"I'm not sure, it certainly wasn't something I'd consciously thought about. But there I was, trying to figure out how we were going to manage, and then somebody, um, at Luralene's said she'd heard there was going to be an opening, and, well, the pieces just sort of fell into place. The manager—Roya Gibbons from church, you remember her?—hired me on the spot. Darryl," she said with one of her exasperated breaths.

"What?"

"I'm only goin' to work at the Homeland, not runnin' off with the circus." She hitched the baby higher up on her hip. "This is a good thing, okay? Go with it."

Darryl lightly banged the heel of his hand against the front fender, then looked at his wife, his muscles pulling at his temples. "Did I miss something? I thought you always said you didn't *want* to work outside the house?"

"We don't exactly have any choice in the

matter, do we? And I'm not about to watch my children starve because of some macho pride thing about you being the designated breadwinner."

"We're not in any immediate danger of starving, Faith. Maybe we've got to cut back on the frills right now—"

"Like what? The gas bill? The mortgage? Lord, Darryl—when's the last time we all went to the movies? Or out to eat someplace other than Ruby's? We were already riding about as fine a line as you could get. Of course... I suppose we could let my parents help—"

"Don't even *say* that."

"Well, then, buddy, it's me or them. Take your pick."

"It's just...this seems so, I don't know. Upside down."

"You really don't get it, do you?" she said in that tone of voice that sends chills up a man's spine, and not in a good way. Against his better judgment, Darryl faced her.

"What's that supposed to mean?"

"It means I feel good about this, you know? Real good, in fact. That I'll be doing something concrete instead of sitting around and worrying to death about the situation. And for another thing…"

She lowered the baby to his feet, keeping her fingers curled in his hood so he wouldn't topple over. "Look—I haven't regretted a single moment I've been home with the kids," she said, "and that's the God's honest truth. And I doubt seriously I would have considered looking for outside work if this crisis hadn't pushed me into it. But…oh, it's hard to explain." She drew a deep breath, then turned to him, her brow crinkled. "It's like…never going hungry, but never getting dessert, either. After a while you begin to feel…well, a little cheated, I guess."

"And you're blaming me for that?"

"No," she said immediately. "How could I, when…?" She sucked in a breath, as if trying to regroup. "It's just that you've always been sure of who you were, what you wanted to do…" Her sentence ended in a half-assed shrug.

A million and one emotions churning inside him, Darryl looked out over the yard, trying desperately to wrap his head around what she was saying. "Well," he said at last, "I suppose if it's dessert you're looking for, a grocery store would be a logical place to look for it."

A soft laugh drifted from her lips. "At least it's a chance to be somebody besides 'Mom' for a few hours a day."

"I thought that's what you wanted," he said, stubbornly.

"I did. Do. It just not *all* I want. Not anymore." Her gaze flicked in his direction. "And then there's Heather."

"Heather...? Oh. You mean her dancing?"

"I know you think it's foolishness—" Faith touched his arm when he blew out a breath "—and maybe nothing ever will come of it. Then again, I don't see anybody with a crystal ball around here, do you? So who knows? But the point is, the child's never asked for anything else her entire life."

"We've already had this conversation."

"So we're having it again." Faith reached over to stroke the Bird's front fender; Darryl had to wrestle with envy for a second or two, but he got over it. "You remember telling me how badly you wanted this car," Faith said, "and what you had to do to get it? Well, did you know your daughter's been trolling for odd jobs herself, anything to earn a few dollars to pay for her lessons?"

His gaze snapped to hers. "On her own?"

"Of course, on her own, You don't think I'd put the child up to it, do you? And guess what? She's got herself two little jobs, helping Heddy Lancaster up at the library shelve books on Saturday mornings and reading to Minnie Hawkins's old mother a couple hours a week."

"Good Lord. How's she think she's gonna do all that and her schoolwork, and take dance lessons besides?"

"Exactly what I asked her. But she's got it all figured out, showed me a schedule and everything."

Feeling woefully left behind, Darryl walked over to the open garage door, leaning his good arm up against the frame. "Lord, Faithie... everything's changing, isn't it?"

"It was bound to happen eventually, I suppose," she said softly behind him.

He grunted, then twisted to look at her. "You really think this job thing will make you happy?"

Long moments passed before she spoke. "I've never been *un*happy, Darryl," she said at last. "It's just lately I've been feeling... I don't know. Unsettled. Itchy. Like...like I needed to give birth to myself, or something."

How anybody could look determined and

vulnerable at the same time, Darryl had no idea. But his gut constricted with the urge to touch her, to draw her close and bury his cheek in all that bouncy hair, to let her soft scent both soothe and inflame the hunger gnawing at his insides. Only that's when it hit him like an avalanche that he had no idea who his wife was anymore. Or worse, how he fit in with this new life she envisioned for herself.

"What do you want from me, Faith?" he said quietly, and her eyes veered to his. Finally, her mouth tilted into a small smile.

"Patience?"

Darryl shoved his good hand into his jeans pocket and let his gaze roam the yard. "Don't you sometimes wish we could turn back the clock? To when we were still too young and dumb to know how hard it was gonna be?"

"Oh, Lord, no," she said with a low laugh, her curls gleaming in the waning light when she shook her head. "I may not know who I am now, but for sure I don't want to be that clueless eighteen-year-old again." She shivered, then bent down to heft the baby into her arms, smiling for him when he grabbed her face with his pudgy little mitts and gurgled at her. "I need to grow, Darryl," she said, her voice soft as a breeze. "*We* need to grow.

So maybe this challenge has come along so we can do just that. Land sakes, it's cold out here…c'mon, baby," she called to Sierra. "Let's get inside."

Pretty sure it wasn't his still sore ribs constricting his breathing, Darryl watched them troop back to the house before he slowly drew the tarp back up over the T-bird. He didn't get it— one of the things that had drawn him to Faith from the beginning was how uncomplicated she'd been. Easygoing. Like him. How their roles had been so neatly defined— protector, protectee. Simple. Predictable.

Although, if he thought about it for more than two seconds, he didn't suppose he could blame her for feeling whatever she was feeling. Hell, her entire world had just been turned ass over teakettle, what else was she supposed to feel? Except…except she'd said she'd already begun to feel this way long before the tornado.

Dammit! Hadn't he been doing all along just what he'd promised? To be there for her and the kids, to provide for them, to put them first… If that had been enough at the beginning, why wasn't it enough now? Because he knew it hadn't been his imagination that once upon a time she'd looked at him as if he'd been her world. When he and the kids had been all she'd needed, when she'd found the same comfort in routine that he did. Only, since he had no idea what he'd done to earn those looks at the outset, he had even less of an idea how to go about getting them back now.

The knot in his chest tightened, rising to lodge in his throat as he stood in the open doorway to the garage, the icy air making his cheeks tingle. Slowly, steadily, he breathed out the temptation to panic, that his marriage— hell, his *life*—had hit a slippery patch and was skidding out of control.

Right toward the edge of a cliff.

Except…except a good driver, a *smart* driver, knows to turn *with* the skid, not against it, in order to get straightened out again.

Huh.

He flicked off the light switch, plunging Marilyn into darkness, then clanged shut the garage door. His cowboy boots, which he'd taken to wearing because they were a helluva lot easier to get on single-handed than his lace-up work boots, crunched the brittle, frosted grass as he crossed the yard. The sky was cottony and heavy, as if it was fixing to snow. He hoped not—shoveling snow one-handed was going to be a real bitch.

Again the panic rose in his throat. Again he refused to let it get a foothold. Because right now, he was steering with the skid. Avoiding tailspins. Focusing on nothing except getting back to normal, on doing whatever it took to win back that look of adoration he used to see in his wife's eyes.

She was in the kitchen, fixing graham crackers and peanut butter for after-school snacks. Her cheeks were still flushed from the cold, making her blue eyes even brighter when she looked over at him. Tenderness, mixed with a healthy dose of anxiety, stole his breath. The one thing he feared most in the world was letting this woman down, of not being the man she needed him to be.

"So…what will I have to do?"

Her brows dipped. "Excuse me?"

"Around the house. Taking care of the kids. While you're at work." He rubbed his cast, as if he could will life back into his arm. "You think I can manage one-handed?"

Her expression thoughtful, Faith set the knife on top of the open jar, licked a smudge of peanut butter off her thumb. Even after all this time, even with two kids and a dog there with them, the gesture was enough to mess with his breathing. "With some modifications, I'm sure you'd do fine."

"Okay, then. If me being Mr. Mom for a couple months is what it's gonna take to...to get us through this, then I'll just have to do the best job I can."

Slowly, Faith smiled. And Darryl felt the tires once again grip the road, heading in the right direction. Except then she said, "By the way, your mother called a little bit ago, inviting us all to supper on Friday night," and Darryl realized he didn't dare relax behind the wheel just yet.

Try as she might, Faith couldn't actually remember Darryl ever being afraid to go inside his parents' house before this. Well, maybe *afraid* was too strong a word. Reluctant, maybe. But then, in his shoes, she'd be halfway to the next county by now.

She hauled Nicky out of his car seat, then joined her husband, standing in front of the house. The sky was already twilight-bruised, dark enough for his folks to have already turned on their Christmas lights. Thousands of them, outlining the roof, snaking up the porch posts, smothering every tree and bush in the yard, flashing and twinkling and glowing with irritating cheerfulness. Still, the kids were beside themselves, oohing and ahhing and jumping around like fleas, squealing their little hearts out. And that's what was important, not her disgruntled mood. Even Heather, who being nearly twelve was far too dignified to run around and act like a *child,* stood in the center of the yard with her arms wrapped around herself, awestruck.

"Look, Mama!" Sierra yelled. "The horsie moves his head!"

A few feet away, Darryl chuckled. It was the first time he'd looked even remotely relaxed since they'd left the house. "That's a reindeer, sweet pea. You know, like Santa has on his sleigh?" He pointed to the roof, where a lighted St. Nick and more deer precariously perched. Along with an angel, a snowman and a three-piece Nativity scene. L.B. and Renee believed in covering all the bases.

The front door swung open, instantly sucking all the kids into the house, trading them, it seemed, for the scent of roast pork and cornbread and some kind of pie. "Y'all coming in?" L.B. bellowed, but Darryl said they'd be there in a minute, Nicky wanted to see the lights. Actually, Nicky was giving Faith that "Uh…

should I be scared?" look, but that was beside the point. The door closed again, bouncing the plastic holly wreath. Anxiety once more vibrated from her husband, vaporizing what little sense of peace she'd been able to hang on to.

For all they seemed to have gotten over the immediate hurdle of Darryl's accepting their temporary role reversal, tension still clung to their marriage like baked-on grease. Not really a surprise, considering it had taken her about ten seconds to figure out he was only going along with her as a means to get back in her good graces. Or at least in her bed. Or her back in his, whatever. But that was Darryl for you. She'd never seen a person so set in his ways, so content to live his life the same way, day in and day out. For somebody who refused to give up an article of clothing until it literally disintegrated off his body, or who had a fit when his favorite TV show changed to a new night, that tornado had flattened a lot more than his business.

But that was nothing compared with the hell of having your wife put your sex life on hold.

Not a conscious decision on Faith's part, but with everything going on, she just hadn't been in the mood, for one thing. Which was very strange for her, because in theory, sex ranked right up there with long hot baths and Baskin-Robbins Jamoca Almond Fudge ice cream as one of God's great gifts. Okay, in practice it did, too. So why she was in this I'd-rather-sit-on-an-anthill mood, she had no idea. She just was.

And she was losing the feeling in her cheeks from the cold.

She looked over, frowning. There he stood, staring at the lights. "Darryl?"

"I know, I'm working up to it."

Faith sighed. "Or we could just wait until your mother sees me standing behind the cash register, let her draw her own conclusions."

"I already told L.B. about you going to work," he said, which was news to her. "Which is why I'm still out here."

"When'd you do that?"

"Yesterday, actually."

"I see." Her gaze swung to the blinding house. "You know, this is not exactly a groundbreaking event. Me going to work, I mean."

"Tell that to L.B. Besides, it's not about you going to work. It's *why* you have to go to work that's the problem."

"Only if you let him make it one."

"Easy for you to say. You're not the one who got reamed for not having a backup plan."

"Oh, and he *did*?"

"Actually, yeah. He was insured up the wazoo."

"When he was just starting out, when you guys were still babies?" She shook her head. "I somehow doubt it. He was lucky, Darryl. Real lucky, that nothing happened. I do know where your father's coming from," she said gently. "I always have. But this isn't about him, it's about us. How *we* decide to work through *our* challenges. And besides, you most certainly do have a backup plan."

"Oh, yeah? And what might that be?"

"Me," she said. "Now can we go inside before my ears fall off?"

Although the conversation stayed in safe territory all through supper, Darryl didn't miss the glances passing between his parents, the unspoken worry like an untouched side dish planted on his mother's Sears-issue maple dining table right between the mashed potatoes and the three-bean salad. The meal over, it was as if his father'd just scooped it right up and carted it into the TV room, where he was clearly determined to force several helpings down Darryl's throat, never mind that he'd already had more than his fill before he got there.

The kids were all in the living room, helping his mother decorate the new artificial tree they'd carted home from the Wal-Mart in Claremore earlier, while Faith was down the hall, changing Nicky's diaper on his parents' bed. Over the past day or so, the initial panic in the aftermath of the tornado's damage had given way to something far more terrifying—a sense of foreboding that things were never going to be the same, no matter how much he might want it. Not in his work, and not in his marriage.

At this point, he wasn't sure which scared the bejesus out of him more.

He wondered now why he'd thought that proving his willingness to handle the house and kids while Faith was at work would be enough to lure her back into their bed. But nope. Not even after he'd told her he'd figured out how to sleep on one side so he wouldn't snore. So he'd finally ditched the subtle approach and just flat out asked her if she wanted to fool around.

She'd said she was too tired.

Too tired? Since when? In all the time they'd been together, she'd never avoided sex, unless it was that time of the month, she had the flu or something, or she'd just had a baby. Or one of the kids was sick. Other than that, every Tuesday and Friday night, like clockwork, she'd be there in bed, all naked and sweet-smelling, waiting for him. And he'd prided himself on learning where all her sweet spots were, on what each little moan and hitched breath meant, on making himself hold off until she was satisfied. In fact, he had it down to a damn science, is what. Now, suddenly, she didn't want it anymore? What the—?

"You look like you could use this," his father said, jerking him out of his thoughts. Darryl almost smiled at the sight of the pair of longnecks in L.B.'s hands. "Or are you still on those painkillers?"

"Hell, no," he said, relieving his father of the extra bottle. "I stopped those after the first day." They both took long swallows before Darryl said quietly, "This some kind of peace offering?"

With a grunt, L.B. sank into the worn corduroy recliner that had probably grown roots into the sculpted pile carpet. The "den," they euphemistically called the converted, fake-paneled half of his parents' double garage. What it was was a sanctuary for Y chromosomes. His mother's idea, actually, to keep everybody from "stinking up" the rest of the house. Whatever. Barcaloungers, a pool table and oversize electronics were the order of the day, the air permanently stained with the scent of nachos and hops.

"Maybe," L.B. said. "I feel bad about coming down on you so hard. It's just…you know how I feel about…about how it's going to look, is all."

So much for the peace offering. Leaning stiffly against the door frame between the den and the kitchen, Darryl forced another swallow of his beer down a tight throat. "To whom?" he finally asked. As if he didn't know.

"Her parents, for one thing."

"Dammit, L.B.," Darryl said quietly, "it wasn't like I asked that tornado to rip apart the garage. Or my arm. And you know something—I've busted my butt these past twelve years to prove myself to Faith and earn her parents' respect. So how come I can't seem to get yours?"

His father's eyebrows shot up. "What the hell are you talking about?"

"I'm talking about the fact that you're so all-fired concerned about what everybody else is gonna think, you haven't stopped to consider what I might be going through. Because, believe me, the last thing I want is to look like a failure in Faith's eyes."

The words had escaped before he'd even known they were there. Silently swearing, Darryl pushed himself away from the doorway and walked over to the window, staring out at the glittering reindeer on his parents' front lawn.

"You two having problems?"

The worry in his father's voice scraped through him. He hesitated, then said, "All I'm saying is that it's going to be a lot easier for Faith and me to sort through this mess without having to deal with your old-fashioned ideas about who's supposed to do what, on top of everything else. No, maybe I don't like it either, but right now, I'm up the creek without a paddle. Or much of a boat, for that matter. I can't work, I have no place *to* work and…" He stopped.

"And what?"

"Nothing."

"Cut the bull, Darryl. What's goin' on?"

Darryl walked over to lower himself onto the edge of the second recliner, glaring balefully at the cast before lifting his eyes to L.B.'s. "The doctors think I might have some nerve damage in my arm."

His father stared at him for a good long time before he finally said, "But it'll go away, won't it?"

"That's the part nobody knows."

"Are you saying…you might not be able to work again?"

"How many one-handed mechanics do you know?"

L.B. let out a curse.

"Yeah, that's about the size of it," Darryl concurred. "The ironic thing is, of course, if I'd died, Faith would at least have gotten the life insurance money. This way…well, frankly, I'm not sure what she's got."

"And you can stop that talk right now," L.B. said, thunking his empty beer bottle on the end table beside the recliner. "It's a setback, son. Not the end of the world."

The world, no. *His* world was something else again. Fixing cars was the only thing he knew how to do. Only thing he'd ever wanted to do, ever since L.B.'d hauled him up to get a look under the hood of their old Ford pickup when Darryl was four years old. He scrubbed a hand down his face and said. "True. But I got an awful lot of 'I don't knows' to work through. Ryan said we can start with therapy soon as this cast gets off, maybe even sooner. I might get better, might even have a full recovery, but I can't count on it. He said nobody really knew what caused these things, so there was no way to predict what might happen. All we can do is hope for the best."

L.B. sagged back against the chair. "I take it Faith doesn't know?"

"No. And I'd like to keep it that way for now. No sense worrying her any more than she already is, especially if the condition clears up on its own in a few weeks. So don't you tell Mama, either."

After a moment, his father nodded, then said, "So, what is this, exactly? A numbness or something?"

Darryl shrugged. "Sometimes. Other times my arm hurts like a bitch."

"So that's a good sign, right?"

A tight smile stretched across Darryl's face. "I suppose." He stood, walking over to stand by the door, listening to his kids' laughter spilling from the living room on the other side of the kitchen. "You know, everybody says we're a lot alike, you and me."

"And how's that?"

"I don't really know how to let a woman take care of me, either. It feels…backwards. Unnatural. Like I'm not holding up my end of the bargain."

His father pushed himself out of the chair and came to stand beside him, planting a firm hand on his shoulder. "Now you listen to me—I don't care what those doctors say. They don't know what they're talkin' about half the time, anyway. You remember how that hotshot in Tulsa told Edie Samson she had six months to live? That was, what? Ten years ago? And she's still goin' strong. So you're gonna lick this, you know you are. Son, look at me."

After Darryl carefully twisted around to meet his father's gaze, L.B. said, "It's not always easy for me to put my feelings into words, so I probably don't say this as often as I should, but I'm proud of you. Real proud. You've done good by Faith and your kids, as good as any man could have, if not better. And since I didn't exactly have a shining example of what a father was supposed to be when I was growing up, I can't take credit for how you turned out, that's just who you are. And all I know is, whatever it is inside you that's made you like that, it's not gonna let you down now."

It wasn't until some time later, though, after they were back home, the kids all in bed, that L.B.'s words got through. Darryl had gone to the kitchen to get a snack when the murmuring of the ten-o'clock news lured him to the living room doorway. Already in her robe and pajamas, Faith sat cross-legged on the pulled out sofa bed, the steely light from the TV slicking over her face and arms and breasts as she swiftly folded the mountain of fragrant laundry in front of her, the routine so familiar he could predict her every move— sorting everything into piles like a card shark, snapping out every T-shirt before she folded it so there wouldn't be any wrinkles, her fingers a blur as she tucked pairs of socks into tight little balls. He stood there, watching, letting the ordinariness, the consistency of the moment seep into his soul, easing the various nagging aches in his battered body. Maybe it wasn't much, this life of his, but it was *his* life. And it was *real*.

Oh, they'd known about each other from toddlerhood; in a town the size of Haven, that went without saying. But oddly enough, their paths hadn't really crossed all that much. Now and then at church, maybe, or when her mama or daddy came into the filling station and she'd be in the car. She hadn't struck him as the kind of girl to be stuck up, but she never exactly went out of her way to be friendly, either. So he'd been more than a little amazed when she'd started flirting with him once they reached high school. Didn't believe it at first, frankly, thinking maybe she'd been put up to it by some of the other girls. Or that maybe she'd turned into one of those people who got off on making the conquest without any intention of following through.

Oh, how wrong he'd been. Because Faith had followed through, all right. Every chance they could get. Not right off the bat—there'd been a whole lot of cold showers in those early days. And Darryl had never once pressured her to go any further than she wanted to. In fact, more often than not, it was him calling a halt to things, if for no other reason than he wanted her respect every bit as much as he wanted her to know she had his. Although the truth of it was, he didn't just respect her, he'd come about as close to worshipping her as a person could, and still retain at least some ability to function.

Eventually, though, nature won out, and Darryl'd found himself sneaking off to Claremore for condoms. Guess he should've read the fine print, though, 'cause that first box was still half-full when Faith told him she was pregnant. Man, he'd been scared. Couldn't breathe properly for two weeks. Still and all, at least he knew he had something to offer her. Maybe it wasn't much, by some folks' standards, but he knew they'd never starve. Cars and trucks always broke down, eventually, especially around here where folks weren't inclined to trade up every two years, just because. And as long as cars and trucks broke down, they'd need fixing. And that, he was good at. Damn good. So even though the timing hadn't been ideal, there'd never been a question about him being able to support Faith and the baby. As well as all the babies that had come along afterward.

But if he lost the use of his arm, what then? If the only thing he knew how to do was ripped from him, what did he have to offer her?

As if sensing his presence, Faith glanced over, the silvery light skimming over her neck, dipping into the V of her robe. She'd brushed out her hair; it floated wild around her face, teasing. Making him ache. If he concentrated, he could smell her lotion. Could imagine the feel of those soft hands against his skin.

"Thought you'd gone to bed," she said, resuming her folding.

"Couldn't sleep."

Her brows dipped. "You in pain?"

"No," he lied. "But I got hungry, thought I'd get a snack."

"How about a piece of pie?" she said, unfolding herself from the sofa.

"You don't have to get up, I can get it—"

"It's okay," she said, tightening the robe's belt as she passed him, "your mother's lemon meringue's been callin' me for the past half hour."

Now her fragrance barreled through his senses, hurtling him back to the first time they'd made out. For a week, Darryl had hidden the shirt he'd been wearing, which smelled like her, under his pillow, only to nearly cry when his mother had washed it, having found it when she'd gone to change the bed. He'd been a lot more careful about hiding the condoms. Although, considering the outcome, he didn't suppose it had mattered anyway, in the long run.

Underneath his cast, his arm itched so bad it felt like a burn, but that was nothing compared to how bad he wanted to lose himself in all that sweet-smelling softness, to remember and forget, both. Or, barring that, to untie her robe and peel back her pajama top, just to look at her breasts. Oh, my Lord, Faith had the prettiest breasts in the world, as pale and smooth as that lotion she used. That first time she'd taken off her bra for him, he couldn't stop staring, which had made her laugh. But between Faith's being the first set of breasts he'd ever seen outside a magazine, and his being eighteen, who could blame him for being mesmerized? He couldn't decide whether his finding them still mesmerizing after all this time meant he was not a person inclined to bore easily, or that in some ways he'd never grown up.

Of course, thinking along these lines was only making him ache even more, which in turn made him wonder if Faith wasn't right about their relationship being based mostly on sex. Not that he fully understood why this was the problem she seemed to think it was, but if he had a shot in hell of solving whatever was going on between them, he supposed he needed to respect her opinion on the matter, just as he used to when they were first dating.

The dog swung her head around, her ears pitched forward, at his heartfelt sigh.

Faith heard Darryl's heavy sigh behind her as she cut two pieces of pie and set them on plates. No need to ask what that was all about; any woman who'd shared breathing room with a man for more than ten minutes knew an I-want-sex sigh when she heard one.

Feeling unaccountably cruel—not to mention conflicted, since she was feeling somewhat beset by physical desire herself—she set the two plates, then two glasses of milk, on the plastic tablecloth. Darryl lowered himself into the chair opposite, his gaze blatantly sliding over her chest. She wrapped her robe more tightly around herself before sitting across from him, hoping he couldn't see her nipples' response to his heated perusal. A blush stole across her cheeks as she remembered his reaction the first time she'd been naked in front of him. Only once before had she seen that look on a man's face, when Hootch Atkins swore he'd bumped into Jesus Himself on the road to Bushyhead, complete with a blinding light that had left his vision impaired for a good hour or two afterward. Granted, most folks chalked up his "vision" to one too many beers, a bearded vagrant and a passing car with its brights on, but she didn't suppose the facts of the situation rendered Hootch's religious experience any less profound.

"We haven't talked about Christmas yet," Darryl said, startling her. "We should probably keep things simple this year, don't you think?"

She hadn't expected him to embark on a practical discussion, and for some reason she found herself oddly irritated. The heat clicked on; she got up to turn down the thermostat before it woke up the kids. As she did, she caught Darryl slipping Dot a piece of crust underneath the table. They all spoiled the dog something terrible—how anybody could just drive off and leave a pet behind was incomprehensible to her—but at this rate, the poor thing was going to be bigger than the town's water tank. Of course, so was Faith, but that was beside the point.

"Actually," she said, returning to the table, averting her gaze so as to not notice the way the light was dancing over the muscles in Darryl's chest and uncasted arm, "I've already done most of the shopping, so the kids probably won't even notice the difference."

Darryl lowered his glass of milk to the table, frowning. "When did you do that?"

"Off and on since the summer." She slipped a bite of the tart-sweet lemon filling into her mouth; her taste buds did a little happy dance. "It's all stashed in my mother's garage."

"You went shopping by yourself?"

"I didn't set out to do it without you," she said, the hurt in his voice surprising her. "It just sort of happened. Oh, come on, Darryl," she said when he got this disappointed look on his face, "you hate shopping. I figured since I was making all the decisions, anyway, I might as well do it without listening to all your grumbling and mumbling."

"I do not grumble and mumble," he said, so indignantly she had to smile.

"Uh-huh." She lowered her voice, pretending to be him. "'How much longer you think this is gonna be, Faith? Can't we do it all at one store? It's up to you, I don't know anything about any of this, anyway.'"

Now he looked sheepish. "At least I went."

"With about as much enthusiasm as Dot when I take her to the vet. You finished?" When he nodded, she got up and removed his plate, dispatching his left-behind crumbs before setting it in the dishwasher. "Oh, don't

look so hangdog, it's okay. I just finally realized it was silly forcing you to go along. In
any case, the kids' presents are taken care of,
more or less. And paid for. I didn't put anything on the card. Funny, how I did it early
this year," she said, closing the dishwasher.
"Almost as if I knew or something. Except..."

She turned to face him, her breath stutter-
ing slightly at the set of his mouth. Darryl
had one fine mouth, and that was the God's
honest truth. And he'd been blessed with a
natural talent for knowing how to use it, a
thought that sent a shiver hopscotching up
her back and down to...other areas. She gave
everything a second to settle down, then said,
"I hadn't gotten anything for you yet. And
considering...things, I think we should forget about you and me exchanging presents
this year, okay?"

"Damn," he said softly. "Guess this means
I'll have to cancel the order for the Mercedes."

She turned around to put the dishwasher on,
a smile tugging at her mouth. "Well, shoot.
Now it won't be a surprise when you give it
to me next year," she said, only to let out a little yelp of surprise when she twisted back to
find him standing right in front of her, a look
of yearning on his face such as she'd never

seen before. Need blossomed low in her belly, even as she inwardly swore. After all, just like cheap chocolate was better than no chocolate, so was perfunctory sex better than none. What did it matter if he took the same route every time, as long as they always reached their destination? Still, was it such a horrible thing— was she such a horrible person?—to want a short time out from the hormonal oblivion in which they'd spent most of the past dozen years?

His mouth began a sure descent to hers, and she thought, *Oh, hell*, but the hand that lifted to his chest didn't seem terribly inclined to push him away. In five seconds, less, she'd be consumed by not only his desire, but her own as well, because that's how it always was and always had been. Nevertheless, she did everything she could to steady her breathing so he wouldn't know how much she wanted him, to cling to at least a tiny scrap of control over the situation. And wasn't that a joke, considering how long it had been since there'd been much need to guess each other's thoughts or moves? Theirs was a marriage with few surprises left, she thought as her eyes drifted shut, as her lips yielded to his, as they had from the first time he kissed her all those years ago.

And yet, as his mouth moved over hers, a faint "Huh?" went off in some distant part of her brain when his free hand didn't find its way to her breast or slip around to cup her behind and press them together. Somehow, this kiss seemed as tender and hesitant and sweet as that first kiss had been.... And with that, tingles of bittersweet longing tendrilled through her, for something she knew was foolish to even try to recapture.

He was, however, close enough for her to feel his excitement, even as, yep, she responded, right on cue. Only then, right when things looked most hopeless, he pulled back, touching her hair.

"Been a long time since I just kissed you good night," he said, then walked away, leaving her with the disconcerting realization that maybe she didn't know her husband quite as well as she thought she did.

Chapter Five

"Paper or plastic?"

Hunched over her flowered, plastic change purse as she rooted inside it for her debit card, Hazel Dinwiddy smiled up at Faith, her dull-red lipstick fighting a losing battle to stay within the lines.

"Whatever's easiest, honey, I'm not picky. One uses up trees, the other petroleum, so I don't see that one's any better than the other. Oh, would you mind not putting all the cans in one bag? It gets so heavy, you know, and my back just gives me five fits if I lift too much at one time."

"Yes, ma'am. You want your potatoes in a sack?"

She could feel Hazel scrutinizing her with the same unnerving mixture of curiosity and pity she'd seen on nearly every face that had passed through her line since she'd started work four days ago. After the first day, she had forced herself not to let the looks get to her.

"No, don't bother, seems a waste, don't you think?" Hazel said. Her debit card posed like a quivering hummingbird over the terminal, the older woman peered through her crooked glasses at the little box for several seconds before finally dragging her card through the slot. "That was such a shame, what happened to your husband. He's gettin' on okay, I hope?"

Faith flicked a smile at the woman. "Yes, ma'am, he is."

"Well, thank God for that! But the garage! Oh, my goodness, there's barely anything left, is there? Although I noticed that great big old Dumpster when I passed by, so I guess that means they'll start cleaning it up pretty soon."

"Dumpster?" Faith said over the scanner's beep.

"Oh, yes, big as a house. Saw Darryl and his daddy, too, tossin' stuff into it right and left, although Darryl looked to be having quite a time of it, what with one arm bein' in a cast and all. A *real* shame. Not that it means anything one way or the other to me, since I haven't driven since, Lord, I don't even remember when, but other folks are probably pretty anxious to see Darryl back in business. I'll tell you what, though, I sure wish they'd get rid of that tree sittin' in the middle of Ivy Gardner's roof. It's downright dangerous, with all those loose limbs. Every time the wind blows I hold my breath one of 'em doesn't come crashing through my window. You'd think, with her being the mayor-elect and all, she'd be more on top of things, but I don't know. Back in '86, when that big thunderstorm uprooted our fifty-foot ash—You remember that? No, I don't suppose you do, you would've been too little. I don't care what anybody says, that was a twister, sure as the day is long. Anyway, my Stanley had that tree cut up for firewood the next day. But folks these days… I don't know, guess nobody feels like they need to hurry about anything, anymore…."

"I'm sorry, Hazel, you need to swipe your card again, it didn't take the first time."

While the old woman went on about how silly it was, wasn't it, that you had to swipe your card a different way in every store, you'd think they'd come up with one machine that'd work the same everywhere, Faith nodded and said "Uh-huh," a couple of times as she bagged the old woman's Banquet frozen dinners and canned grapefruit juice and Wonder bread, wondering herself about Dumpsters and mule-headed husbands, all the while thinking if she heard "Jingle Bell Rock" once more she'd scream. How she was going to maintain her sanity for the nearly three weeks left before Christmas, she had no idea.

Not that she wasn't grateful. They needed the money, the job wasn't exactly mentally taxing and all the employees seemed to get along well enough. Heaven knew there were a lot worse things she could be doing. But once the initial thrill of landing a job wore off, she quickly realized that in the dessert department, this job was like being served a bowl of canned fruit cocktail instead of, say, chocolate cream pie.

Faith loaded Hazel's purchases into her little red wagon, taking care to keep the potatoes away from the bread, and the old woman trundled off, her muddied, ankle-high boots barely visible underneath her worn wool coat.

"So how *is* it going with getting the garage up and running again?" Faith heard behind her.

Leaning over to relieve her aching back—for the first time in an hour, her line was empty, hallelujah—Faith glanced at Rosie Chavez, the cashier in the next lane. A fixture at the store ever since Faith could remember—a conservative guess would put her at twice both Faith's age and weight—Rosie dug a pen into the dark-rooted center of her long, blond corkscrew curls. "Because, I'm tellin' you, Manny's fit to be tied, havin' to go all the way to Claremore to fill up."

Faith swallowed down her sigh. To a person, everybody she ran into seemed to be taking her and Darryl's misfortune personally.

"Depends on when we get the insurance money, I guess. And how fast Darryl heals. The office wasn't hit too bad, though, and the pumps passed inspection, so I expect the gas station'll be up and running pretty soon—"

"Faith? Honey?"

Her stomach fell. Not that it should; she and her mother-in-law had always gotten on just fine, even if they weren't exactly close. Even so, a body could only take so much goodwill and not crack under the pressure.

"Well, hey, Renee! You want paper or plastic today?"

"Oh…plastic, I suppose," Renee said in her

soft voice, the light slanting through the front window glinting in the whorls of one of Luralene's finer hairstyling creations as she set a plastic bag of fresh green beans on the belt. A staunch subscriber to the school of "never letting herself go," Darryl's mama was one of those women who somehow managed to look older and younger than her real age at the same time. Faith had never seen the petite, trim-figured woman that her honey-blond hair wasn't done within an inch of its life or that her outfits weren't flawlessly coordinated, in their own way. Today's ensemble involved a fuzzy, pink turtleneck sweater and a white fake fur jacket. Stiletto heels, too, most likely.

A smile flickered in Faith's direction. "I guess this is going to take a little getting used to. Seeing you here. I mean—" she unloaded a six-pack of Bud, two cans of store-brand tuna in water, a bag of egg noodles "—for you, too. You must be missing your babies something fierce."

"Oh, well, you know…" Faith scanned the tuna. "Most of 'em are in school now. And Darryl'll be with them, so I imagine they'll be okay."

"But with him still in his cast…"

Smiling brightly, she met her mother-in-law's worried gold-green eyes, half-hidden under wispy, but stiff, bangs. Renee wore her hair swept up off her neck today with several loose pieces floating around her face, à la Dolly Parton circa 1978.

"You'd be surprised," Faith said, her eyes on her task. "About the only thing he can't do is change diapers, so the baby's with my mother while I'm here. Didn't Darryl tell you how we worked everything out? I even left him a schedule."

A net bag of oranges, three boxes of Wheaties and a rump roast trundled past. "Oh, he did. But it's just…such a change. And you know how men are when it comes to domestic chores—half the time you end up cleaning up their messes, anyway, to the point where it's just easier to do it yourself to begin with. I mean, heaven knows, Darryl's a good father…." She laughed a little nervously. "But I'm not so sure he's cut out to be a mama!"

Faith laughed, too, mainly because it was either that or cry. Her own mother was reasonably domestic, insofar as they'd never been in any real danger of starving or being swallowed up by dust bunnies; but the first time Faith set foot in Renee's house, she'd felt as if she'd entered a holy shrine. The house wasn't just clean, it *gleamed*. And cooking... oh, my word. Every pot, pan and kitchen gadget known to man. An entire bookcase devoted to cookbooks. Faith did well to follow the recipe on the back of a soup can. That Darryl had gone all these years without once comparing Faith to his mother—at least, not out loud—was a true testament to his character. Nor had Renee ever overtly criticized her. Still, a young wife knew when a challenge had been issued, no matter how subtle.

"I know this isn't ideal, Renee," Faith said levelly, "but it's not like we asked to have the rug yanked out from under us." She jerked a head of lettuce across the scanner and dumped it into the waiting bag. "I'm sure we'll come through just fine, with a little support here and there."

"Oh, you can count on that, honey! In fact, I told Darryl he can bring the kids over anytime, it's no bother, although he said he'd already made arrangements for your mother to take care of Sierra today." Faith's eyes shot to hers. "Because he obviously couldn't have the baby around all that debris? Oh, my goodness, honey—didn't he tell you about getting the Dumpster?"

Right. With a sigh, Faith resumed her scanning, since another customer had pulled in behind Renee and probably wouldn't be too pleased about being kept waiting while her cashier dealt with assorted family issues.

"Actually, no, he didn't. Although Hazel went through a little bit ago and she'd told me about it." She flashed a smile. "I'd just forgotten, that's all."

"Now, don't be put out with him, honey. If you ask me, it'll do him good, being proactive and all. Anyway. I thought maybe I'd drop off a couple of casseroles later, since he said you told him he's to see to supper when you're working. All he has to do is heat 'em up in the oven, no problem. Although you know, it's easy as pie to throw a chicken in the Crock-Pot before you leave—"

"Okay, your total is $34.56. And thanks, Renee, that's real nice of you. I'm sure Darryl will be very grateful."

Except, as she validated Renee's check, she thought back to all those endless days when she'd been home alone with a houseful of babies, when Darryl had been at work from seven in the morning until long after it got dark. Not that Faith had ever expected either of their mothers to rescue her—after all, the babies had been her idea. Hers and Darryl's. Sure, a couple of 'em had been surprises, but they'd all been eagerly welcomed. And ninety-five percent of the time Faith had coped on her own just fine. But that other five percent…well, she would have appreciated the occasional offer to take the kids off *Faith's* hands for a couple hours, or a casserole now and again so *Faith* wouldn't have had to cook.

However, since it wasn't in her nature to be small, she let it go.

The register spat out Renee's receipt, which Faith handed to her, jumping a little when the other woman clasped her wrist.

"I'm sure nobody understands more than you the blessings that can come out of trials, but still… I'm praying every day that things get back to normal for you and Darryl as soon as possible. It must be drivin' the boy nuts, having things all topsy-turvy like this. And between you and me…" She leaned closer, her words clearly intended for Faith's ears alone. Unlike her perfume, which was clearly intended for half the county. "It can put a real strain on a marriage when a man feels, you know. Like he's lost control of his life. They get scared, Faithie."

Faith reared back, frowning. "Of what?"

One side of her mouth lifted. "Of finding out we don't need them nearly as much as they need us." Renee gave Faith's hand a brief, final squeeze, then tucked her wallet back inside her purse. "Okay, honey…don't work too hard. And I'll swing those casseroles by a little later, if that's okay. Oh! And Darryl asked me to pick Heather up from school and take her to dance class. It seems forever since she and I spent any time together, just the two of us."

Faith thought she heard a wistfulness in her mother-in-law's voice that took her a little by surprise, prompting her to say, "You know, Renee, anytime you want to take Heather for a little while, all you have to do is ask. I'm sure she'd be thrilled to have a break from her brothers and sisters now and again." She smiled. "Not to mention her mother. She's getting to that stage, you know."

"Well, that's what I was thinking, honey, but I didn't want to presume." The older woman's face brightened. "Maybe she'd like me to start teachin' her how to cook!"

Knock yourself out, Faith thought but did not say.

Speaking of knocking somebody out…

As soon as she went on break, she headed to the garage. As she got closer she could see Darryl and his father tossing junk into the Dumpster, the bangs and clangs muffled by the howl of the wind. She saw L.B. poke Darryl, who looked in her direction.

"Hey, honey," he said, straightening up. Even though it was barely thirty degrees, he was only wearing a long-sleeved T-shirt, one they'd slit the seam on to get it over the cast. The last thing he needed was to come down with pneumonia on top of everything else. "I thought you were at work?"

"I'm on break. I have to be back in ten minutes. Hazel Dinwiddy came through my line, told me y'all were over here." L.B., she noticed, picked that moment to find something to do elsewhere. "What's goin' on?"

"I'm cleaning up, that's what's goin' on."

"With a broken arm?"

"That's not the arm I'm using. And don't start in about how I'm supposed to be home with Sierra. Your mother told me to bring her on over to the day care until the other kids got off school."

"I'm not concerned about Sierra, I'm concerned about you. I heard the doctor flat out tell you to take it easy for at least a few weeks, give yourself a chance to heal."

Darryl turned away and hefted another splintered chunk of wood into the Dumpster. "That's exactly what I'm doing."

"By strainin' yourself like this? For heaven's sake, Darryl, your ribs—"

"Are fine."

"Uh-huh. Like I can't see how slowly you move when you don't think I'm looking. Besides, I remember when I fell off my bike when I was twelve and banged up my rib cage something terrible. Took six weeks before I could even breathe normally, let alone do anything strenuous. So don't give me this song and dance about how it doesn't hurt."

"Didn't say they didn't hurt." Another splintered two-by-four flew into the Dumpster. "That doesn't mean I'm ready to be put down yet."

She caught a whiff of something in his words that made her frown. "Nobody's talkin' about putting you down, for pity's sake," she said. "But you're not going to be any good to me or anybody else if you aggravate your injuries and end up being out of commission even longer!"

He wheeled on her then, the effort not to wince plain on his face.

"Would it kill you to at least let me enjoy the *illusion* that I've got some control over the situation? Why are you trying to make me feel worse about this than I already do?"

"I'm not! What happened isn't your fault, but neither is it your responsibility to fix it all by yourself, either!"

"And you know I can't just sit around, Faith, doin' nothing," he said, his voice as harsh as the wind whipping her hair around her face. "Anyway, L.B. and I figured we may as well get as much of this cleared away while the weather holds. God alone knows when the insurance money's going to come in, but we can probably get the office fixed up, at least, so I can start selling gas again. The sooner I do that, the sooner we can get back to normal."

For a moment, the word hovered between them, like a partially deflated balloon, only to be whisked away by the wind.

"I'll be home around eight," Faith said flatly. "Your mother said she's bringin' over a couple of casseroles. Could you make sure the kids are fed and have their homework done by seven?"

"I'll do my best," he said.

She smiled weakly. "You always do," she said, then walked away, her hands stuffed in her pockets.

Darryl stared after her, feeling like he'd swallowed a hunk of that chewed-up wood. Control over the situation? Who the hell was he kidding? But then, even he had said it was only an illusion.

But Faith and him…had that all been an illusion, too? And if so, what the hell was he supposed to do about it?

He swallowed past the knot in his throat as he watched her bright orange coat fade into the distance.

Do you still need me, Faithie?
Do you?

Having arrived early to fetch Heather, Renee took up the latest women's fiction novel her online book club had been reading over the past couple weeks. She wasn't sure she liked it all that much, to be truthful—the characters could stand a little lightening up, in her opinion—but she was a firm believer in improving one's mind, even if it was sometimes uncomfortable. As far as she was concerned, a day without learning at least one new thing was a day wasted, a goal she found much easier to attain since they'd gotten Internet hookup. Of course, she sometimes learned about things she'd just as soon not, but she supposed knowledge wasn't always something you could pick and choose, like bunches of broccoli or a pair of shoes.

It was cold in the car, but keeping the heat on wasted gas. Something else she'd learned on the internet. Along with the fact that SUVs were terrible gas hogs. Unfortunately, L.B. had just bought her an almost-new Ford Expedition, and she couldn't very well tell him to take it back, could she? So she assuaged her conscience by conserving where she could.

Realizing she'd read the same paragraph three times, Renee shoved the book back into her purse, then blew out a breath, tapping her fingernails on the steering wheel. She hated waiting, but she hated being late worse. Getting places early gave her a sense of control over the situation, something not easily come by these days. Oh, my goodness, it was eating her alive, wondering what was going on with Faith and Darryl. *Really* going on, not whatever this front was they were putting on for everybody. She'd been tempted to ask Didi, but she and Faith's mother had never really been close. Nobody's fault, she and Didi were just too different in personality and temperament, that was all.

In any case, she only hoped it was the strain of current circumstances and not something more far-reaching causing the worried, slightly confused look on Darryl's face, the reluctance on Faith's part to look Renee right in the eye. She told herself it wouldn't be the end of the world if the marriage didn't work out—people got divorced right and left these days, and most seemed to survive it okay—but it would just about kill L.B. Therefore, since Renee wasn't ready to be a widow just yet, she felt impelled to get to the heart of the problem before it took root. As far as she could tell, her oldest granddaughter was probably the quickest and most expedient route to the information she sought.

Oh! There was the bell. Not three seconds later, the doors burst open and a flood of kids poured out of the building, making Renee even more glad she'd gotten there early enough to park right in front. Spotting Heather, she got out to wave the girl over, warmth flooding her chest when the girl smiled hugely in response. To be honest,

Renee hadn't been all that sure she was ready to be a grandmother at forty-two, but from the moment she'd laid eyes on her first granddaughter she'd been completely and hopelessly smitten. L.B. had given her untold grief about her inability to resist every little dress and pair of lace-trimmed booties she laid her eyes on, but after three sons, she couldn't help it. Besides, Darryl and Faith went on to have two more girls, anyway, so Renee regarded the purchases as an investment. L.B. had only grunted when she'd pointed this out.

"There's a sandwich and a carton of chocolate milk in the bag, there," she said when the child got in and buckled her seat belt. "I thought you might be hungry."

"Cool! I'm starving. Thanks, Nanny!"

Renee consoled herself with the knowledge that at least she didn't *look* like a goat.

As her granddaughter devoured the sandwich like she hadn't eaten in three years—thank goodness the child hadn't fallen victim to all those silly fad diets the young girls seemed so keen on these days—Renee eased out into the traffic, the V-8 purring like an overfed, contented cat.

"I saw your mama earlier, when I was out doing my grocery shopping."

Heather shrugged, taking a big swig from the carton. For all her long legs and budding breasts, she was still a little girl, and Renee was in no big hurry to see her grow up. She did, however, sometimes worry about the child, who tended to take more on her slender shoulders than she should. Why, Renee had nearly fallen over when Darryl had told her about the girl's finding work, just so she could take her ballet classes. And her only being eleven years old. No doubt about it, Heather was going to make something of herself, a thought that sent a spurt of pride through Renee, enough to at least somewhat mitigate the worry.

"How are you and the other kids doing, with your mama goin' to work these days?"

Another shrug. "Okay, I guess." Heather stuffed the last corner of the sandwich in her mouth and said around it, "Better than I thought, actually. Considering that Daddy's, like, totally clueless." She swallowed. "I'm here to tell you, if I ever have boys? You better believe they're going to know their way around the kitchen and laundry room."

"But other than that," Renee said, vaguely irritated, "things are…okay?"

Much too smart for her own good, the child

turned to her, a neat little crease settled between her light brows. "Okay how?"

"Well, I don't know, do I?" Renee said, trying to keep the exasperation out of her voice. Honestly, fishing for information shouldn't be this hard, especially considering her years of experience. "I just meant...do things seem, I don't know. Normal." She glanced over at the frowning face, then back at the road, finally spitting out, "Between your mama and daddy, I mean."

The girl turned back around, her mouth tucked down at the corners. That she hadn't immediately replied told Renee more than she realized she wanted to know, after all. Except it was too late now, wasn't it? So she reached over and patted her granddaughter's knee.

"It's okay, baby. You know you can tell me anything."

Another several seconds followed before Heather finally said, "Mama's been sleeping out in the living room since the accident."

Renee sucked in a breath. Oh, dear. If Darryl was anything like his father—and she strongly suspected he was, which was why he and Faith had had to get married to begin with, not to mention why they had five children—this was not a welcome turn of events. Not at all. Not that Renee believed that a woman was obligated to have sex with her husband just because, but L.B. had always been grumpy as a bear if he'd had to go for more than a week or so without. The Andrews men might be prone to elevated cholesterol levels, but a lack of testosterone had never been an issue.

"Are you sure?"

"Yes, ma'am. I don't think Daddy's real happy about it, either. Also…"

"What?"

"I don't know, I can't exactly explain it. It's just…when they talk to each other? The words don't sound any different, I guess, but they *feel* different. Like there's lots of stuff they're not saying. Ohmigosh, Nanny— *please* don't say anything! I don't think they want anybody to know."

"I won't say a word, honey," Renee said, lowering her left hand to cross her fingers. "But you know, this business with the tornado and all…" She glanced over. "I imagine your parents are just real worried about how everything's gonna work out. And that often makes things tense. But they love each other, you know they do, so you just have to be as supportive as you know how to help them get through this."

"So you think things'll be okay?" Heather asked, and the worry in her voice nearly broke Renee's heart. They pulled into the rutted yard fronting the barn where Carly Stewart ran her dance school; Renee put the car in Park, then reached over to give her grandbaby a big hug.

"I'm sure of it, sweetie. Now you better get," she said, releasing her. "And Daddy'll be here at five-thirty to pick you up," she added, her words lost in the slam of the passenger door.

Instead of driving off right away, though, Renee sat in the car, her hands clamped around her first-ever leather-covered steering wheel, trying to order her thought—a process that seemed harder and harder to do as she got older, right when she needed the ability the most. It seemed as though every time she turned around, one part of her life or another was undergoing some sort of upheaval. Of course, she supposed that was true for most people, but this time, she felt as though something deep inside her was shifting, as well.

She shut her eyes, thinking, *Honestly.* Her son's marriage could be in jeopardy, and here she was, thinking of herself. And she really was worried about Faith and Darryl, especially after catching that look today in her daughter-in-law's eyes. The eye thing was like some kind of code women had developed over thousands of years, obeying some unspoken rule that one simply did not speak of one's domestic troubles. Renee finally put the Expedition into Reverse, wondering what on earth they were all so afraid of that they couldn't just come out and admit when they were having marital difficulties.

Because nobody wants to look like a failure, she thought with a sigh, executing a three-point turn and pulling back out onto the road. But then, men were even worse, weren't they? Take L.B., for instance. Oh, my, Renee's mother had nearly had kittens when Renee took up with the tall, rough-looking young man (thirty years and fifty pounds ago, L.B. had been almost unbearably handsome, at least in Renee's eyes), the son of a man her mother openly called a "no-account bum."

"Mark my words," Mama had said, "once trailer trash, always trailer trash."

Well, Renee had proved her mother wrong, hadn't she? Or rather, L.B. had. There'd been a few boyfriends before L.B., but not a one of them had worshipped her like he did. And that hadn't changed in more than thirty years of marriage. Right from the outset, L.B. had made sure Renee never had to worry about anything, working his fingers to the bone so she could stay home with their boys, a luxury neither of their mothers had. Oh, no, L.B. was nothing like his daddy. And Renee, whose own father had more or less vanished from her life after her parents' divorce when she was five, was hardly going to find fault with a man whose every thought and action were geared to making sure she was taken care of.

She frowned as something like a shadow flitted through her brain. Now why do you suppose her thoughts had chosen to go down that particular path?

Realizing it was only a hop, skip and a jump to the Double Arrow, the motel-turned-resort where her youngest son, Danny, was a part-time manager, she decided to make a quick stop.

What had once been a dingy, run-down motel with a few rattletrap cabins dotting the woods behind was now a real pretty little resort, thanks to the combined efforts of Hank Logan, a retired cop and the eldest of the three Logan brothers, and his partner, Joe Salazar. It being December, the landscape was bare and brown, but the newly renovated main building, with its bright white stucco walls and red-tiled roof, glittered in the late afternoon sun. As she slid out of the car, Renee spotted Jenna Logan, Hank's new wife, up on a ladder draping Christmas greens along the edge of the roof, her shoulder-length, light-blond hair blowing softly in the chilly breeze.

Even in jeans and one of those big fisherman sweaters, the trim, forty-something Easterner exuded a sophistication that Renee wouldn't be able to pull off in a million years. Apparently sensing Renee's approach, Jenna twisted on the ladder, her face splitting into a wide smile. "How's it look so far?"

Blushing at being asked her opinion, she nodded in approval. "Those folks who decorate the White House could take a lesson from you," she said, and Jenna laughed. "So you're not working on a book?" Renee asked.

Jenna was a popular mystery author, making her something of a local celebrity, although she was not one to put on airs. "Yeah, but I'm stuck," she sighed. "So I'm hoping this will jar something loose in my brain." She descended the ladder, moved it over. "How's Darryl doing? I saw Faith when I was in the store the other day, but I didn't get in her lane so we didn't talk."

"Oh, Darryl's getting on okay," Renee said, holding her coat a little more tightly around her. The breeze had begun to pick up, a damp one that bit right through her. "And Faith's just working at the store temporarily, you know, until Darryl gets the business back up and running."

She thought maybe Jenna tossed her a funny look, but it might have been a trick of the light. More boughs in tow, the blonde climbed back up the ladder. "Well, please give them my best, if you see them before I do." She shoved a hunk of greens in place, adding, "Darryl's a damn good mechanic, so here's hoping both he and the garage get fixed soon!"

Renee said she certainly hoped so, too, then scurried into the office before her teeth started chattering, sighing in pleasure as warmth from the snapping blaze in the new fireplace washed over her icy skin. The place sure looked nothing like Renee remembered. The previous typical motel decor—cheap paneling, tacky gold, brown and green geometric patterned carpeting, a scarred check-in counter—had given way to Southwest pastels, a tile floor with real Native American carpets, troweled walls, whitewashed wood.

And the fireplace, in front of which a pair of tan leather chairs beckoned.

"Renee! Hi!"

She turned, smiling at her daughter-in-law SueEllen, who'd apparently come out from the back at Renee's entrance. With her long, straight hair, her slender figure inside a cropped sweater and a pair of close-fitting bell bottom jeans, the gal hardly looked old enough to be working, let alone a wife and mother, as well. Renee had to remind herself that she hadn't been older when David, her oldest, had come along, and she'd done okay.

"Where's the baby?" Renee said, her high heels clicking on the tile as she crossed to the front desk.

"Oh, I'm sorry…he's asleep." A wrinkle marred the space between her daughter-in-law's eyebrows. "Do…do you want me to get him up?"

"Bite your tongue, honey—first rule of motherhood is never wake a baby before it's time to." She noticed SueEllen's silver laptop open on a counter against the back wall. Her daughter-in-law had taken several courses on designing websites and in the past few months had started her own business doing just that. How she juggled that, manning the front desk and taking care of a baby, Renee had no idea. "Is Danny here?"

"No, he's gone up to Tulsa to do some research on a big project he's doin'," SueEllen said, referring to Danny's working toward his architecture degree, Renee supposed. My goodness, the child looked pale. Sue-Ellen was a darling girl, but Renee sometimes wished she'd put on a little makeup now and again to give herself some color. One thing about Faithie, she never left the house without makeup. And maybe she'd put on a few pounds with all those pregnancies, but Renee sincerely doubted that Faith was one of those women who would let herself go. Unlike David's wife, Brenda, who after two kids had just ballooned, there was no other word for it. And her being a corporate executive, too. David didn't seem to care, which was honorable of him, but Renee was a firm believer than a wife owed it to her husband to make as much of herself as she could.

In any case, SueEllen was obviously busy, so Renee said to give Danny and Scottie her love, and walked back outside, feeling slightly unfocused.

Which was ridiculous, since she had casseroles to make, didn't she?

Once back home, she changed into clothes more suited for kitchen chores, then set about gathering ingredients—tuna, noodles, cream of mushroom soup. After more than thirty years, her hands knew what to do with barely a prompt from her brain. Normally, she found the orderly routine soothing. But today the house was just too darn quiet and her brain was just too darn agitated.

She clicked on the small kitchen TV L.B. had given her for Christmas a few years ago, so she could cook and not miss her soaps. She knew they were silly and completely unrealistic, but really, there was only so much drama to be found in making a tuna noodle casserole.

Except today, try as she might, she just couldn't keep her mind on the goings on in Llanview. Instead her thoughts kept bouncing from one thing to another like the boys used to do with their beds when they'd been little. Drove her nuts then, too.

The casseroles assembled, she put them in the oven, then wandered out into her living room, although she had no idea what to do with herself once she got there. It had been nearly two years since Danny had left, and she still hadn't gotten used to not having anybody to do for. Oh, she still had L.B., of course, but that was different. And then, with a surge of heat great enough to make her cheeks burn, it struck her that she was the only woman she knew without any sense of purpose whatsoever outside of keeping her house spotless and her husband happy.

Oh, my.

Frowning, Renee flapped the hem of her sweater until the hot flash dissipated, wondering if, along with the physical and emotional upheaval of menopause, all this hormone shifting could bring about a complete personality change, as well. She'd been completely content with her life for more than thirty years. Now, suddenly, she realized she had nothing to show for those thirty years that couldn't be defined in terms of what she'd done for somebody else.

She sank into the edge of her flowered sofa, completely and utterly exhausted.

Chapter Six

"C'n we put the tree up tonight, Daddy? Pleeease?"

At least, that's what Darryl thought Jake said over all the high-pitched hollering going on out in the living room. Sierra tormenting Crystal, most likely. Dot was barking her head off, too, although Darryl couldn't quite tell if the dog was egging 'em on or trying to get 'em to shut up. He shoved the casserole into the oven—thank God for his mother, was all he had to say—banging the door shut with his hip. Nicky was still at the church day-care center with Didi, Heather at dance class, but that still left three kids to drive him nuts.

These past four days had been among the longest in his life. Doing this for months—or worse, from here on in—was enough to make his blood run cold.

Out in the other room, the hollering turned to wails. Two seconds later, his eight-year-old appeared, struggling under the weight of her sobbing baby sister. A red face and scrawny arms jutted out from over Crystal's stranglehold around Sierra's chest.

"She fell and banged her head on the coffee table," Crystal yelled over the caterwauling. "She's not bleedin', though," the older girl said calmly as Darryl lunged to scoop Sierra out of Crystal's arms before she choked to death. "She just makes a lot of noise, is all. I don't think she's used to where stuff is yet from when Mama moved everything around. *Again*," she added with a huff.

Yeah, Faith did have this thing about rearranging the furniture every few months. Made him crazy, too. Darryl dropped onto one of the kitchen chairs, ignoring the wildfire racing up his bum arm. "Hold her still so I can get a look at this," he barked at Crystal, then gently lifted curly wisps of white-blond hair away from the tiny girl's forehead. Damn. That was gonna be one nasty goose egg. The three-year-old's sobs had already begun to subside, thanks to her thumb stopping up her mouth, Darryl suspected. But the way she looked at him with those huge, water-logged green eyes just tore him to pieces.

"She gonna be okay?" Jake said at his elbow.

"Sure she is." Although Darryl doubted *he'd* be, once his wife got a load of that knot on her baby's head.

"Kiss it," Sierra said around her thumb, so Darryl did. Barely. Last thing he wanted was to set her off again.

He carted the toddler back out to the living room and set her down, shoved all the magazines and crap off the coffee table, grabbed one end and dragged it through the kitchen and out to the garage. Three kids and the dog trailed him, tripping over each other. Crisis clearly over, Jake said, "So…about the tree?"

"What tree?" Crystal asked in her breathy little voice.

"The Christmas tree, dummy," he said, and Crystal's blue eyes bounced up to Darryl, her mouth in a perfect little *O*. Between that and the mess of blond curls quivering around her face, she looked just like an angel. Until her hands slammed onto skinny little hips, lost somewhere underneath one of her older sister's hand-me-down sweatshirts.

"Yeah, what's up with that?" she said. "Mama always puts it up right after Thanksgiving. We *never* go this long without a tree."

Darryl sighed. Then led them all back into the kitchen, where he valiantly fought against sitting back down. Because he knew if he stopped moving, he'd *stop moving*. Not that he'd ever admit this to Faith, but he'd definitely overdone it with the cleaning up today. What hadn't hurt before sure as hell hurt now. At the moment, he barely had the energy to look at a tree, let alone set one up. And just how was he supposed to put it together with one hand? "Christmas isn't for another three weeks yet. What's the rush?"

"Two-and-a-half weeks," Crystal said, her arms now crossed over her flat little chest. "I counted. And the rush is, if we don't get the tree up, Santa's gonna think we've turned Muslim or Jewish or something and then he won't put us on his Stop Here list."

Jake spun around and headed back toward the garage. "C'mon, Crys, I know 'xactly where it is, it's in that big box over in the corner...hey!" he yelped when Darryl snagged him by the back of his plaid shirt.

"I got a better idea—how about you guys help me get this place at least somewhat cleaned up before your mother gets home from work? You can start by collecting the two hundred or so plates and glasses and what-all you managed to use in the past two hours, and load the dishwasher. Even you, ladybug," he said to Sierra, who'd obviously recuperated from the Attack of the Killer Coffee Table. "You can put all your toys in your basket, okay? What?" he added when he realized three sets of eyes were burning holes into him.

"I hate this," Crystal said softly, tears pooling over her lower lashes.

"That I asked you to help clean up?"

She shook her head, looking down at her sneakers. Dot wedged herself between the kids, licking first Crystal's fingers, then Jake's. With a sigh, Darryl squatted in front of them, fighting to keep his balance when Sierra tried to climb up on his knee.

"This is hard on all of us," he said. "I miss Mama, too."

Crystal nailed him with her gaze. "You don't even know how to cook."

"Neither does Mama," Jake said, and Crystal slugged him.

"She does, too, bug brain. Whaddya call hot dogs an' spaghetti and all that stuff?"

"Well, you know," Darryl said, "Mama's had lots of years to perfect her…skills. I've only been doing this for a few days. And with one arm, to boot." He tapped her nose. "So you think maybe you could cut me a little slack?"

Apparently, that merited a couple seconds of consideration before she finally let out a long, solemn sigh. "Yeah, I guess. But I still wish things were the way they used to be," she said, then drifted out to the living room, her brother and sister in tow.

"Yeah," Darryl muttered as he got to his feet. "Me, too." Then he glanced at the kitchen clock and nearly choked. Holy crap! How did it get to be that late?

"Crys, Jake! Grab your coats, we've gotta get out of here, like, yesterday!"

"That's okay," his son called from the living room. "Me and Crystal can stay here."

Darryl charged into the room to find all three kids sprawled on their stomachs in front of the TV, watching…something. Jake half rolled over to look up at him. "She can watch us. Huh, Crys?"

"Sure, no sweat," the eight-year-old said, chin braced in the V of her hands.

"Yeah, that'd work," Darryl said, tossing them their coats from where they'd dumped them on the couch after school. "If the authorities didn't string me up, your mother sure as heck would. Crys, Jake, anybody—get Sierra into her coat so we can get outta here!"

A half hour or so later, all five of his chicks gathered, he pulled into the driveway, the older kids out of the Suburban before he could even get his seat belt undone, each one determined to beat the others to the front door. He'd just about gotten Nicky out of his car seat—it was truly amazing what a man could do with only one arm if he put his mind to it—when the constant, high-pitched *eeeeee* of the smoke alarm registered. He backed out of the car so fast he banged his head, spinning around just as Heather appeared in a cloud of smoke—and stars—at the front door.

"Uh, Daddy...? Did you leave something in the oven?"

The word he let loose would probably scar the kids for life.

Sometime after eight, Faith pulled into her driveway, cut the engine and draped herself over the steering wheel, listening to assorted pings and ticks and clunks as the engine in

Darryl's pickup cooled down. Bone-tired didn't even begin to describe how she felt. All she wanted was to sleep for about three years. Right here. Except then she'd freeze to death. Besides, there'd be food in the house. Real food. Food she hadn't had to cook.

Finally, her arm muscles obeyed her brain's message to open the truck door, just as her house belched forth an assortment of extremely energetic little people, all yelling "Mama! Mama! Mama!" at the tops of their lungs as they rocketed toward the truck. Tears sprang to her eyes, and not from joy. Sucking in a deep breath, Faith slid to the ground, half surprised that her legs supported her. Instantly a host of small arms strangled her waist and thighs as three unbelievably shrill little voices assaulted her eardrums. Honestly, you'd think she'd been lost at sea for six months, not gone since this morning—

"Mama! Daddy forgot to—"

"—an' my eyes hurted, Mama—"

"—all black. It was so cool!"

"Hold on, hold on, I can't understand you when you're all talking at once...." But by this time Faith and her parasites had gotten inside, where the acrid stench of charred tuna and noodles smacked her in the face. An arctic gale blew through the house, courtesy of every window being open.

And that was just the opening act.

From his playpen in the living room, Nicky let out a squealed "Ma!" and hauled himself to his feet. His unpajama'd feet. In fact, nobody was in their pjs. The Christmas tree lay in pieces all over the floor; there were plates and glasses and shoes and backpacks and boxes of decorations everywhere; the damn dog was barking her fool head off because Jake was now singing "Jingle Bells" loud enough to wake the dead. Crystal had launched into a tearful saga about how Billy Magee kept calling her dumb, so she went to tell her teacher, only then *she* got into trouble, not Billy. And Faith's back hurt and her head throbbed and just where the Sam Hill was her husband?

"Mama?" Heather asked, her voice saturated with worry, just as Darryl appeared, wearing the pleading, lost expression of a man clearly in over his head.

"I'm really sorry about the casserole. I guess I'm not used to keepin' tabs when something's in the oven. I gave the kids graham crackers so they wouldn't starve, but I thought I'd wait and see what you wanted to do about supper. And where do you keep the paper towels? We're all out."

Faith felt her eyes pop wide open. "It's eight-thirty and the kids haven't had *dinner yet?* And where do you *think* I keep the paper towels? In the pantry where we've kept all the paper supplies for the entire *ten years we've lived in this house!*" The last words came out on enough of a shriek to shut up everybody, including the dog.

After several seconds of profound silence, Nicky burst into tears. Faith took in five other horrified expressions before she spun around and stomped down the hall, slamming the bedroom door shut behind her.

"Maybe you shouldn't've asked her about the towels," Heather said, scooping a howling Nicky out of his playpen, and Darryl said, "We got any chocolate in the house?"

Jake dashed back to his room, returning ten seconds later with a half-eaten chocolate bunny from Easter that had apparently been keeping the fuzzier ones under his bed company. Fortunately, Crystal coughed up her leftover Halloween stash—Darryl made sure they were talking *this* Halloween—which contained an assortment of dust-free, miniature chocolate bars. After crossing his heart to Crystal and swearing he'd replace them (with interest), Darryl grabbed the plastic pumpkin and marched down the hall, flinching when he reached the bedroom door and something thudded against it.

After a glance toward his wide-eyed offspring clustered at the end of the hall, and praying he had enough candy (wondering if there was enough candy in the world), he knocked. Loud, unladylike nose-blowing ensued for several seconds before he heard: "*What?*"

"I've got chocolate."

He jumped again when the door swung open, revealing one very puffy-eyed, red-nosed, seriously annoyed woman. "What kind and how much?"

He showed her, like a jeweler offering pieces for her inspection. The first bar was stripped and crammed into her mouth before she said, "How much did you pay Crystal for this?"

"She volunteered it, I swear."

Tears clung to Faith's lashes like dewdrops. "Our Crystal?" she said, chewing. "Voluntarily gave up her candy?"

"Only 'cause it was an emergency!" came from down the hall.

"They're all there?" Faith said, unwrapping another piece.

"Yep."

She sighed, then peeked around the door frame. "Go on back to the living room, I need to talk to Daddy alone for a minute."

They all shuffled off. Faith walked over to her nightstand and snagged a tissue out of the box, blowing her nose again.

"How'd you know the candy was Crystal's?" Darryl asked.

"'Cause everybody else's is long gone."

"Oh."

He wasn't quite sure what was expected of him, but he didn't think a hug would be remiss.

He was wrong.

"I really don't want to be touched right now," Faith said, sidestepping. "And no, I don't know why, so don't bother askin'."

Darryl tried not to take it personally, but it wasn't working. Used to be, wrapping Faith up in his arms could pretty much cajole her out of anything. Her rejecting him ripped away the only weapon in his arsenal he'd been able to count on, besides the chocolate. So now what?

"You want me to leave you alone?" he asked.

After a moment, she shook her head. "No," she said, sniffling a little, then sighing like she'd been holding it in for weeks. Maybe years. *Wrecked* was the only word to describe her expression when she looked up at him. "Oh, Lord… I am so sorry."

"For what?"

"Losing it."

"You had cause," he said. She muttered something about that being beside the point, which wasn't making him feel any better… *oh, crap.* If she didn't let him touch her, they might actually have to talk. Not exactly his strong suit.

"Bad day?" he said.

Her gaze bounced off his. "Not particularly, no. I'm just worn out, is all, just like you are when *you* get home from work. Only my period started, to boot, which is something you never had to deal with. And I'm not used to standing on my feet all day, or fielding prying questions about my personal life every ten minutes, or worrying about whether the kids are being properly taken care of in my absence. And I know I'm overreacting, which is making me feel terrible because this is still all new to you, but—"

A new flood of tears shimmered in her eyes, provoking a flare of annoyance in Darryl's gut. Not at Faith for crying, but because everything was upside down. Because she shouldn't have to stand on her feet all day and because he wasn't sure he could handle the house and kids any more than Faith, who was the least mechanically inclined human being he'd ever met, would suddenly know how to rebuild an engine. Because he resented being forced to come at everything from a new angle when the old way had been working just fine.

"This is a lot harder than it looks," he finally said.

She actually laughed, although it was a dried-up little sound. "If there's a compliment in there somewhere," she said, "feel free to let it out."

He frowned. "That your way of telling me you haven't felt appreciated? Because if that's what you think, it's not true. It's not true at all. I've always appreciated you, Faith. You, and everything you do. And believe me, after these past few days, I appreciate you more than ever."

He reached out to steady himself on the chest of drawers, his impassioned declaration having left him feeling dizzy. And a little embarrassed that, outside of Mother's Day cards every year, he'd never actually told her how he felt.

She watched him for a long moment, then said very softly, "Thank you. Still…" She unwrapped another piece of candy and popped it into her mouth. "I don't think it's out of line for me to expect to not walk into total chaos at the end of the day any more than you expected to when I was home with the kids. And how on earth could you have lived in this house for ten years and not know where we kept the paper towels?"

Darryl decided it wasn't in his best interest to point out that there had, in fact, been plenty of evenings when he'd come home to total chaos. When the kids'd been screaming, and the house had looked like a Category Four twister had swept through, and dinner had been cold cuts or eggs and toast. He did, however, feel compelled to point out that she hadn't started out with five kids and a broken arm. "I'm not saying that makes your day-to-day load any lighter," he added, wondering how anybody came out of a discussion like

this alive, "just that at least you had a chance
to ease into it, which I didn't."

At that, she frowned at the pumpkin, then
lifted her eyes to him again, looking as confused as he felt. "You're absolutely right," she
said with yet another sigh. "Lord knows, this
entire turn of events is upsettin' for all of us.
But wishin' things were back to the way they
were before the tornado isn't going to make
it so. And if we all don't learn to adapt, this
family's gonna fall completely apart."

And there it was. Simple and basic and ir-
refutable. The credo of the species—adapt
or die.

He'd made a promise to her, and he'd let
her down. Simple fact. Didn't matter if he
was tired, didn't matter if his arm hurt...he'd
screwed up. So he strode out of the room and
down the hall, where he did what he should've
done from the beginning—took charge of the
situation. After all, there was more than one
way to prove to Faith he was man enough to
do what needed to be done.

"Heather," he said on his way to the kitchen,
"get Nicky changed and ready for bed. Crystal
and Jake, get your pjs on and see that Sierra's
in hers." He opened the freezer and scanned
the contents, pulling out a box of chicken

nuggets, a bag of frozen corn, another bag of green beans. "Supper's in…" He scanned the instructions on all three bags. "Ten minutes."

"What about the tree?" Jake said.

"It's too late to put the tree up tonight. It'll have to wait until after school tomorrow," he said, ripping open the bag of corn with his teeth.

"Ohmigod…what happened to Sierra?" he heard from the living room just as Jake mumbled, "I hate corn."

"Don't go there," said Darryl, spitting out a piece of plastic.

"What the hell are you doing?"

"What's it look like I'm doing?" Faith answered her husband, jamming the last branch into the Christmas tree. She'd only meant to get it out of the way while Darryl herded the kids to bed, but one thing had led to another, as these things do, and before she knew it she had an eight-foot-tall tree in her living room.

"Thought you were about to drop?"

"Supper revived me."

"I'm not sure how. It wasn't anything to write home about."

At the apology in Darryl's voice, Faith turned, wiping her hands on her butt. To be honest, she was still half-irked that it had taken a near meltdown on her part to finally light the fire under him. But she also felt guilty for shaming him into action, as if she had deliberately manipulated him. She knew she had a tendency toward the melodramatic—heaven knows enough people had accused her of it as a child—although she preferred to think of it as earnestness. Still, even she knew there was a fine line between the two, a line a woman often found herself obliged to cross if she had any hope whatsoever of seeing results. But wouldn't it be nice, just once, to be able to revel in the satisfaction of accomplishment without feeling bad about it, too?

Men, Faith had long since decided, did not have this problem of being unable to decide between conflicting emotions. Not that she didn't believe they experienced all the same emotions as a woman, they just never seemed to experience them all at the same time.

"Believe me," she said, "if I didn't have to cook it, it was great. Besides, it was no different from what I've served you probably a thousand times over the years, and you never complained. So I'm hardly about to, am I?"

"That doesn't mean you don't deserve better," he said, throwing her. "We should have been able to go out, at least get pizza or something."

Faith turned back to the tree, even though there was nothing left to do. "It's okay, I really didn't feel like going out," she said, although even she had to admit that next to chicken nuggets and frozen corn, pizza sounded like heaven.

Well. She could hardly stand there and stare at the naked tree forever, could she? But it was either that or stare at her husband, who seemed to be asking her for something she couldn't give him.

Something he more than deserved.

Not only had Darryl finally pulled it together with supper and the kids, but then he'd lectured them all about how, now that Faith was working, they had to stop looking to her to do things for them they could do perfectly well for themselves. He'd stopped her protest, too, when she tried to take at least some of the blame for that, since she'd made them all so dependent on her to begin with. This was a huge turning point for him, and she knew it. And a very necessary one, if they were ever going to get through this.

Even so, the guilt was about to eat her alive.

In her robe and pajamas, Heather appeared,

a grin lighting up her face at the sight of the tree. "You set it up anyway?" she said in a squeal to her father, who pointed to Faith.

"Um…that mean you're feelin' better?" When Faith nodded, Heather said, "So could I show you some of the steps I learned today in dance class?"

"Sure, baby," she said, settling onto the sofa, not quite sure how to react when Darryl sat beside her. Really beside her. Close enough for her skin to start crackling. And oh, did Heather's eyes dart between the two of them, chockful of curiosity.

Anyway, Faith decided to concentrate on watching her daughter, willing herself not to gravitate toward Darryl's solid warmth, or react to his scent, a smell that always crawled right through her and made her go all gooey inside—

Stop it. Right now.

She got up to light a cinnamon-scented candle, one of those great big things with four wicks, figuring that should do the trick. It did. Made the house smell all Christmasy, too, which was a nice bonus. Except she no sooner solved that problem when she found herself faced with another one.

Because tonight, for some untold reason,

Heather's bubbly excitement about her dancing stirred a longing inside Faith she would
have sworn had been long since dead and
buried.

And with the longing came a razor-sharp
tang of envy so seductive it stole her breath.
She even pressed one hand over her mouth, as
if doing so would keep her feelings locked inside so they couldn't poison the atmosphere—

"Mama? You okay?"

Of course she was, she assured her daughter.

Of *course* she was.

Because whatever this was all about, this
upheaval going on inside her, no way did it
have anything to do with choices she'd made
before Heather's birth. No *way*. Why, it was
absurd to think... For pity's sake, she hadn't
even *wanted*...

No. *No.* She'd walked into the life she'd
chosen with her eyes wide open. Joyously.
Eagerly. And even if an occasional, infini-
tesimal bubble of *What if...?* floated through
her brain...well. Bubbles popped, didn't they?

After Heather had gone to bed, though,
Darryl followed her into the kitchen, leaning against the counter and scratching the
dog's head while she finished up the clean-

ing. "Okay…you gonna tell me what that was all about?"

His low, rough voice dipped inside her, tugging at things she didn't want tugged. That she *did* want tugged. Because it had always been far easier, hadn't it, to take *him* inside her than to get inside *herself*? Well, no more.

So she eased away and said, "I just got overwhelmed for a second at how fast Heather's growing up, that's all. You need anything before you go to bed?"

The silence behind her was sharp enough to hurt her ears. "No, I'm good," he said at last. "Well. 'Night, then," he said, turning to leave.

"'Night," she said through a throat so tight she wasn't sure how she was breathing, only to start when Darryl wheeled back, his eyes probing hers….

…only he finally shook his head and walked away, leaving Faith behind, waiting for the snick of the bedroom door closing.

Faith grabbed the baggie of leftover chicken nuggets out of the fridge, scarfing them down like there was no tomorrow, neither she nor Dot caring one whit that they were stone cold.

Chapter Seven

Jacqui Stevens, who owned the Better Read Than Dead bookstore (her husband, Everest, ran the funeral parlor, which probably accounted for Jacqui's offbeat sense of humor) waved from the back of the shoe-box size store when Renee pushed open the heavy wood-and-glass door. Renee never used to shop on Saturday mornings, wanting to be home with L.B. when he was off work, but now that he was retired the point was moot. And anyway, her book club had just announced their new pick and she wanted to start in right away so she'd be finished before they started discussing it. Not that she participated directly in the discussions, but reading the others' comments often made her think about things in a different light.

She found the book easily enough—right up front on Jacqui's bestsellers rack—only to grimace when she saw it was over six hundred pages long. My goodness, she couldn't imagine having that much to say in her entire lifetime—

"Renee? Hey, honey—I thought that was you!"

She looked up to see Didi Meyerhauser bearing down on her, all round and bubbly in a baby-blue down vest nearly as bright as her eyes over a heavy white sweater and blue jeans. Tucked against her side were a half dozen or so paperbacks, none of which were half as thick as the book Renee was holding. With her free arm, Didi gave her a brief, almost crushing hug around the shoulders. For a small woman, she was remarkably strong. And her smile was so bright Renee almost wished she'd left her sunglasses on. It wasn't that Renee didn't like her son's mother-in-law—she did—but all that cheerfulness was wearing on a body this early in the morning.

"I was meaning to call you anyway, about Christmas...oh, my, that coffee smells good.

You want a cup?" Since Didi was already edging toward one of the two tiny tables Jacqui had set up between the self-help and travel sections, her attempt at competing with the big chain bookstores, Renee had no choice but to follow. They both helped themselves from the Mr. Coffee on the counter—Hazelnut Creme today, judging from the aroma—Didi picking up the tab by plunking two quarters into the jelly jar designated for that purpose.

They squeezed in at one of the tables, carefully setting their foam cups of coffee on the wobbly surface. Didi nodded toward the book Renee was still clutching to her chest. "Whatcha got there?"

"Oh…" She turned it around so Didi could see. "For my book club."

"What's it about?" the other woman said, taking a sip of her coffee.

"I'm not sure. Somebody goin' through some sort of crisis, probably. Leastwise, that's the kind of books they usually pick."

"Does it end happily?"

"I doubt it. Last time I was depressed for three days after I finished."

"Then why on earth do you read them?"

"To improve my mind," she said, staring balefully at the book.

"Not sure I see how depressing yourself *improves* your mind."

Renee had nothing to say to that. Only Didi went on about how she liked to relax when she read, take her mind off all the awful things going on in the world. "Give me a happy ending any day," she said, splaying her selection so Renee could see them—brightly colored paperbacks like Renee's mother used to read, mostly mysteries and romances. "One where the good guys win and the boy gets the girl. And if I can laugh along the way, so much the better."

It was then that Renee noticed one of Jenna Logan's books in among Didi's choices. Renee picked it up, skimming her fingers over Jenna's name embossed in gold—well, it was Jennifer Phillips, her pen name—like it was a piece of jewelry she couldn't afford.

"That's the one that came out in hardback last year," Didi said. "I'm getting this one to send to my sister out in California."

Renee handed it back. She was probably the only person in town who hadn't read Jenna's books, although she honestly had no idea why. And she was very grateful that Didi didn't press the issue, but instead switched the subject to Christmas dinner, which she was hosting at her house, since Renee was giving Nicky his first birthday party two days before.

But after they hashed out the particulars (Renee being determined to win the rights to do the ham and dessert without hurting Didi's feelings—the woman was as good as the day was long, but it was easy to see why Faith wasn't particularly talented in the kitchen), Renee heard herself say, "Actually, I've been thinkin' of calling you, too," although she'd hadn't realized before that very moment that she had.

And worse, that the second Didi said, "About what?" she was in grave danger of violating Heather's confidence. But since Heather had given no indication over the past week or so that things had changed in regards to her parents' sleeping arrangements, Renee felt impelled to either find out what Didi knew or at least enlist her aid in remedying the situation.

She glanced around to make sure no one could hear them, then leaned forward and said, "Has Faith said anything to you about…" She cleared her throat. "About how she and Darryl are, um, getting on since the tornado?"

Didi took another sip of her coffee and said, flat out, "You mean, in bed?"

In spite of being relieved at not having to

spell out the problem, Renee felt heat flood her cheeks. "Yes," she said, and Didi sighed.

"Not directly, no. Why? Has Darryl said something to you?"

"Oh, no. But…" Renee lowered her eyes to her coffee, then lifted them again. "Promise me you won't breathe a word of this to anyone, especially not Faith. Or Heather, since I promised her I wouldn't say anything…but Heather told me—" she lowered her voice even more "—that Faith's been sleeping out in the living room since the accident."

"Oh," Didi said. "Well…it could be simply logistics, you know. Because of Darryl's cast and all."

"You really believe that?"

That got another sigh. "Knowing those two?" She shook her head.

"What do you think we should do?"

Didi's brows popped up from behind her glasses. "*We* can't do anything. And don't go getting ideas in your head that we can. All marriages have bumpy patches, you know that as well as I do. But I've never yet seen one recover when other people have butted in. If they're having problems, they're the ones who have to work it out. All we can do is be there. Just like when they were kids."

Renee and Didi looked at each other for several seconds. Didi and Chuck had been the epitome of graciousness when Darryl and Faith had announced her pregnancy, but embarrassment still lingered in the air whenever the subject came up. Now she jumped a little when Didi's soft, plump hand covered hers. "They love each other, Renee. But I think Faith…" Her mouth pulled tight. "I think a few things have caught up to her, that's all. Things she should've dealt with a long time ago." She let go of Renee's hand to pick up her coffee. "I went through something similar when Faith was a little girl, round about the time I turned forty. I swear, I woke up one morning and thought, 'How did I get here?' I felt…trapped. Like I was suffocating."

Renee felt a twinge of what felt almost like alarm. "What happened?"

Didi chuckled. "My period started. But I also realized I had to get off my duff and start taking a more active role in my own life. That's when I got the day-care center going. And stopped taking myself so seriously," she said, getting to her feet and scooping the books into the crook of her arm.

Renee stood as well, gathering her purse

and the book. "So you think we shouldn't worry? About Darryl and Faith?"

"I think we have to trust them to make their own decisions. And now I've got to run—I've got a redecorating meeting for the church at one. You should come along," she added, as if struck by the thought. "You've got more talent for decorating in your little finger than the rest of us put together!"

Renee blushed at the compliment, but declined, citing plans for the afternoon. Although the truth of the matter was, something inside her had always kept her from getting too deeply involved with groups like that. One day she needed to sit down and figure out why that was.

But not today, she thought as Didi gave her another hug and went up to the register to pay for her purchases. Today she had enough on her mind worrying about her son and his marriage—she just didn't have it in her to be quite as laid-back about it all as Didi—and Christmas coming up and Nicky's birthday and getting this book read in time for the discussion in January.

Reassured that her life was as full as it could possibly be, she toted the novel up to the register…only to turn back around and snatch up Jenna's book, as well. Just to see what all the fuss was about, you know. And after all, one book was hardly going to turn her into her mother, was it?

"You hear from the insurance company yet?"

Darryl sent up a silent prayer that the lunch-time clattering and chattering at Ruby's had probably drowned out his father's question to anybody but him. For a man so protective of his own privacy, L.B. sure had no qualms about spreading anybody else's out for the rest of the world to pick over like items at a yard sale. What particularly annoyed Darryl was that all he wanted right now was five minutes to just enjoy his enchiladas—Ruby had gone on about getting the recipe from Joe Salazar's mother—without thinking about the garage or Faith or his arm or anything else. Five lousy minutes. Was that too much to ask?

A glance across the booth at his father told him apparently it was.

"Talked to 'em just the other day. 'Soon,' the gal said." Darryl shrugged, ignoring the annoying tingle in his fingers. "Whatever the hell that means."

"You want me to call 'em?"

Darryl shoveled in a large bite of enchilada, savoring the explosion of green chili against his tongue. "No, I do not need you to call anybody, L.B. I'm perfectly capable of handling this myself."

"I know you are," his father said. "It's just, with everything else you've got on your plate, I thought you might not mind some help."

At the obvious hurt in his father's voice, Darryl's eyes lifted to L.B.'s. Damn. Probably he wasn't trying to interfere as much as looking for a way to feel useful. L.B. had retired way too soon, in Darryl's opinion. But he'd insisted it was time to turn over the reins to his son, and there was no talking him out of it—

Darryl's eyes narrowed as the most crucial part of that sentence worked its way through. "And what *everything else* would that be?"

"Oh, don't go gettin' paranoid on me. I mean with your arm and all. And…other things. You know," he said when Darryl squinted harder. L.B. glanced around, then said in a low voice, "At home."

So much for him not interfering. Suddenly the enchiladas were burning a hole in Darryl's mouth. He grabbed his glass of water and chugged half of it down, a move that brought

Charmaine, the day waitress, zipping over to the table, her smile nearly as blinding as her bright pink uniform. As a single mother, Charmaine—who'd gone to school with Darryl and Faith but had never been what you'd call close—believed in keeping her options open, even if the options themselves weren't. Once the brunette had finally determined there really was no more she could do for either of them, she drifted off, and Darryl leaned forward.

"For your information, 'at home' is just fine."

"You sure?"

Hell, no, Darryl wasn't sure, hadn't been sure about much of anything for weeks. Especially since the night of Faith's meltdown, when she'd gotten that weird look on her face while she'd been watching Heather dance, a look that clearly said she'd gone someplace Darryl didn't have a hope in hell of reaching. A fact only confirmed when she'd put him off when he'd tried to get her to talk afterward.

But no way was he getting into any of this with his father. Especially in public.

"I'm sure," he said.

"So how come you and Faith aren't sleeping in the same room?"

Darryl's head snapped up so quickly he nearly ruptured something. "Where'd you hear that? And why in the hell are you bringing this up here?"

"From your mother. Who heard it from Heather. And I'm bringin' it up here because I know you won't get up and walk out and risk drawing more attention to yourself." Now L.B. leaned closer, his double-patty cheeseburger clamped in his hand. Darryl tucked that away as future blackmail bait—his mother would have five fits if she knew that's what L.B. had ordered. "You might be able to keep things under wraps with the younger kids," he said in a low voice, "but that oldest gal of yours doesn't miss a trick. And according to your mother, that is one troubled little girl."

Breathing out a frustrated sigh, Darryl leaned back in the booth, gazing blankly at the same tinsel stars Ruby'd put up for Christmas every year since he could remember. You'd think by now he'd've figured out that just because a kid doesn't say something, that doesn't mean she's okay. And Heather always had had this thing about keeping her worries to herself.

At least, she used to.

Darryl's gaze swung back to his father's. "Faith's been sleepin' out on the couch because I have to sleep on my back, on account of my arm. She says I snore. I guess I thought Faith'd explained it to the kids. Heather, anyway."

"Apparently not. Or if she did, the gal's not buyin' it." His father stuffed a French fry in his mouth, saying, "And frankly, neither do I."

Darryl felt his neck get hot. "And frankly, L.B.," he said quietly, "this is none of your business. So can we just drop it?"

Except his father added, "So what you're sayin' is this isn't just about sleeping?"

"For crying out loud, L.B.—"

"Women go too long without, then tend to get real cranky. That's all I'm sayin'." Which was far more than Darryl wished to hear, thank you.

"L.B.? I don't mean to be disrespectful, and I know you're only concerned about my well-being…but I'm asking you once again to back off. My private life isn't open for discussion, not even with you."

After a moment, his father nodded, although Darryl knew better than to think L.B. was going to stop fretting about it simply because the subject had been declared off-limits. However, he thought maybe he saw a spark of respect in the other man's eyes that he hadn't noticed before, so that was something.

For the rest of the meal, the conversation stayed on relatively safer subjects, mainly plans for rebuilding the garage, L.B. clearly in denial about the possibility that Darryl might not be able to work again, at least not the way he had. They'd already gotten a couple of estimates from local builders—the insurance company insisted on sending out their own people, which Darryl knew bugged L.B. no end—although with all the other damage in the area it didn't look good for getting started on any real repair work until well into the New Year.

By which time, Darryl mused, the cast would be off and he'd maybe have a better idea of what was really going on with his arm. At his last checkup, the bones appeared to be healing just fine, but the nerve business was something else again. As before, sometimes he couldn't feel a thing, other times his hand and arm felt like it was on fire. He hated taking the pain meds, but there were days when it was either that or lose his mind. He also felt bad about keeping the truth from Faith, but he just couldn't bring himself to add to her stress…and whether she wanted to admit it or not, she was definitely stressed.

Which only made L.B.'s commenting on their current situation all the more irritating, since nobody knew more than Darryl how far a little action in the sack could go toward smoothing the rough edges off life. Hell, just thinking about being naked with his wife produced a hopeful tingling low in his belly…

A glance at his watch propelled him out of the booth. "No, no, you go ahead and finish your lunch, L.B., I have to pick the kids up from school. They get out early today for some reason…"

But L.B. said, no, that was okay, he was finished anyway and to put that wallet away, this was his treat.

Once outside, his father put a hand on his arm, stopping him.

"I've really gotta go, L.B—"

"This won't take but a second. And I know you don't want me to stick my nose in, but…" He let go, shoving his hands into his back pockets underneath his plaid jacket, concern creasing his features. "Used to be a woman'd stick by her man, no matter what. Many times when she probably shouldn't've," he said with a grimace, and Darryl knew L.B. was talking about his own parents. "But these days, they expect more. And if they don't get what they need, they look elsewhere. You hear what I'm saying?"

Darryl's gaze tangled with his father's for several seconds before he said, "You're not tellin' me anything I don't already know, L.B."

"I didn't figure I was. But it never hurts to be reminded. Don't let her get away, boy," he said gently, and Darryl said, "Believe me, I don't intend to."

Only it was getting harder and harder to figure out how, exactly, to do that.

The kids collected, he stopped by his mother's to pick up a pan of lasagna, making the rug rats swear not to kill each other while he went inside. As usual, the house smelled like furniture polish and—in keeping with the holiday theme—pine-scented air freshener. He scooped up a handful of cellophane-wrapped Christmas mints for the kids from a ruby-red candy dish and stuffed them in his jacket pocket, taking care not to stray from the plastic runner stretched across the just-vacuumed, pale beige wall-to-wall. His mother kept a beautiful house, no doubt about it, but sometimes he wondered how he and his brothers had survived growing up here without becoming freaks.

"Mama?"

"Kitchen! And don't you dare walk on the carpet, I just ran the Bissell on it."

Renee was sitting at the kitchen table, snapping beans, her eyes glued to some soap or other. Teddy bears in assorted Christmas getups pranced across her red sweatshirt, dangled from her ears and grinned at Darryl from every pot holder, kitchen towel and place mat in the room. He'd have nightmares for a week.

"I'm here to get—" he started, but she shushed him with one bean-filled hand, so he went over to the refrigerator and retrieved the foil-covered pan himself. The music swelled, signaling the commercial break, at which point his mother shook herself as if coming out of a spell. She always had taken her programs very seriously, often talking about the characters as if she knew them personally. Sure enough, she started in about some couple and how awful it was that their marriage had fallen apart, you know, that they were only together because of the kids, really, but (she leaned forward and whispered) absolutely *nothing* was happening in the bedroom anymore. Then she stared pointedly at him for several seconds.

Darryl stared pointedly right back. His mother spooked him from time to time, but she did not intimidate him. He rested the lasagna on the edge of the table and said, "So I hear Heather's been tellin' tales out of school," and Renee said, "I don't think you realize how kids pick up on these things," and he said, "She doesn't even know what she's picking up *on*," and his mother gave him much the same look his father had.

"Unless you want to end up like Nicole and Trent," she added.

"Who the hell are Nicole and Trent?"

"The people I was just tellin' you about. On my soap," she finished with some exasperation.

"You do know those aren't real people, right?"

"Well, of course I know those aren't real people," she said, the teddy bears in her ears swinging wildly. "What do you take me for? But that doesn't mean a person can't learn a thing or two from them."

"You know," Darryl said with no small amount of exasperation of his own, "I already heard this from one parent today."

"Well, now you're hearing it from the other one," she said, lobbing the two halves of a broken bean into the bowl.

Darryl sighed. Again.

"Okay," he said, "since it's obvious neither of you are gonna let this rest…whatever's goin' on between Faith and me—not that it's any of your business—isn't gonna be cleared up simply by her moving back into our bedroom."

His mother's eyes zinged to his. "Meaning?"

"Meaning, Faith's goin' through some kind of… I don't know what you'd call it. Like she isn't sure who she is or something. And whatever it is, it's been coming on for some time. Since before the tornado. She said…" Darryl frowned, trying to remember. "Something about…wanting dessert?"

Renee got a funny look on her face. "Oh," she said, then seemed to shake herself again, swatting away his comment. "She's just reassessin' her place in life, that's all. All women go through that, but it passes…" Her voice kind of drifted off, then her gaze swung back to his. "It's funny, where the seeds of discontent can spring up. You can have so much, and yet…"

She got up to carry the bowl of beans to the sink, setting them under the spigot and turning on the water. "She just needs reassurin', honey," she said, swishing her hand through the wet beans, then turning to him with a smile that seemed a little tight. "That she's not getting old, you know? That you still, um, *want* her." She pushed the spigot down. "I still say, show that wife of yours how much you love her, and you'll be fine."

He was sorely tempted to argue, but he was even more sorely tempted to believe her, to grab on to the hope that whatever Faith was going through, she would go *through* it and be none the worse for wear once on the other side. So if there was anything Darryl could do to speed up the process, he'd just better get to it, hadn't he?

But he didn't say any of this to his mother, for obvious reasons. Instead, he said, "Thanks for the lasagna. I've got the kids in the car, I can't stay," and hotfooted it out of there, the silver icicles draped all over the Christmas tree fluttering in the breeze left in his wake.

Since the day-care center closed at six, and—as usual—Faith was late picking up Nicky and Sierra, she didn't even bother stopping at the church but went on to her parents' house a block away. Didi had told her over and over not to worry about it, but she couldn't help feeling bad about imposing. Yes, her mother loved her work, but heaven knew she put in enough hours without having her own daughter dumping her kids on her besides.

"There's Mama!" Faith heard her mother say the second she dragged herself inside. Instantly, Sierra wrapped herself around her thighs. "Nicky walked!" the tiny girl chirped. "All by'm'self, wifout holdin' on or anything!"

Faith's head shot up, just in time to see her beaming mother lead an unsteady, grinning baby by the hand out from her kitchen. "Go on, sugar," she said, letting go. "Show Mama what you learned how to do today!"

Nicky wobbled for a second, hands up, then lifted one foot and took a step. Then another. Then, with a stream of giggles, he made it all the way across the floor, not losing his balance until, caught up in his own accomplishment, he tried to clap, at which point he plopped onto the carpet with a squeal of either glee or annoyance, it was hard to tell.

"Oh, my goodness, sugar pie," Faith said over the lump in her throat, this being the only one of the five whose first solo flight she'd missed. "What a big boy! Come here!"

Still, she couldn't help but laugh at the gee-am-I-hot-stuff sparkle in those big brown eyes so much like his daddy's. Lower lip caught between his four teeth, Nicky got to his knees, hesitated, then cautiously pushed up...to his feet...where he teetered and swayed and...

Plop!

"Oops-a-daisy!" Faith's mother said, laughing, which earned her a tiny glower, followed by a little huff, before the baby apparently decided *forget this* and got on his hands and knees to crawl like lightning to Faith. Too weary to get up, she let both kids climb into her lap, at which point she caught the worried look in her mother's eyes.

"I'm fine," she said, preempting the inevitable question.

"Because heaven forbid you should actually *admit* when you're having a hard time of it."

Faith gave her mother a not-in-front-of-the-kids look, then hauled herself to a standing position, no mean feat with twenty pounds of solid, squirming baby in her arms. "I'm fine," she repeated. But after they got the kids in their coats, Didi followed her out to the car, her arms wrapped around herself to ward off the merciless wind.

"And how's Darryl gettin' on with the house and kids? Or is he leavin' most of it to you, anyway, even though you're going out to work now?"

"Darryl's doin' the best he can, Mama," Faith said, opening the back door of the truck to toss in the kids' diaper bags and what-all. "But it would be unreasonable to expect him to figure out how to do in a couple of weeks what I've been doing for more than ten years."

"Which means," her mom said as Faith strapped Nicky into his car seat, "you're runnin' yourself into the ground trying to do it all."

Faith grabbed Sierra's hand to steer her around to the other side. "I'm not," she called over her shoulder as she went, although she didn't have the energy to go into specifics.

"Could've fooled me," Didi stated, in that tone of voice that said she wasn't buying the denial for a second. She followed her around the truck, waiting until Faith had finished buckling up Sierra as well before adding, "Let us help, honey. Please."

"You *are* helping, Mama." Faith grabbed her mother's warm, soft hand, as if she might derive enough strength from her touch to ward off at least some of the mental ambivalence threatening to pull her under far more than the physical demands of her job. "Without you taking care of the babies, I don't know how we'd've gotten through this. Besides, it's not forever."

She let go, a little more reluctantly than she expected, and climbed up into the truck. As the engine roared to life, she lowered the window long enough to tell her that all they needed was their love and support—really, they were fine. But she never had been any good at lying to her mother—she suspected not even during all those months before she and Darryl were married, when they'd become remarkably adept at finding any number of opportunities to enjoy each other—so why on earth would her mom believe her now?

Whatever. That was her story and she was sticking to it. Just like she'd so brazenly lied about all those times she and Darryl had sneaked off, way back when. My, my, my— what a wicked girl she'd turned out to be, Faith thought with a wry smile as she backed the truck into the street. But for sure she'd been one of the happiest wicked girls in history.

Just as she was wondering what had happened to that girl, she heard from behind her, "Is Nicky still a baby?"

Real life, Faith thought with a rueful smile. *That's* what happened to that girl. "Sure, he's still a baby for a little while." She glanced at her daughter in the rearview mirror, although she couldn't really see her in the dark. "Just a baby who can walk."

"Oh. I like babies."

"Me, too, sweetie."

"So c'n we get another one?"

"No, honey," Faith managed to reply with a choked laugh. "We're all done with having babies in this family."

"How come?"

"'Cause Daddy and I think five kids is enough." *And have taken appropriate steps to make sure we don't change our minds.*

"So Nicky's *always* gonna be the baby?"

"Well, yes. But you know, somebody has to be, in every family. And anyway, someday all of you guys are going to grow up and get married and have kids of your own, so there will be more babies. Probably lots of babies," she said, only to think, *Ohmigod, I'm going to be a grandmother.* And if Heather followed in her footsteps, that could be in…

Seven years.

"Mama, why'd you make the truck do that?"

"It's…it's okay, sweetie, I just, um…"

Nearly gave myself a heart attack, is what.

"Where's the lights?" Sierra asked as they turned into their driveway, referring to the Vegas-worthy display L.B. had strung up the previous Saturday. Faith had thought for sure they'd short out half the neighborhood when they first turned them on. Or inadvertently signal aliens to land.

"Don't know," she said, cutting the engine. "Guess Daddy forgot."

"Bad Daddy."

Faith climbed out of the truck and opened Sierra's door to spring her from her seat. "Daddy's not bad, honey," she said. "He's just got a lot on his mind. Taking care of you guys demands a lot of concentration."

"What's that?"

"Hard thinking."

"Oh." The little princess slid to the ground. "Daddy's okay, but you're better," she said solemnly, then marched off toward the house.

Faith shut her eyes for a second, then reached in and scooped Nicky out of his seat, setting him on the ground so he could practice walking from the truck to the house. Except the lights suddenly flashed on—Faith guessed Sierra had gotten on her daddy's case—and he stopped, openmouthed and wide-eyed, completely uninterested in moving another step. After several seconds of stunned silence, he let loose with a streak of very excited…something. Hungarian, maybe. And for a moment, Faith wished for a little of her baby's innocence, the unbridled delight in a million glittering lights, in being able to stand on your own two feet. And once there, to actually get somewhere.

Why did life have to be so blamed complicated?

She scooped up her squealing, quasi-lingual child and carted him into the house. A house that smelled like something Italian. And not burned, hallelujah. The whole gang was in the kitchen, the kids at the table making snowflakes like there was no tomorrow. As tired as she was, as befuddled as she was, the sound of her husband's deep, gentle voice as he supervised their elves nudged to life old feelings, making her feel even more befuddled. And definitely more tired.

"Okay, big stuff…" She set Nicky down. "Show Daddy what you can do."

Questioning brown eyes touched hers just

long enough to make her question, well, everything, basically, before swinging toward his youngest child. "Hey, bud," he said, crouching. "What's up?"

At that, the baby let out a shriek, let go of Faith's pant leg and took five unsteady steps into Darryl's arm. All the other kids let out whoops of approval and clapped their hands, and the baby ate it up. Even the dog got into the act, sticking her slobbery face in Nicky's and giving him a juicy kiss of approval.

And naturally, Faith burst into tears.

"...Only then it occurred to me," Renee said as she cleared away L.B.'s supper dishes, "that it might be easier for Darryl and Faith to, um, reconnect—" considering how good her and L.B.'s sex life had always been, she never had figured out why she had so much trouble talking about it in plain terms "—if they didn't have the kids around all the time."

"I suppose so," L.B. said. And that was it.

Honestly, men could be so clueless sometimes.

The dishes scraped, Renee set them in the dishwasher, then turned around. "So what do you think we should do?" she said, thinking,

Oh, for pity's sake, this isn't higher mathematics—catch on, already.

He'd been watching the local news on the little TV; now his head slowly swiveled in her direction, his forehead crumpled. "Do?"

"About Darryl and Faith? And the kids?" she added, in case she hadn't planted the idea firmly enough.

L.B. sat back, his arms crossed over his chest. "Well, I don't know.... I suppose maybe we could take 'em for the night or somethin'."

"That's a terrific idea!" Renee said. "In fact, why don't we just go on over there right now? It's Friday night. We could take 'em into Tulsa tomorrow to see Santa Claus—it'll be Nicky's first time, since his birthday's the 23rd!"

"Tonight?" L.B. said, not moving.

"Why not? Unless you've got hot plans I don't know about?"

"Would it make any difference if I did?"

"Probably not, no. So come on—" She was already in her coat, her purse hugged to her chest. "Let's get a move on!"

L.B. watched her for a moment, frowning. Then a slow, deep chuckle wandered over to wrap itself around her heart. "Why do I get the feeling I was just railroaded?" he said, pushing himself to his feet.

"Don't talk crazy, L.B.," Renee said, pushing his coat at him. "How could I railroad you when it was your idea to begin with?"

"Uh-huh," he said, steering her toward the back door, his hand at the small of her back like always.

Chapter Eight

What now? Darryl thought, gawking at his weepy wife, even as she shook her head, waving away everyone's concern.

"It's just me gettin' all sentimental," she said, grabbing a napkin to blow her nose, and Darryl thought *Uh-huh*. "Smells good," she said, smiling way too brightly, making him want to go bang his head against the nearest wall.

Or his wife, a thought that nearly made his eyes glaze over. All that softness wrapped tight around him, trusting him not to let her fall. Those sweet little moans she made when—

"Look at my snowflake, Daddy!"

Darryl had to blink several times before his oldest son's holey grin came into focus, a mangled piece of paper thrust out for his approval.

Okay, maybe this wasn't the best train of thought to be entertaining in a kitchen full of kids. Not to mention a feat he had a hope of accomplishing as long as his arm was in this damn cast. Still, the idea definitely brightened his outlook on life, especially when he caught Faith's gaze and saw her cheeks redden and guessed she was thinking along the same lines. Maybe not the wall part—although you never knew; she used to have some pretty wild ideas once upon a time—but close enough to count. And hell, it was his arm that was broken, not what was currently bitching about being confined beneath a thick layer of denim.

All afternoon, his parents' words had played over and over in his head like a tune you couldn't forget. Maybe Darryl wasn't exactly a deep thinker, but it didn't take an Einstein to figure out that as long as he and Faith had been having sex, they'd been okay. And that the longer they went without, the further apart they seemed to be getting. So why on earth would they throw out the one thing that did work between them?

The doorbell rang, raising an instant chorus of "I'll get its!," followed by the thunder of many little feet hoofing it to the door. "Um, I should see who it is," Faith said, turning, but Darryl spun her back around, feeling very smug when her eyes got all big and unfocused.

"Seems to me four kids are more than enough to determine who it is," he said, tugging her close enough, and fast enough, and hard enough, to elicit a little grunt. "Now kiss me, dammit, before one or the other of us explodes."

"I don't think—"

"Kiss now. Think later."

Except five seconds really wasn't enough time to do much in the way of persuading, even for him. It was, however, more than enough time to rally the troops in his bloodstream and make him remember exactly why kissing his wife made life worth living.

"It's L.B. an' Nanny!" at least three kids yelled, at which point Faith took a giant step backward, glaring at him.

"There you are!" his mother said breathlessly, bursting into the kitchen, all those little dangling pieces of hair sticking straight out from static electricity. "I know this is short notice, but L.B. and I were sitting at the table after supper, and all of a sudden he's going on about how long it's been since we've had the kids spend the night, and one thing led to another, and, well…" She clasped her hands together, huffing out a breath. "Here we are!"

"You're…taking the kids for the night?" Faith asked, the way you might to someone intent on telling you about the time they spent with the little green men.

"That's right!"

"*All* of them?"

"Well, of course, all of them, honey! Unless you think it'd be better to leave the littlest ones behind—"

"No!" Darryl said, probably too quickly. Especially when Faith shot him a narrow-eyed look. "I mean," he said to his mother, "if you and L.B. are really sure you want to do this—"

"They haven't had their supper yet," Faith said.

"Oh, we've got tons of food at home…don't we, L.B.?" she said when Darryl's father finally got to the kitchen, Nicky in his arms, Sierra and Jake clamped to his thighs. But instead of waiting for an answer, she corralled Faith—who tossed Darryl another dirty look on her way out—and Heather into gathering up pajamas and toothbrushes and such, so they could get out of there and let Faith and Darryl have a nice, romantic supper all by themselves, for once.

"Subtle," Darryl said to his father once the women and most of the kids had left the kitchen.

L.B. chuckled. "Rumor has it this was my idea."

"L.B., really, if you don't want to do this, you don't have to—"

"And you should see the look on your face right now. Trust me, it doesn't even come close to matching your words."

Releasing a breath, Darryl swiped his hand through his hair, then grinned sheepishly at his father. "Thanks."

"Don't thank me, thank your mother. Although…" L.B. tickled Nicky, who let out a husky chortle. "I can't say I'm gonna suffer any, havin' these critters all to myself for the next little while."

"Yeah, well, before you get too excited, you might want to wait until after you've *had* 'em for a little while."

"Oh, come on—I survived you and your

brothers, I suppose I'll be okay with my own grandkids."

Darryl angled his head at his father. "I don't recall you ever doing much of the day-to-day stuff, though."

"What are you talkin' about? Not a day went by that I wasn't around for you boys."

"I don't mean that. I mean, you know…" He circled his hand. "The *stuff*. The cleaning up and the making sure we didn't kill ourselves and that we ate right, and the tears and nose and butt wiping. That was Mama's world, not yours."

L.B. frowned at him. "I was at work all day, you know that. So yeah, I guess that side of things was your mother's department. But she was better at it than I was, anyway, so it worked out just fine. And why are you bringin' this up now? It getting to you, being a whaddyacallit, a househusband?"

"Hell, yeah, it gets to me. But now I understand why Faith would sometimes shove whoever the youngest one was at the moment in my arms the second I walked in the door after work, then take off to her mother's for an hour or so. This…this is *hard*."

L.B. looked down at the baby, who was chewing on one of his buttons, then back at

Darryl. "I guess I'm not what you call a nat-ural-born nurturer."

"Is anybody?" Darryl replied just as Faith and everybody returned, assorted stuffed backpacks in tow. A few minutes later, after they'd traded vehicles rather than go through the hassle of switching car seats, he and his wife were completely alone in their house for the first time since…actually, Darryl couldn't remember how long it had been. Nor was he about to waste the opportunity. But this time, when he tried pulling Faith close, she backed away, arms crossed, mouth set, and a chorus of *Oh, hells* went off in Darryl's brain.

"Do you think I'm stupid or what? You *planned* this!"

Darryl barked out a laugh. "You're a lot of things, Faith, but stupid is not one of them. And for sure *I'm* not dumb enough to try pulling one over on you. So trust me, I was just as surprised as you when my parents walked through that door. Although…" He lowered his head to peer into her eyes. "I'm not real sure what you're so ticked about."

"Think about it," she said, spinning around and stomping out of the room.

"I am thinking about it!" Darryl said, following her. She'd plopped down on the sofa, crossing her legs to match the crossed arms. The reflection from the blinking Christmas tree lights kept catching in her hair, making it look like the anger was bursting off her in little multicolored sparks. "In fact, I've been doing nothing but thinking about it for weeks!"

"*It* being sex, I assume."

"Honey, I'm a guy. I think about sex every fourteen seconds. Except when I'm around you, then it's pretty much constant."

He thought he might have seen the beginnings of a smile, but he wouldn't bet his life on it. Only then she said, "So, what? You told your parents we weren't sleeping together?"

"Of course not! But apparently Heather said something to my mother. Who naturally told L.B."

Faith groaned, then said, "I may ground her till she's thirty."

"Works for me," Darryl said, wondering if he dared take a seat beside her, deciding no, this was a woman in serious need of her space.

"I suppose," she said, "this led to the consensus that I should move back into our bedroom to assuage Heather's concerns."

Darryl finally decided to sit down, although in the chair opposite the sofa. The dog took this as a signal to shove her butt against his knee in order to get scratched. "No, more like you should move back into our bedroom to keep our marriage from falling apart."

She looked at him steadily for a long time before finally saying, "Sex being what's always held it together, you mean?"

Words that should have by rights sliced straight through him...if they'd been aimed at him to begin with. The pain in her voice, her eyes, told another story, though, one that made his gut clench with wanting to do whatever it took to make it better.

"You really think there's nothing else going on here except sex?"

"Says the man who just admitted he thinks about it every fourteen seconds."

Darryl leaned back in the chair. "It's a compliment, dammit," he said softly, even though he felt like he was about to implode from frustration. "I'm a simple man, Faithie. Which you knew from the outset. Providin' for you and the kids and makin' love to you are the only ways I've got of showing you how much I love you." He waited until her eyes were hooked on his before continuing. "Except I *can't* support you and the kids right now, so that kinda limits my options, doesn't it? If you won't let me make love to you, how the hell am I supposed to make you happy? Tell me, Faith, because I really want to know."

Her eyes teared up again. "But that's just it. It's not up to you to make me happy. Or save me. Or even protect me."

"But I thought that's what you wanted."

"I thought that's what I wanted, too," she whispered, looking at the tree.

He waited until he could breathe again before asking, "Is this a recent conclusion?"

She folded her legs under her, her gaze fixed on the dog, who'd abandoned Darryl for her. "Yes and no."

"What the hell is that supposed to mean?"

Finally, her eyes lifted to his, swimming with apology. "That I knew it all along, but chose to ignore it when remembering wasn't…convenient."

Darryl watched her for a good long while, then sprang from the chair, desperate for something, anything, to distract him. A sagging light strand on the tree would have to do for the moment. "So you're shutting me out?" he asked, rewinding the strand one-handed around the branch.

"Of course not," she said, sounding about

as miserable as a human being could. "But I can't resume relations with you just to get your parents off our case."

He spun around so fast the dog tripped over herself trying to get out of the way. "This has nothing to do with my parents, dammit! This is about us! *Us!* For cryin' out loud, Faith— the one place we never had any problem communicating was in bed! And these days we don't even have to worry about you getting pregnant anymore! Not to mention that you started this, not me! Cripes, that first time we went out? I hardly knew what hit me, the way you were all over me!"

"I *know* I started this!" She pressed one hand to her chest. "I…*know*. Which is what makes this whole thing so…nuts. And hard. And, yeah, unfair," she added, getting to her feet, "because it sounds like I'm trying to change the ground rules. But…" She swallowed. "But sometimes I think I use sex almost like a drug, to avoid facing reality. And I just can't do that anymore. At least, not until I figure a few things out…"

"Where are you going?"

She'd headed back to the kitchen, where he found her punching her arms into the sleeves of an old sweater as she snatched the garage keys off a hook by the back door.

"I brought the kids' gifts over from my mother's the other day," she said, yanking open the door. "May as well get them wrapped while they're gone."

Darryl wasn't sure whether to be relieved she wasn't leaving or ticked that she'd arbitrarily decided the conversation was over. Since it wasn't, not by a long shot, he followed her as she strode across the frozen yard toward the second garage, her breath leaving her mouth in tiny, frosted bursts as she walked.

"You hid them in Marilyn?" he said when she ripped the tarp off the car, sending waves of lust crashing through him, although whether for her or the car, he couldn't be sure. He thought maybe both, which sparked an idea, which in turn provoked what he knew was probably a dumb-ass grin.

"Seemed as good a place as any," she said, hauling bag after bag out of the back seat. Her arms so full you could barely see her face, she turned to him. "What?"

The grin broadened. Bags crinkled as he backed her up against the car, bracketing her as well as he could with one arm. "Two words— *back seat.*"

That got a blank stare for a second or two before she said, "Oh, right. It's barely twenty degrees in here and you're in a cast. Yeah, that'd work." Faith pushed past him and started back, the bags crackling indignantly as she walked.

"Where's your sense of adventure?" he shouted after her.

"Not in an unheated garage," floated back to him over the wind.

Darryl quickly replaced the tarp, killed the lights and slammed shut the garage door; by the time he got back to the house, Faith already had the first present—an aircraft carrier complete with about a million planes guaranteed to cause at least that many curses over the next ten years as they found their way under Darryl's bare feet—set on a huge piece of wrapping paper in the middle of the kitchen table. She glanced at him as he came in.

"You don't give up, do you?" she said quietly, her scissors skimming across the paper.

Darryl pulled out a chair and sank into it, ignoring the tiny flames of heat spiking through his arm. Not to mention the not-so-tiny ones spiking through other places. He wouldn't go so far as to say he was desperate, but the tightness in his chest told him he was a lot closer that he would have liked.

"About getting you naked again?" He shook his head. "Not in this lifetime." He covered her hand with his, earning him a muffled curse when the scissors slipped, messing up her perfectly straight cutting line. "I want you, Faith," he said in a low voice. "Worse now than I think I even did in the beginning, and that's going some. In fact, I think it's pretty safe to say I'm still gonna want you when I'm so old I'd probably have to prop up my best friend with string and Popsicle sticks."

He lifted her hand to his mouth, skimming her knuckles against his lower lip, smiling slightly when he noticed her breathing go all shallow. Then he let go, getting to his feet. "But if you need some space, you go right ahead and take it. I'll be waiting right here— or wherever—when you're done," he said, crossing to the back door and pulling on his jacket.

"Where are you going? We haven't had supper yet—"

"I'm not hungry," he said, letting in a blast of frigid air when he wrestled open the door. "No, that's not true, I'm just not hungry for lasagna. But since what I'm hankerin' for isn't on the menu…" He let his gaze linger on hers for a good, long moment before he called the dog and disappeared into the dark.

Her throat constricted, Faith blinked at the present, then tossed the scissors onto the table with a clatter. So much for that. So much for all of it, she thought with a snort as she stomped across the kitchen to remove the lasagna from the oven. Not that she was at all interested in eating it, but no sense letting it burn.

This whole crisis thing would be a lot easier if she'd married a jerk. Then at least she'd have an excuse for going headfirst off the deep end, right into all this…muck. She'd never envied Darryl his uncomplicated approach to life more than she did at that moment. Nor had she ever appreciated him more for standing by her all these years, for putting up with her moods and foibles and bad cooking without a word of complaint. No, whatever else might be going on inside her head, this sense of everything being out of whack wasn't about her choice of mate. Her husband wasn't the problem, and never had been.

The "whatever else," however, was about to drive her right over the edge.

* * *

The damp, frigid air welcome against his heated skin, Darryl stood across the street from what was left of the garage—which looked even more devastated with all the debris cleared away. He wasn't sure why he was here, even less sure what he was supposed to be thinking. Weak light from the Christmas decorations strung up on Main Street glanced off the pumps, the skeleton of the buildings, the dog's sleek coat as she darted in and out of the wreckage, stopping every few feet to sniff. Nothing much left at this point except memories and shadows.

His chest felt like somebody was stepping on it—was that happening to his marriage, too? At least the garage could be rebuilt. To his specifications. True, he didn't have control over what might or might not happen with his arm, but at least he had control over this part of his life. But Faith...

Yes, he'd wait. And hell, yes, he'd be patient. But what if—?

"Darryl?"

With a slight jerk, he turned at the sound of the familiar, friendly voice, forcing a smile for Cal Logan, Dawn's husband, as the tall, lanky man approached. The two men briefly clasped hands, after which Cal squatted to make over Dot, who about wriggled herself into a frenzy. Darryl and Cal had known each other all their lives, being around the same age, but they'd never really been friends. Certainly nothing near what Dawn and Faith had been. There'd been a time, way back, when Darryl had wondered why Faith hadn't gone after Cal instead of him—it would have been a far more sensible match, at least on paper—except that Cal had only had eyes for Dawn ever since they were kids. Eyes that hadn't strayed nearly as much as some folks would have you believe during the ten years that Dawn had been back East.

"What are you doin' here?" the men asked each other at the same time, making Darryl smile.

"Just out for a walk," he said, noncommittally. "You?"

Cal pulled the collar of his coat higher up around his neck. "We're temporarily down a vehicle—my truck's out of commission—so I'm playing chauffeur for Dawn, gettin' her to and from work, until it's fixed. 'Cept she wasn't ready, as usual. 'Come back in fifteen minutes,' she said. So here I am, cooling my heels. Not to mention my backside and everything else."

"Sorry to hear about the truck." Darryl knew the old Chevy intimately. "What's wrong with it this time?"

"It's old, that's what's wrong with it. Put 150,000 miles on me, I probably wouldn't be much use to anyone, either."

"Don't you kid yourself, she's still got another twenty thou in her, easy."

"Yeah, with you lookin' after her, maybe. Not according to the guy in Claremore I had to take her to."

"Who's probably gettin' kickbacks from all the dealerships in town if he steers folks in their direction."

Cal chuckled. "You might have a point at that. He sure did seem hot to convince me I needed to trade the old gal in. Not that it would take much convincing at this point. Although I'd probably have to pay somebody to take her off my hands... Darryl? You okay?"

"What? Oh, sure. I'm fine."

Cal glanced across the street and blew out a breath, mumbling something about being an idiot. "Like I don't know what it feels like, thinking you might lose everything. When I wondered how in the hell I was gonna keep the farm going last year, if I was gonna have to sell the horses for whatever I could get…" He shook his head. "Nothin's scarier than thinking everything you've worked for your entire life could slip through your fingers."

"Tell me about it."

Off in the distance, a train whistle sliced through the creaking of the lone stoplight swinging in the wind. "Hey," Cal said, "you want to go get a cup of coffee at Ruby's before we freeze our tails off?"

"Can't. I've got the dog, but you go on ahead—"

"No, that's okay, it was just an idea."

Darryl frowned at him. "You don't need to stick around on my account, you know."

The other man shoved his hands into his pockets again, his breath clouding around his face. "If that's your way of saying you'd rather be alone, I'm outta here." His gaze swung to Darryl's. "If, on the other hand, you're just trying to give me an out because you think I don't care about whatever's making your shoulders slump like that, that's something else again."

"We're not close, Cal."

The other man shrugged. "Sometimes 'close' can be a liability. And if you're worried about me carrying tales back to Dawn..." He adjusted his broad-brimmed hat on his head. "Ain't gonna happen."

That almost got a smile. "So you keep secrets from your wife?"

"I keep *other* people's secrets from my wife, if they ask me to."

Darryl chewed this over for a couple of seconds, then nodded in the direction of the Victorian across the way where Dawn had her law office. "How'd you do it?" he said softly.

"How'd I do what?"

"Keep Dawn from going back to New York."

"Oh." He rubbed the side of his jaw with his thumb. "I didn't. In fact, I was fully prepared to let her go."

"Even though she'd just had your kid?"

"I didn't say it wouldn't've killed me," Cal said. "But Dawn had to make up her own mind. And if Sherman hadn't've left his practice to her..." He shook his head, looking up at the light in the second-story window. "She might've stuck around for a while, because of Max if nothing else. Maybe even because of me," he added with a crooked smile. "But eventually... I have no doubt she would have withered and died without an outlet for her

talents, you know? Which means she probably would have left me, anyway."

"You don't know that."

"No, but I know Dawn." Cal's eyes cut to
him. "So what's this all about?"

"Oh, nothing. Just…thinking."

Then the light across the street blinked
out, apparently Cal's signal that his wife was
done for the night. He clapped a hand on Darryl's arm, reminded Darryl he knew where
to find him if he needed a sounding board,
then strode across the street, whistling, the
sound irritatingly upbeat to a man whose life
seemed to be slipping further out of his reach
with every passing moment.

Darryl called the dog and headed back
home, head bent against the wind, not sure
what to expect when he got there. And for
sure he didn't know why he stopped in to
take another look at Marilyn, just for a minute, just to reassure himself that the car, at
least, hadn't changed on him in his absence.
That was one thing about cars—you could
put your heart and soul and sweat into them,
but at least you knew what you had when you
were done. Marriage was something else entirely. For not the first time, he considered
how much easier life would be if women were

like cars. But then, Darryl thought as he and
the dog crossed back to the house, it was the
very unpredictability of women's natures that
kept men from keeling over in sheer boredom.
One of those no-win situations, he guessed.

He opened the back door to find the
kitchen table set for two, Christmas music
coming from the living room. He walked
into the room to see a whole mess of presents
wrapped and neatly arranged under the tree,
those scented candles Faith liked so much
burning in clusters on every surface.

"I made biscuits," she said softly behind
him. Darryl turned to see her standing in the
kitchen doorway—she must've been in the
pantry when he'd come in—her hands fisted
in the pockets of her favorite big sweater. A
tiny smile flickered over her mouth. "Those
big fluffy ones you like so much? I found a
can in the refrigerator door I'd forgotten we
had. The bottoms got a little scorched, and
they don't exactly go with lasagna, but…"

"But, nothing." His lips curved up, though
his insides had gone all trembly. "Biscuits go
with everything. Didn't your mama teach you
anything?"

Her smile flickered a little brighter, only
to dim again as she tucked a curl behind her

ear. And met his gaze dead-on. "If you think this is about me doubting the choices I made twelve years ago…" Her head wagged slowly from side to side. "It isn't."

"I see." Darryl reached over to tweak a light back into place on the tree. "So what you're saying is…if you could go back and do things differently, you wouldn't?"

The dog bumped her hand; she lowered her eyes to scratch the beast's head. "Even if I could…" A long, slow breath left her lips. "The only thing that matters is *now,* Darryl. And now…" Bottomless, watery blue eyes met his. "I hope to heaven I'm not so much of a fool that I'd throw away something a lot of women never even come close to having."

And Darryl wasn't enough of a fool to demand anything more from her, just at the moment.

"Come here," he whispered, holding out his arm. She crossed the room and snuggled up against his chest, and he felt something shift inside him, although he couldn't have defined it if you'd paid him. He tugged her closer, as well as he could, rubbing his cheek in her soft, fragrant hair. "I don't suppose this means…" he said, and she swatted him and pulled out of his arms.

"Be grateful you're getting biscuits," she said, walking away.

But she was smiling. So for now, the elephant was still locked in its cage, safely out of sight. And if she refused to acknowledge it, then so would he.

Which didn't mean he didn't have his work cut out for him to make good and sure things stayed that way. And if previous methods of persuasion were currently off the table, then he'd better for damn sure come up with something else.

Something, anything, to prevent even the slightest doubt from taking root in her mind that she should've chosen Door #1, after all.

Chapter Nine

The Sunday before Christmas, Darryl was rudely awakened by a shaft of bright winter sunshine slashing across his face, courtesy of Faith's yanking up the miniblinds. Mumbling "What the hell…?" he tried to burrow underneath an extra pillow, only to have Faith snatch it out of his hands. He blearily noticed she was already perfumed and made up and dressed in a short, thigh-hugging skirt and a loose, not-hugging-anything sweater.

"You need to get moving or we're gonna be late for church," she said. "And you promised to go, so don't even think about groaning."

"You plied me—" he yawned hugely "—with biscuits."

"Like that would hold up in court," she said. "Get up."

Darryl blinked at her. Outside their room, the kids sounded like they were gonna kill each other for sure. "When was the last time I went to church with you guys?"

"Too long ago," she said, pawing through his clothes in the closet. "Here," she said, pulling a long-sleeved corduroy shirt off a hanger and tossing it at him. "That looks like the sleeve'd be large enough to fit the cast through."

"I hate this shirt," he muttered, but Faith, who was making noises about how she should've ironed his khakis, and guessed he'd have to wear jeans, anyway, didn't appear to notice. Darryl frowned up at her. "You never pushed me about going to church before. So how come now?"

"Because it's the Sunday before Christmas, for one thing." The mattress trembled when she sat on her side of the bed to put on her boots. "And Jake's singing in the children's choir for the first time, for another."

"Did I know that?" he said to her back, thinking R-rated thoughts involving his hand, the warm skin just on the other side of that fuzzy sweater and unhooking her bra.

"I told you, but whether or not it registered—" she bent over, grunting a little with the effort of getting the zipper done up "—I couldn't say. So I was going to put the screws in, anyway, but you saved me the trouble by offering."

"I'm never eating biscuits again," he said, and she snorted. But it was a sad snort. A snort with a lot of heavy meaning underlying it. Darryl pushed himself over on his side, the pillow squashed under his head.

"And this is about more than Jake and it being close to Christmas, isn't it?"

Faith huffed out a breath, then twisted around, her mouth all funny. "Okay, so I thought maybe a little damage control wouldn't be remiss."

Darryl's forehead cramped. "Tongues are wagging?"

"Like a hound dog's tail."

Slowly, he sat up, glowering at the shirt, a years-ago Christmas gift from her mother. It was bright yellow. And two sizes too big. He was gonna look like a damn school bus. "You know, maybe people should mind their own business."

"And how long have you lived in this town?"

Grumbling, Darryl hauled himself out of bed. His arm tingled today, the sensation close enough to pain to make him testy. Once on his feet, he plodded into the bathroom, half shutting the door to take care of immediate business, then opening it again to glower at his wife. "So what are *people* saying, exactly?"

She'd moved to the dresser to brush out her hair in front of the mirror, and now looked at him in the reflection. "Speculation, mostly. About how well we're holdin' up under the strain."

"I see. Has it gotten to bet-taking status yet?"

"Wouldn't surprise me. Especially since—"

"What?"

She shook her head.

Darryl sighed. "Especially since half the town's been *speculatin' about us since we got married, right?*"

He saw her chest rise, then fall. "I'd just like us to show up at church as a family, for once. That's all."

"Yeah, that's bound to stop rumors in their tracks, all right."

"It wouldn't hurt," she said, then glared at him. "Okay, then why *did* you offer to go?"

"I told you. Biscuits." When she looked as

if she might lob her brush at him, he added, "And because I figured I could use a few extra points."

Her mouth curved up at the corners then. Just a little.

"With me or God?"

"Either. Both." He walked around the bed, watching her watch him in the mirror, before he lifted her curls off the back of her neck and pressed a kiss into that great spot where her neck met her shoulder. "Especially since," he whispered, "you wouldn't let me earn points in other ways."

"It's not an either-or thing," she said. With a slight shudder.

"Didn't say it had to be. Although…" He slipped his arm around her waist, then lightly rested his chin on her shoulder, his eyes melded with hers in the mirror. "Feeling your soft, naked skin against mine…watching your face when I get you goin'…honey, we are talking *serious* hea*ven-on-earth time."*

He felt her swallow. "Darryl…"

"Or have you forgotten that part of our vows where we promised to worship each other with our bodies?"

She grimaced in the mirror. "How is it you

can remember that, but never, ever where you put the remote?"

"You're a lot more fun than the remote?" he said, kissing her temple. She grunted. "How long do we have?"

She flinched. "What?"

"Before we leave for church?"

"Oh. A good half hour yet."

"I'll be ready," he said, not even bothering to hide his smile when she wobbled slightly after he released her.

Oh, dear Lord.

Faith sailed out the bedroom, hoping against hope that throwing herself into the melee of kids and dog would quickly deflate her swollen, aching libido.

No such luck. Even in the midst of refereeing who got which cereal, and a frantic search for Crystal's favorite shoes, and fixing Heather's hair, which simply would *not* cooperate, and changing Nicky's diaper for the third time that morning—no more creamed spinach for him, boy—every nerve ending she had pulsed and sang and begged and generally made itself a complete and total nuisance. And the worst part of it was, she couldn't decide if she was winning or losing the war.

No, the *worst* part was…she had no earthly idea what the war was even about anymore.

Why was it the harder she tried to get her head screwed on straight, the more confused she got? Was it bugging her that Darryl's sex drive seemed to always be idling on high, or that hers was?

And what, exactly, was the problem with that again?

"Mama! Nicky won't stop flushing the toilet!"

Ah, yes. Now she remembered. *Babies*. Except that was a non-issue now, wasn't it?

She grabbed Nicky's coat and tromped down the hall to the bathroom, scooping up the screeching baby to stuff pudgy, uncooperative arms into tight, equally uncooperative sleeves.

Because, really, what was the freaking point? Was she any closer to some sort of conclusion about who she was/what she wanted/ what she was going to do about any of it after several weeks of abstinence than she would have been if she and Darryl had been boinking like bunnies all along? Somehow, she doubted it. A revelation that ticked her off, frankly—

"Everybody in the car! Heather, quit primp-

ing and get out here! Jake, don't forget your
choir robe, it's hangin' on the back of your
door! Darryl, we have to leave *now* or Jake's
gonna miss his warm-up!"

—because it meant she'd been putting herself (not to mention her husband) through the
wringer for nothing.

They all piled into the Suburban and took
off, Darryl's freshly showered and shaved
scent pure torment to her battered senses, and
she thought, great, now she was going to be
sitting in church all hot and bothered, beset
by all manner of wayward thoughts.

"Something wrong?" he asked, glancing
over, although she barely heard him over the
din of Crystal's and Jake's getting into it over
God-knew-what from the back seat. Then
Jake let one rip, which of course he found
immensely amusing, especially when Heather
and Crystal both launched into moans of dis-
may. Faith glanced over and caught Darryl
trying his best to keep a straight face, and the
absurdity of the whole situation hit her like a
water balloon to the face.

She burst out laughing louder than her son,
which provoked pained outbursts of "Mama!
It's not funny!" from her poor, grossed-out
older daughters. So of course, Darryl lost his

battle as well, although he managed to con-
fine his amusement to a grin and a chuckle.

And Faith thought, *You know, you chose
this man. And this life, when all's said and
done, it is a pretty good life at that*. And dissecting the reasons for her choice…after all
this time, what was the point? More often
than not, her marriage worked just fine. As
for the other…well, there'd been no guarantee that would've worked out anyway, right?
So maybe Darryl and her mother and everybody else was right, maybe it was just the
turbulence brought on by the tornado and its
results that had thrown her off-kilter, and all
she needed was to wait it out until things got
back to normal and this craziness passed.

Because—she reached over to straighten
out Darryl's collar, which he couldn't do one-
handed, and he managed to send a smolder-
ing look in her direction that couldn't have
lasted more than a half-second—she really
didn't want to lose this man, now any more
than she had at eighteen.

Which meant, it occurred to her as they
pulled into the church parking lot, maybe she
hadn't changed as much as she'd thought.

A thought that should have put her mind at
ease a lot more than it did.

* * *

Sitting next to Faith, watching dust motes sparkle in the sunlight streaming through the greenery trimmed, plain glass windows, Darryl thought, you know, this really isn't so bad. In fact, he wasn't sure why he resisted so hard going to church. Faith's daddy injected a lot of humor into his sermons, holding to the idea that people were more likely to think things over if you made them laugh rather than swamping them with guilt. And would you look at Jake up there, belting out "Silent Night" like his entry into heaven depended on it. So all in all, the experience was a whole lot more pleasant than, say, the agony those X-ray people put him through when he went in to have his arm checked. What he hadn't expected, though, was to run into the elephant. Right here, wedged in the pew between him and his wife. Or more to the point, in her throat.

Because this wasn't how she used to sing, back before they were married. Man, it was something else, the way she'd give that sweet, strong voice of hers its head, the sound cutting right through everybody else's, like it was reaching for the stars. Used to turn him on, frankly. In fact, he remembered the first time he really took notice of Faith, when she'd been around thirteen or fourteen and had been standing right where Jake was standing now, singing "O Holy Night" in a manner suggesting she'd actually been present for the actual event.

Seemed like she sang all the time, back then—in the school chorus, at church, sometimes just walking home from school, not caring who heard her. He remembered, too, how she'd sit on her porch now and again, strumming softly on her guitar, her bare feet tucked up underneath her on the porch swing, singing some old, sad ballad from way before their time.

All the talk was how Faith would make a name for herself with that voice, maybe even make it all the way to Nashville. The music teacher up at school—Mrs. Evers, that was her name—had even made a tape of her and sent it on to somebody who knew somebody who knew an agent in Nashville, which was how the man had actually come to Haven to talk to Faith, in person, right around the time Darryl had finally gotten used to calling her his girlfriend.

Only then she got pregnant, and she'd been all excited about the baby and them getting married. And little by little, he now realized, his own good-for-nothin' voice getting stuck in his throat, she'd stopped singing altogether, except for a lullaby to the baby from time to time. Come to think of it, he wasn't even sure he knew where her guitar was. Up in their closet? At her parents'?

And now, listening to her mumble the hymns, Darryl finally came to grips with the simple fact that not acknowledging something didn't make it go away. That Faith could twist herself inside out from now to doomsday, trying to figure out what she was missing, when the truth was it had been looming behind her for years, just waiting for her to turn around and see it.

They sat back down as the organ started up the offertory. Faith dug a five-dollar bill out of her purse and pressed it into his hand, even though she could have just as easily put it into the basket herself. She could be real old-fashioned like that sometimes. In fact, it had been her traditional approach to things that had convinced him they'd make a good fit, right from the start.

After the service, all manner of folks came up to them, to compliment Jake, to express their pleasure at seeing Darryl again after such a long absence, to ask how he was getting on, if the garage would be up and running anytime soon. But more than one person expressed a heartfelt wish to hear Faith sing the solo like she used to, or at least to rejoin the choir. She only laughed and said with the kids and all, she'd let her voice go something terrible and wouldn't dream of inflicting it on the public in such a major way.

Only now, finally, Darryl heard the truth humming underneath her words and smile. A truth that provoked him into wanting to ask a question he wasn't entirely sure he was ready to hear the answer to.

And one probably best not brought up in the car with five kids gyrating behind them like downed power lines. But he knew if he waited, he'd lose his nerve.

When the noise level rose enough to drown out front seat conversation, he said, "It's taken a long time to catch up with you, hasn't it?"

She looked at him, frowning. "For what to catch up with me?"

"That you gave up your singing for me."

When she didn't say anything, he glanced over. He didn't think it was only the harsh midday light making her look paler than usual. Their gazes wrestled for a moment or two before she shifted her attention back out the windshield. "I thought we cleared this up the other night."

"No, what we did was sidestep it."

"Well, then, let me *make* it clear. I lost interest in performing, Darryl. And that's all. I did not give it up for you."

"Lost interest? That's like sayin' a person could lose interest in breathing. Or eating. You'd sung all your life. Everybody said—"

"I know what everybody said," she said quietly. "That I was destined to be a star." A dry laugh left her throat. "Like every year thousands of young girls with the ability to put across a song aren't being told the same thing."

"But that agent—"

"Was some fast-talkin', two-bit nobody lookin' to fill a girl's head full of empty dreams." He felt her gaze warm on the side of his face. "You, on the other hand, were real." She lowered her voice. "Just like our child growing inside me was real. That was a future I could count on. The other…" Her shoulders hitched again. "Not even worth thinking about."

"That still doesn't explain why you stopped singing altogether."

"And maybe you're looking too hard for an explanation that doesn't exist…oh, Jake, for heaven's sake, quit tormenting your sister! Or have you forgotten Santa's watching?"

From Thanksgiving to Christmas, they had Santa. The other eleven months they were screwed. The profound silence behind them following Faith's threat might have brought a smile to Darryl's face if, one, their conversation hadn't left him feeling profoundly annoyed and two, Faith hadn't picked that moment to remind him that she had to go to work at one.

"Did you tell me you had to work today?" he said, pulling into their driveway, the older kids exploding from the car before he'd even cut the engine.

"My schedule's right on the refrigerator. Where it's been for the past two weeks. Besides…" She unhooked her seat belt. "I told you from the beginning I'd have to work on weekends, being low man on the totem pole and all."

"And when're you gonna admit how much you hate it?"

Her head whipped around. "Where on earth did you get that idea?"

"Come on, Faithie…you come home beat every night, you never talk about work, you look like you're going to your execution every time you walk out the door...you think I haven't figured it out?"

With her purse hugged to her chest, she finally said, "Okay, so it's not exactly a dream job. But come on, weren't there times when you didn't want to go to work, either?"

"No." He hesitated, then laid a hand on her knee. "It's not dessert, is it?"

"I've got to get a move on," she said, shoving open the door and striding toward the house, head bent, arms crossed tightly over her middle.

Well, he had his answer, didn't he? And if he felt like somebody'd stomped all over his stomach, he had nobody to blame but himself. Because even a blind man could see straight through that "losing interest" line. Why Faith had spent the majority of their married life denying an elemental part of who she was, why she was *still* denying it, he had no idea.

But if this wasn't a time bomb waiting to explode, he didn't know what was.

All through lunch, Faith felt a lot like she had a couple years ago when some idiot in a pickup pulled out right in front of her when she was taking the kids to school, making her slam the breaks so hard the Suburban nearly skidded off the road. Nobody'd been hurt, but it was a good week or two before she could get behind the wheel without having a near panic attack. Coming way too close to disaster would do that to a person.

Of course, anyone with half a brain would think she'd lost hers, to be comparing narrowly escaping a car crash with her jitters now. And anyway, she saw no point in dissecting the reasons behind a decision that was for all intents and purposes irreversible. After enough time, and enough children, what did it matter whether her desire to sing had given up the ghost on its own or she'd suffocated it?

She'd just zipped her black jeans and was getting ready to freshen up her makeup when Heather poked her head inside their bedroom.

"Hey, sugar—what's up?"

"Nothin'," the girl said, drifting into the room and flopping crosswise on the bed. "I just put Nicky down for his nap. He went right down without a fuss."

"Thanks, sweetie. You get your homework done?"

"I told you Friday, I didn't have any this weekend. Remember?"

"Oh, right. Where's Daddy?"

"In the living room, watching some dumb

football game. I think maybe his arm's hur-
tin' him."

Faith's brow knotted. "Why do you say that?"

"Jake banged into it when he and Daddy
were tussling, and Daddy made this really
scary face for a few seconds. You don't think
Jake could've broken it again or something?"

"No, honey," Faith said over the sensation
of her stomach dropping to her knees. "It's
been a month, the bones are already pretty
much set."

"Then why's he still wearing a cast?"

"To give everything a chance to get strong
again."

"But what if his arm doesn't heal right?
How's he going to be able to work?"

Faith turned around, her lipstick in her
hand. "For heaven's sake, what are you going
on about? Why do you think his arm's not
going to heal properly?"

"Carly's knee won't ever get well enough
for her to dance again. And look at old Miss
Ida—she's never been able to walk right since
she broke her hip."

"Miss Ida is in her late eighties, sugar, her
bones were probably like shredded wheat. And
she refused to do her exercises, according to
her daughter. And Carly's case is different—

her injury has nothing to do with breaking anything." Faith turned back to the mirror, swiping the lipstick across her mouth. "For goodness' sake, people break bones all the time and they heal just fine. In fact, your father broke his arm before, when he was a teenager, with no aftereffects whatsoever. Why should this time be any different?"

"Because he's old now."

Faith laughed. "Oh, I bet he'd just love to hear that."

"But what if his arm doesn't heal? What would happen?"

"Boy, you are like a terrier with a rat today, aren't you? Like I said, I don't see that happening. But if it should…" She twisted the cap off her mascara, then leaned forward to apply a fresh coat. "I guess we'd just have to deal with the situation when it comes up. It's pointless fretting about something that *might* happen, don't you think?"

Heather didn't look convinced, but at least she let the subject drop. Then she said, "When do you have to go to work?"

"In a few minutes. I'm really sorry, I know you guys are used to having me around all the time. I'm hoping I can switch my schedule after Christmas so I don't have to work in the evenings, at least—"

"I was only askin', Mama, chill." The girl rolled onto her stomach, her hair puddled on the bed on either side of her shoulders when she rested her chin on her folded hands. "Most everybody else's mother works, you know. It's not like it's any big deal or anything."

"Nice to know I'm missed."

"That's not what I mean, geez." A faint crease tried to lodge between the child's eyebrows. "I don't want you to worry, that's all."

As if. Heather's propensity for fretting didn't come out of nowhere.

"All I know is," she said, "I sure as heck don't intend to give up my career if *I* have kids."

Faith's eyes zinged to her daughter's in the mirror. "Um…good for you. But what brought that on?"

There was a long pause, then a sigh. "Okay, so I heard you and Daddy talking in the car when we were coming home from church."

"Over all the ruckus your brothers and sisters were making?"

The girl shrugged. "We were talking in class the other day about how species develop whatever abilities they need to survive. In my case, I think my hearing's so good because otherwise I'd miss out on all the good stuff."

"I don't think you were supposed to tell me that."

Her shoulders bumped upwards. "So do you really hate your job?"

"I'm grateful for it," Faith said, dodging. "And we need the money."

"That's not answering my question."

Brother, Faith thought, recapping her mascara. "No," she said. "I don't like it very much. But you do what you gotta, you know?" At the girl's silence, Faith looked into the mirror and said, "What?"

"Grandma says you sang all the time, always won talent contests and stuff. She said you loved to sing more'n just about anything."

"So you heard that part of the conversation, too."

"Enough."

Faith sighed. "It was a kid thing. I got over it."

Heather watched her intently for a long time. "Like Daddy thinks I'm gonna get over wanting to dance?"

Faith shook her head, which only shook the truth awake even more. "Not the same thing."

More intense staring. "No, I guess not.

'Cause I can't imagine not wanting to dance anymore. It would be like cuttin' out a piece of my heart."

Oh, the drama of being eleven.

"Did you…did you stop singing because of me?"

Honest to Pete, what was with everybody today?

"No, Heather, I did not stop singing because of you. Or because of your daddy or anybody else. I stopped singing because I didn't want to do it anymore." That much, at least, was true. "And if I don't get out of here, I'm going to be late."

"You think it'd be okay if I went over to Patrice's for a couple hours? I'll be back in time to get Nicky up from his nap and change his diaper."

"It's okay with me, but check with your father first."

The girl scooted out of the room; Faith followed a few minutes later, peeking in to say goodbye to Sierra and Crystal, who were playing with an entire beauty pageant's worth of Barbies in their disaster of a room. Jake, however, was outside with Dot, determined to build a snowman out of the whole inch of snow that had fallen the night before.

"You leaving?" Darryl asked when she crossed the living room to the front door. The way his eyes were glued to the TV, she probably could've walked by him stark naked and he wouldn't have noticed.

"In a minute or two," she said, digging her own coat out of the pile dumped on the chair nearest to the front door. "Make sure Jake doesn't track up the floor when he comes in."

"Yeah, okay." Faith bit her tongue to keep from asking him to repeat what she'd just said. "Heather went over to Patrice's for a little while," Darryl added. "She said you said it was okay."

"Only if it was okay with you," she stated, and he grunted, the sound of a man who's been hoodwinked but who would die before admitting it. Faith slipped into her jacket, yanking her hair out of the collar before swinging her purse over her shoulder. "Heather said Jake crashed into your arm earlier. You all right?"

"Sure. Why wouldn't I be?"

"She thought maybe you'd gotten hurt."

He aimed the remote at the TV to change the channel. Oh, Lord—*two* games? "Nope, I'm fine," he said.

One day, Faith mused, men were gonna figure out that women were naturally hardwired to know when they were lying. Especially this man, she thought as annoyance rippled through her.

"Darryl?"

Finally, he tore his gaze away from the TV, wearing that slightly irritated expression of a man who's just had his testosterone flow interrupted.

"Are you keeping something from me?" she asked, straight out. Which wasn't like her, not at all, but she really was going to be late for work if she didn't get a move on, so her pussyfooting time was at a premium.

His eyebrows pulled together, but other than that, he wasn't giving anything away. "About what?"

"What did they say about your arm the last time you had it x-rayed?"

Underneath the frown, wariness clouded his eyes. "Nothing. Other than the bones are knitting back together exactly the way they should. Why?"

"I just wondered. Since you hadn't said anything. But aren't you supposed to be doin' some exercises by now, to keep the strength up in the muscles?"

He looked back at the TV. "I have been. You just haven't been around."

"But you'd tell me, wouldn't you, if something wasn't right?"

Once more, he dragged his attention away from the TV, scowling. "If I had something to tell, yes. Since I don't, this is a pointless discussion—"

The high-pitched shriek of a thwarted three-year-old pierced the air as Crystal, her face the picture of *I have* had *it,* lugged a screaming Sierra into the living room. Honestly, Faith thought, swallowing down her annoyance, if they ever got to finish a single conversation, she'd fall over in a dead faint.

"You stay here with Daddy!" Crystal said, unceremoniously dumping her baby sister onto the sofa beside Darryl.

The move clearly didn't sit well with the toddler, who launched herself back at her sister with an eardrum shattering, *"No!"*

"Whoa, whoa, whoa," Darryl said. "What the Sam Hill's going on—?"

"She won't stay out of my stuff, that's what!" Crystal said with a grunt, shoving the littler girl back onto the sofa when she tried to get off. *"No,* Sierra, you stay there!"

"Don't wan' to!" the child screamed, her

face the color of boiled lobster. By now the two girls were a blur of flailing limbs as Sierra aggressively resisted Crystal's attempts to pin her to the sofa. "My room, too!" the younger child yelled, her voice rapidly reaching steel-cutting level as Faith hiked her purse up onto her shoulder and backed toward the front door. "*My room!*"

"What's going on?" Jake asked, a lot more hope than worry in his voice—nothing like the prospect of his sisters coming to blows to stir the blood, boy—as from down the hall came Nicky's sleepy, irritable wail.

"It was my room first!" Crystal bellowed, dodging her sister's attempts to catapult herself off the sofa. "You can't come back... *ow! No,* Sierra! *No hitting!* Mama!" Crystal wheeled around, rubbing her arm. "Tell her no hitting!"

"Sorry, guys, but I've really got to go—"

"*Nooo!*" Sierra wailed, now flying across the room to wrap herself around Faith's knees. "D-don't go, Mama, don't g-go!"

"I'll be back soon, sweetie—"

"*Nononononono—!*"

"Come here, monkey," Darryl said, somehow prying the child off her legs with his good arm. "Go on," he said to Faith, the wriggling, ticked-off child firmly grasped around the waist, facing away from him. "It's okay— cut it out, Sierra!—I can handle it."

"I'm sure you can," Faith said, slamming the door shut behind her.

Chapter Ten

The rubber ball sat on the counter, sneering at him. Taunting him. Daring him to squeeze the life out of it. Or even to close his fingers around it.

The rest of the upheaval in Darryl's life had provided a convenient excuse to ignore the arm, to avoid thinking about the what-ifs. But since Faith had obviously picked up the scent of his deception, his days of waiting to see whether or not there was anything to really worry about were numbered. He'd done a pretty good job of faking things for these first few weeks, but Faith was right, he was supposed to be exercising the bum arm. Should have been for a while already. And now that she'd dragged the subject kicking and screaming out into the open, he could be sure she'd bug him to death about it from now on.

He glanced up at the kitchen clock: fifteen minutes before he had to leave to pick Heather up from dance class. Last time he'd checked, the middle two were sprawled at opposite ends of the sofa, watching some holiday movie, thanks to his mother's vast DVD collection. The babies were at Faith's mother's, dinner was in the oven and all was right with the world.

Except for this.

"Don't expect miracles at first," the physical therapist had said. "Just do the best you can."

He put the ball into his left hand with his right. It fell to the floor, barely making it two feet before Dot pounced on it.

"Give it back, you dumb beast," Darryl growled, wresting the now slimy ball out of her mouth. Her bug eyes trained on the ball, she scooted back, rump shimmying, then woofed at him.

He turned away, his eyes burning as he desperately tried to feel the ball in his palm, willing his numb fingers to close around it. It didn't make sense that his arm could hurt so damn bad and yet there be no sensation in his fingers at all. Panic rose in his throat, tightening his chest, as *normal* seemed to be slipping even more out of his grasp—literally—than ever.

Darryl wrenched open the back door and hurled the ball outside with his good arm, sending the dog streaking across the dry, brown grass. Except the yard was all glowing from the last, gold rays of the setting sun, and the air was crisp and clear, and he could hear the kids giggling at the movie, and he thought, *You know, dumb-ass, you've got a lot to be grateful for.*

So he marched out into all that golden light and fought the dog for the ball, stuffing it into his left hand. And it fell out again, and Darryl swore, only the cussing wasn't quite as edged with panic as it had been. He didn't exactly know why, only that he didn't feel quite as hopeless as he had a few minutes before.

Some time later, he stood at the back of Carly Stewart's barn/dance studio, painfully aware he was the only male in the place, other than Jake. A busted axle had brought Carly and her dad, Lane, into Haven to begin with, back sometime in the early fall, when their

camper had gone off into a ditch on their way
through town. Cranky had been his first impression of the gal. Too damn skinny had
been his second. And for sure too citified to
ever take to a podunk town like Haven. But
damned if her daddy didn't take a shine to
Ivy Gardner, which led to his buying the di-
lapidated farm next to Sam Frazier's property,
and damned if the gal didn't end up staying
here, too. Word was that Carly and Sam had
become an item, too, the farmer's six kids
notwithstanding.

All of which accounted for Darryl's standing here watching a bunch of young girls
more or less Heather's age prancing around
in everything from one-piece swimsuits to
bicycle shorts to sweats, all bony elbows
and bent knees, some of them still a little
on the pudgy side, others so skinny a stiff
breeze'd blow 'em away. A few had real ballet shoes on, but most were barefoot. According to Heather, Carly—decked out in a baggy
sweater and what looked like sweater sleeves
on her legs—wasn't picky. The point was to
dance, not make a fashion statement.

"Okay, guys, we have time for one more
combination," Carly shouted, her voice remarkably strong for somebody that puny.

"Slow or fast?" she asked, which got a chorus of mixed answers, but "slow" won out.

The brunette stood for a moment in the center of the room, her curly hair more out of than in the clip holding it up off her neck, then started to move, calling out a bunch of foreign-sounding words as her limbs seemed to float through the air, like they were attached to strings. After that, she had the girls imitate her—kind of—until she was sure they knew what to do. She clicked the CD player back on, some flowery music with lots of violins, and everybody went through the steps again with Carly. Then she turned, continuing to call out the steps as she walked around the room, adjusting an arm here, a tilt of the head there. Not that it made any difference with most of the girls, as far as Darryl could tell, but it impressed him, the way she smiled and encouraged even the ones with two left feet. Somewhere along the way, the cranky woman from a couple months back had disappeared.

Then he caught sight of Heather, who'd been behind a couple other girls where he couldn't see her, and Darryl damn near forgot to breathe.

When had her legs gotten that *long?* He

swallowed hard as a mixture of pride, protectiveness and terror assailed him. And something else. Something he couldn't even name. Heaven knew, Heather didn't look like Carly when she did the steps—her back wasn't quite as straight; her arms bent in places Carly's didn't; her feet weren't as pointed. But she sure as hell didn't look like any of the other girls, either. She moved like…like the music came from inside her. And the look on her face…she *glowed*. Like nothing else mattered but this. Like nothing would *ever* matter but this.

"Heather's real pretty, isn't she?" Jake whispered up at him.

"Yeah, buddy," he said over the knot in his throat that forms when a man realizes his kid has become something apart from him. "She sure is."

The music stopped, all the students clapped, then the scene dissolved into a blur of giggles and gabbing, of limbs being shoved into jeans and heavy coats and sneakers and boots, of feet thundering across the wooden floor. The noise level crescendoed as the girls' chatter blended with their mothers', only to rapidly die out as each family in turn filed outside until nobody was left except Darryl and his brood. And Carly, who was grinning from ear to ear as she walked over to them, slipping into a cardigan big enough to cover three of her. Now the barn reverberated with hollers and the pounding of sneakered feet as Crystal and Jake streaked across the floor, stopping in the middle to spin themselves dizzy.

"So what do you think of your girl?" Carly said, looping one arm around Heather's shoulders and giving her a swift hug. "I know you probably have no idea what you're looking at, but believe me, she's got real potential."

"I can see that," Darryl said, his half smile provoking a shy one in return from his oldest child. "She's really...something."

Carly gave him a funny look for a moment, then said, "Heather, would you mind giving me a second to talk with your dad?"

With a "Sure," his daughter tromped off to join her siblings, which was when Darryl noticed the huge ring on Carly's left hand. She followed his gaze, then laughed, lifting her hand to let the light play off the rectangular pink stone.

"Isn't it gorgeous? Fifteen bucks at Macy's. Sam's kids picked it out."

"So it's not just a rumor?"

"Apparently not. Although you can tell

Faith I'm counting on her to give me lots of pointers on dealing with a batch of kids. But that's not what I want to talk to you about." Carly hesitated, then said, "Look, I know things are tough for you guys right now. Heather's already told me how she's earning her own money to pay for some of her lessons. Which is pretty damn remarkable for a kid of her age. For a kid of *any* age, actually."

"She's a remarkable kid."

Carly smiled. "Yeah, she is. But she's going to be an exhausted kid if she's not careful. Eleven-year-olds have an amazing well of energy to draw on, but it's not unlimited. I don't see any way she can go to school, dance *and* work and not end up completely wasted within a few months."

"I agree. But she's got her heart set on doing this."

"Then let me teach her for free. At least until you get on your feet again?"

Darryl blew a harsh breath through his nose. "My wife put you up to this?"

"No. I swear. And Heather doesn't know anything about it, either. This is completely my idea."

"Why? Pardon me for saying this, but what are her chances of—"

"Success? I don't know. It's way too soon to be making any predictions. All I can go on is what I see, and I see an incredible natural talent that could conceivably be a spectacular talent one day, with the right training. And Heather's desire to make the most of that talent."

Darryl pushed out another breath, then looked into the brunette's weird, pale blue eyes. "Just doesn't seem right, you taking such a huge risk, spending all that time and not getting paid for it."

"Why? Because there aren't any guarantees?" She shrugged. "It's my risk to take, I suppose. And Heather's. Besides, sometimes it's not about the getting, it's about the *trying*." Heather joined them again; smiling, Carly linked her arm through his daughter's. "There are lots of gifted people in the world," she said. "But precious few of them ever get a chance to really make the most of those talents. Just seems like such a waste, don't you think?"

At that, Heather looked up at him with those big, hopeful eyes, and it hit Darryl right between his that he didn't have it in him to stand between her and the moon. Especially when, this time, he knew damn well that's what he'd be doing.

"I'll…think about it," he said.

Carly grinned. "Can't ask for more than that."

That didn't mean, however, he thought on the way home as Heather talked his ear off about something that happened at school that day, that he still had any stomach for the idea of letting Carly teach Heather for free. But where the hell was he supposed to get the money?

Only before the question was even completely formed in his brain, he had his answer. Not an answer he liked a whole lot, to be honest. In fact, the *"No! Anything but that!"* that clanged inside his brain actually made him flinch so hard Heather asked him if he was okay.

But when he glanced over at his daughter, into those eyes full of fire and trust, the clanging immediately subsided, to be replaced with that sense of calm that comes when a man knows he's doing the right thing.

Or knows when he's doomed, maybe.

Having a kid with a birthday two days before Christmas, Faith mused as she wrestled

Nicky into the adorable reindeer-covered overalls Renee had given him, was a major inconvenience, to say the least. However, with two sets of grandparents, at least she didn't have to do the actual party. Not that one-year-olds needed a party, for heaven's sake (the pointlessness of that endeavor had made itself more than clear at least three kids ago), but this way all the grown-ups were appeased and all Faith had to do was show up with the kid. And if nothing else, it provided a distraction for the other rug rats, who were about to drive her insane with the pre-Christmas hypers.

Not to mention provide a distraction for her, as well.

She heard the phone ring, heard Heather yell, "Daddy! It's Uncle Danny!"

Again? Faith thought idly, finally snagging one of Nicky's perpetually kicking feet and shoving it into a tiny hiking boot. Darryl and his younger brother had talked to each other more over the past few days than they had in probably the last three months. Whenever she asked about the calls, her husband shrugged and said, "Just family stuff. Nothing important," and changed the subject. She hoped like heck he wasn't planning some sort of Christmas surprise after all, especially since she hadn't gotten anything for him.

Her youngest finally clothed, she trooped out to the living room, hollering to everyone to get their coats—they were already late. Only then, when she finally had the other four actually getting into the Suburban, Darryl threw her for a total loop by saying he'd have to catch up to them later, he needed to go out to the Double Arrow for a bit to see Danny about something.

She handed Nicky over to Heather so she could strap him in, then turned back to her husband, suspicion sprouting like weeds in her brain. "Okay, what's going on?"

But he only gave her this funny I-know-something-you-don't smile and said, "I won't be long, I promise."

"Where the heck have you been?" Faith whispered an hour later when Darryl finally showed up, slipping his right arm around her waist. Everybody was gathered at Renee's dining room table; in his high chair, happily gnawing on the birthday hat that Faith had long since given up trying to keep on his head, Nicky was totally oblivious to what was coming next. "Your mother's about to bring out the cake."

"I know, I know," Darryl whispered back. "Just trust me, okay?"

At that moment, Renee appeared with a gorgeous, perfectly frosted chocolate cake, a huge "1" candle blazing away on the top. Nicky stopped munching on the hat and blinked in interest, only to jump a foot, his eyes huge and wary, when a dozen people burst into singing "Happy Birthday." This, of course, was followed by cutting the first piece for the baby, with the ensuing gales of laughter and camera flashing—Renee was real big on "documenting the moment," as she put it—when he proceeded to gleefully give himself a chocolate frosting facial. Faith already had four other sets of photos exactly like it in a huge plastic bin at home, waiting for that mythical day when she'd actually put them all in albums. It was enough to make a woman very weary.

But before she sank into full-out depression, Darryl took her by the hand and dragged her back into the kitchen, calling Heather as they went. Forking in her cake and ice cream like she was afraid somebody'd take it from her—which, in this family, was a valid worry—the child gave Faith a "What's up?" look as she joined them, to which Faith could only shake her head and shrug in reply.

"I've got an early Christmas present for you," Darryl said, grinning about as broadly as he could without injuring himself. He reached inside his shirt pocket and took out what turned out to be a money order, which he then unfolded and showed to Heather.

Her plastic fork stuck in her mouth, the girl's eyes widened. Then the fork slowly dropped. "Is that as much money as I think it is? Mama…?" she said, turning to Faith as if not sure what she was supposed to do or say next.

Faith could relate. She tore her eyes away from the money order to look at her husband, her heart turning over at the *Do I rate or what?* expression on his face.

"Darryl…where'd you get this?"

"From a very nice man who just bought the Bird off me."

Her mouth dropped open as Heather said, "You sold Marilyn? Why?"

Darryl's gaze shifted to their daughter. "Because I saw you dance, baby. Or more to the point, I saw the look on your face when you danced. And then Carly did her number on me, and..." He shrugged. "I knew I couldn't live with myself until I found some way for you to do this. Some way that didn't involve either Carly teaching you gratis, or you running yourself into the ground. And the other day Carly told me there's a school in Tulsa, a good school. One of the best in the country. She said in a year or so, you might be ready for it. I just thought it wouldn't hurt to plan ahead."

"Oh, Daddy..." The child launched herself at her father, wrapping her arms so tightly around his waist Faith wondered how the man was breathing. How Faith herself was breathing. "This is the best present ever! Thank you, Daddy, thank you, thank you, *thank you!*" Only then she pulled away, her mouth turned down at the corners. "But aren't you gonna miss Marilyn?"

Faith figured it was only because she knew Darryl as well as she did that she even noticed how the joy in his eyes flickered, just for a second, like a candle in a sudden breeze. "I suppose, for a while. But the man who bought her...you should have seen the look on his face when he saw her. I have no doubt he's gonna love her and take care of her and show her off the way she deserves, instead of keepin' her locked up in a garage all the time. And who knows? Maybe someday I'll get another junk heap and start over. Only this time, maybe you can help me, how's that?"

"Really?" the child said, beaming, and Faith gawked at her, thinking, *Good Lord, when did that happen?*

"You bet. Now you better go on back to the party and get some more cake before everybody else eats it all."

It wasn't until after Heather had floated— there was no other word to describe it—out of the room that Darryl's eyes finally found their way back to Faith's, and she thought, *This goes way beyond biscuits.*

Darryl's only thought at the moment of impact was amazement at how something so soft and round and short could pack such a wallop. In fact, he might've let out a wince when his hip glanced off the edge of the counter but for Faith's mouth keeping his otherwise occupied. Catching on *real* quick, he cuffed her neck and encouraged the kiss to go as deep and hot as she wanted. Which was apparently pretty deep and hot, sending every nerve ending he had into a tizzy of excitement. Except for the ones in his left hand, which didn't seem to be getting the message, but damned if he was going to let that rain on what was shaping up to be one doozy of a parade.

He broke for air long enough to say, "Welcome back?"

She laughed, then started nuzzling the hollow of his throat. Oh, man. "You really sold Marilyn?" she said, looking up at him again with that "My Hero" look in her eyes that every man dreams about, and Darryl knew right then and there he'd racked up major points. Hell, he'd won the game, the division title and the entire state championship.

Dilated pupils! *Yes!!!*

"I really did," he said, thinking those dilated pupils must be acting like some sort of anesthetic, considering how quickly the pain of giving up the car was fading.

"How on earth—?"

"The internet." She'd wrapped her arms around his waist, meaning that there was a good two-foot stretch there where everything was touching. Made thinking a real challenge, but never let it be said that he couldn't multitask. "That was what all the calls back and forth between Danny and me were about. SueEllen found a website where I could list

the car, with Danny as the contact 'cause I
didn't want you or Heather to catch wind of
what I was doing until it was a done deal.
I had no idea if it would work or not, but
damned if I didn't get three bites the first
day, including one from this guy from up near
Bartlesville."

"Wow," she said, big-eyed.

"I know. Surprised the hell out of me, too.
Anyway, he wanted to come see it right away,
but I had to put him off until I knew y'all'd
be gone."

"Which would be today."

"Yep. He was hanging out at the Arrow
until I sounded the all clear."

"So that's why you were so late."

"The guy insisted on a test drive. Go figure."

She chuckled, then—no surprise there—
got all shiny-eyed. "That is the most generous, unselfish, incredible…" Her head tilted.
"*Thank you* seems woefully inadequate,
somehow."

"I'm sure we could work something out,"
he said, and lowered his mouth to hers again,
and their tongues got real cozy and his brain
was practically screaming *"Breast! Breast!"*
to his hand, but he somehow didn't think

going at it in his mother's kitchen with the entire family on the other side of the swinging door was such a hot idea. Well, it was a *hot* idea. Just not a real smart one.

Anyway, he broke the kiss before one or the other of them combusted, managing to divert his brain from his aching groin long enough to say, "I know what it feels like, wanting something so much it hurts. I also knew," he said softly into her hair, "there was no way I was gonna let history repeat itself."

She reared back to look at him, her lips all swollen, but the haze clearing some from her eyes. A neat little crease set up camp between her brows. "Huh?"

"Just seemed to me I had some major catching up to do in the sacrificing department, that's all," he said.

He was issuing a challenge, and he knew it. Knew, also, exactly what he'd be sacrificing if she reacted badly. So he held his breath, feeling his heart beat in his chest, seeing in Faith's eyes a thousand thoughts sort themselves out, until, after an agonizingly long time, she again pressed her body to his.

"And I'm telling you once and for all," she said, hanging on tight, "it wasn't even a contest. I also think it's high time I got back to proving that to you."

He stilled, then gently tugged her hair to make her look up at him. "What about needing time to think?"

"All done," she whispered, then stood on tiptoe to kiss him again. Except they no sooner got going when his mother walked into the kitchen, making them spring apart like they were still teenagers.

"Oh, there you two are! Heather just told us about you…selling…the car…" Her eyes bounced back and forth between them before her face lit up like somebody'd flipped a switch. "Ohmigosh—I interrupted something, didn't I?"

Darryl groaned and said, "Mama, for God's sake," only he said it to her back as she disappeared into the den.

"You know what?" she said, returning not five seconds later with their coats, which she practically shoved at them. "I just realized we're all out of Cokes, somebody should really go to the Git-n-Go for some. Only you'll probably have to go all the way out to the one near Pryor, you know, since the one here is all out."

"Now why the hell would they be out of Cokes, Mama?" he said.

But Faith slugged him in the arm and said, "Don't argue with your mother," right about the time the older woman yanked open the back door and more or less pushed them outside.

"But you better drive *real* slowly, you know, because it's snowing? I mean…" She wrapped herself in her sweater and peered up at the sky, a snowflake or two catching in her hair like white glitter, before returning her gaze to his. "Could take, oh, an hour. Or more. You never can tell. But you better get a move on, honey, what with Faith already being in the car and all."

Darryl stopped just long enough to kiss his mother on her cheek.

Chapter Eleven

Darryl barely got his seat belt latched before Faith gunned the motor, zooming out of the driveway like she was driving a getaway car.

"Thought we were supposed to drive slow?" he said, and she grunted, taking a right instead of a left at the corner. The snow swirled and spun in the headlight beams, landing in splotches on the windshield. Darryl frowned. "You got a new way to get home I don't know about?"

"Not goin' home. Not *that* home, anyway." She glanced over, a slight smile curving her lips. "Trust me."

"Your *parents*' house?" he said as they

pulled into the Meyerhausers' driveway less than a minute later. The yard was dark, except for a softly glowing, knee-high Nativity scene on the front lawn. No reindeers or Santas for the Meyerhausers, boy.

Faith unlatched her seat belt and pushed open her door, her eyes fixed on the house in a way that made a shiver crawl up Darryl's back. "It was the closest warm place I could think of," she said, but something told him there was more to it than she was letting on.

Only his gaze snagged on that Nativity scene again and he said, "Aw, Faith...how'm I supposed to do what I assume we came here to do with the baby Jesus right outside the window?"

"I don't recall it ever stopping my parents. Come on."

Great. Now he had that image to get out of his head, as well. With a sigh, Darryl got out of the Suburban as Faith sprinted across the yard, raising a ruckus from several of the neighborhood dogs. A few seconds of frantic rustling underneath the euonymus bushes fronting the house produced the fake rock with the key, after which she bounded up the porch steps and unlocked the door. They practically fell inside, a mad tangle of limbs and tongues and assorted clothing, Darryl thinking if he didn't feel her bare skin against his bare skin within the next few seconds, he was going to expire. They didn't bother turning on a light, the only illumination the paltry glow coming from an under-the-counter fixture in the kitchen.

"I take it you figured out a way to say thank you?" Darryl said against her lips, fighting her sweater in his quest for breast, only to run into what felt like a bulletproof bra. *What the hell*…?

"Since I can't cook," she said breathlessly, yanking his sweatshirt sleeve off his cast, "this will have to do." Was it his imagination, or was she even more frantic than he was?

Tongue…over his nipple…hot, wet, moving down, cool air colliding with the heat, making his muscles jump, making him groan, making him lose what little brain function he had left…

"Lord, Faithie," he rasped, "if anybody walks in right now—" he buried his good hand in her hair "—I'll have to kill them. Or myself."

Chuckling, she unsnapped his jeans. He thought he'd pass out.

"Uh, honey? Not that this isn't fun and all, but my options are kinda limited standing up."

"Oh, you might be surprised," Faith murmured into his navel, only to apparently take pity on him at his pained laugh, grabbing him by the hand to lead him upstairs. But the trip was too long, *way* too long, and the wall shook when he backed her up against it and kissed her, hard, and for a moment he was seventeen again and brand-new in love, shuddering with wanting, scared and excited and disbelieving all at once. She bit his lip, lightly, just enough to catch him off guard and escape, running up the stairs, trailing laughter and perfume. Darryl followed, two steps at a time, hesitating when he reached the landing.

"Over here," she said. "My room."

This time when he hesitated—by unspoken agreement, they'd never done it in her room—he heard her chuckle. "It's okay, we have a license."

"Yeah, *now*," he said, following her voice.

"Funny, that's exactly the word I was thinking."

But when he reached the doorway, there was nothing but darkness. And a little heavy breathing, though he couldn't tell where it was coming from.

"Where are you?" he whispered, only to let out a *whoomph* when she wrapped herself around him again. He fumbled behind him, found the dresser, hoped there was a lamp on it—

"Don't turn on the light—"

"Have…to…see you…"

"You've…seen me…a time or two—oh!—before… And the walls, remember the purple walls…?"

"Like I give a damn about the damn walls!"

"But they're hideous, they'll—ohmigosh, are you *sure* you're only operating with one hand?—destroy the mood—"

"Honey, the only thing that would destroy my mood right now is death. *I have to see you*," he said, desperate, hitting pay dirt when his flailing hand accidentally smacked what turned out to be one of those touch-sensitive lamps.

And boy, was there a lot to see.

She rolled her eyes. "After all this time, you still get that goony expression on your face."

He tried to look hurt. "That's called *appreciation*."

"Yeah, whatever. Lose the pants."

No problem.

"Ohmigosh, I've *missed* you," she said. Only she wasn't talking to his face.

Darryl glanced down, then back up. "I think it's safe to say we've missed you, too," he said. "Especially naked." Because while Faith clothed was enough to make a man run into things, Faith naked was enough to make him weep. Even though there was no mistaking that this was a woman who had carried five babies. Everything was…looser. Softer. More fun to sink into.

Which, judging from the look in her eyes, he figured on happening sometime in the next, oh, ten minutes.

Or maybe five. Because sometimes you just gotta have dessert first.

And then he was on his back, and Faith had straddled him, her hands braced on either side of his head, and the walls faded and the room faded and all the crap of the past month no longer existed, nothing existed but his wife naked and warm and giving on top of him, her moans when he suckled her nipple like that sharp, first pull of a ice-cold beer, all the sweeter for the expectedness of it. The thought crossed his mind to see if he could bring her to climax that way—he had before, on more than one occasion—but she didn't give him the chance, shifting to slide down his body, licking and nibbling, kissing and stroking and damn near taking *him* over the edge, especially when her mouth closed around him, just long enough to tease.

When he groaned, she laughed, then sat up, her curls tumbling around her face as she took him inside her, just as he knew she would…and she rode him slowly at first, her back arched, just as he knew she would…and the knowing what came next nearly made him crazy…just as *she* knew it would.

Except he reached out, palming right above where they were joined, his thumb finding the sweet little bit of flesh she'd once said was more than adequate compensation for pregnancy and childbirth, and she gasped and looked down, then back into his eyes, her expression suddenly almost solemn.

"Yesss," she hissed, the sound pleading, and he lifted his thumb to see what would happen. Instantly her hand covered his, pushing it back down, and he chuckled and said, "Gotcha," which earned him as sharp a look as she could give him, under the circumstances, considering how close she probably was.

She kept her hand over his, showing him

exactly what she wanted, what made her feel good, until it was impossible to tell who was in control, who had the power. All the while she was getting hotter and slicker around him, and then she let out a cry that did him proud, boy, right before the strongest contractions he'd ever felt in his *life* pulled a damn good one out of him, as well, setting the empty house to ringing with the sounds of a husband and wife gettin' reacquainted in the best of ways.

She collapsed on top of him, breathing hard, her heart pounding against him, and Darryl cupped the back of her neck and kissed her forehead, over and over, until the stinging sensation behind his eyeballs passed. Finally she sat up, smoothing his hair off his forehead, her own all crinkled. "I didn't hurt you, did I?" she asked, touching his cast, and he let out a laugh.

"Almost killed me, yeah. Hurt me, no. Although…" He waited until those hazy blue eyes veered back to his, then said, "Are you telling me all it took to get you back into bed was a check with five zeros after it?"

Slowly, her swollen lips spread into a smile. "What can I tell you?" she said. "I don't come cheap."

* * *

They made love again that night, in their own house, their own bed, in that deep hush that settles over the world after midnight, when even the most wired child can no longer fight the pull of sleep. Outside their window, the snow continued to fall in soft, silent flakes from a platinum sky that seemed to seep right into their bedroom, cloistering them.

Save for an occasional whisper, the slight creak of the bedsprings, the sibilant rustling of the sheets as Faith settled into Darryl's lap, there was nothing but the quiet. And each other. *And this*, Faith thought, taking her husband deep inside her once more, surrendering herself to the pure joy and delight of his solid, sure predictability. Once again turning to what she knew, and what she knew she could trust. She was safe here, in this room, in her husband's arms. She—

Wrapping her arms more tightly around Darryl's shoulders, she swallowed her cries as spasm after sweet spasm shuddered through her, as if by keeping the sound from escaping, she could somehow keep the moment prisoner as well. Because this was real, this was right, this was all she would ever have and would *ever need*…

Her heart pounding, Faith molded herself to her husband's torso, her face buried in his neck. Her nostrils flared at his scent; aroused, possessive, she felt her nipples tighten. Faith grazed her teeth over his skin, making him tremble, then licked it, making him chuckle. But only for a moment, because he then tangled his fingers in her hair to look into her eyes.

"So what's going on? Because for damn sure this isn't only about me selling the car."

"And what if I said it was?" she said, smiling.

"Then you'd be lying."

Her mouth pulling tight, she forked her fingers through his hair. "Fine. So I caved."

With a cocky grin, he leaned back against the pillows, his good arm propped underneath his head. "You tellin' me I'm too hot to resist?"

"This is news?" she said, and he laughed. Only the laugh faded as he took his hand out from under his head to stroke her arm.

"Not that I'm not flattered and all, but what happened to all that crap you were so intent on dealing with not so long ago?"

"I'm dealing," was all she said, then leaned forward to nip at his mouth. Playful, teasing, dead serious. "I'm here because I want to be here," she whispered, willing it to be true. Willing the past to stay in the past, where she'd left it without a backward glance so long ago. "Because this is where I belong."

Darryl wrapped his arm around her and pulled her down to lie against his side, resting his chin in her hair. "You got any idea how much I love you?"

"I think I get the idea. But you know..." She trailed her hand across his stomach. "You feel the need to reassure me about that, you go right ahead, anytime you want."

"Deal," he said, kissing her on top of her head. And yawning. "But as much as it pains me to admit this, that last time just about did me in." He squeezed her shoulder. "Guess I'm not eighteen anymore."

"Could've fooled me," she said, only he was already making that whuffly, brain-gone sound of a post-orgasmic man on the verge of passing out.

Faith slipped out of bed to quickly put on her nightgown and unlock the door in case they had short visitors, pulling the comforter up over them both when she came back to bed. Almost immediately, Darryl started to snore; Faith softly kissed his shoulder, smiling when he didn't react, then shifted to lie on her side...curled tightly around the gnawing emptiness, tears pooling in her eyes.

"...So it was, like, after...*nine* before... they finally...got up," Heather said, her words punctuated with each push of the marble rolling pin over the piecrust laid out on Renee's counter. "An' then they were all dopey with each other, smiling and givin' each other these dumb looks..." The girl shuddered; biting her lip to keep from grinning too broadly, Renee pretended to be intent on peeling her apples. "Is this okay?" Heather asked. "It came out kinda crooked."

Renee glanced over, wiping her hands on a towel. *Crooked* was an understatement. It looked like a map of Texas. But she just smiled and said, "For a first try, that's not bad at all. And it's the bottom crust, we can always patch it. I'll show you." But all the while her mouth was talking crusts, her brain was processing Heather's news. Well, her slant on the news. Best Christmas present she could've asked for, far as she was concerned.

As it was, she'd had to do some pretty fancy tap dancing last night when, not fifteen minutes after Darryl and Faith's hasty departure, Faith's daddy took it into his head he needed to go back to their house for something. Oh, my—there was a tense moment or two! Not that Renee knew for sure that's where Faith and Darryl were, but when she'd surreptitiously peeked out the front window after they'd left, she did notice they hadn't turned the way they should to get to *their* house. And since there was no way she could come right out and say, "Your daughter and her husband are in all likelihood having sex in your house at this very minute" to a pastor, for goodness' sake, she quick like a bunny found Didi and told *her,* which apparently put an end to whatever Chuck's quest had been.

Anyway, Renee was glowing a bit herself this morning, L.B. having been in a friendly mood as well last night. And if it took him longer to get his engine fired than it used to, well, she certainly had nothing to complain about from her end. So between that and the other and having her oldest grandchild with her, helping with tomorrow's meal, she should have been feeling on top of the world. That she wasn't was causing her no end of annoyance, but dammit, she would not allow herself to feel irritated on Christmas Eve.

L.B. wandered into the kitchen just then,

looking like he needed something to do. He
didn't look directly at Renee, which made her
blush, which in turn made her hope to high
heaven Heather didn't notice. The poor child
would be scandalized.

The poor child was also clearly bored with
flattening Texas, so Renee gave her leave to
go on out to the living room and watch TV,
although she knew the girl was practically
eaten up with curiosity about what was inside her Christmas gifts. Renee knew that
Darryl had thought to buy her some dance
clothes with the money from selling the car,
but Renee had already done it—two black
leotards, three pairs of pink tights and a pair
of pink kid ballet slippers, so pretty and soft
she'd half thought of buying a pair for herself,
just to wear around the house.

L.B. rooted around in the refrigerator for
what seemed like forever until he finally
found the leftover meat loaf from two nights
ago. Reading his mind, Renee abandoned her
apple peeling, snatching the foil package out
of his hand and telling him to sit, she'd make
him a sandwich. L.B. knew better than to
argue.

She set his plate in front of him, then sat
down herself, listening for a moment to make

sure the TV was on before saying, "I think our little crisis has been averted."

Chewing, L.B. frowned over at her. "Which crisis might that be?"

"Well, for heaven's sake, how many crises do we have goin'? The one with Darryl and Faith, of course. Between what I assume transpired last night and Heather's comment's this morning, I think it's safe to say they're back together, if you get my drift. So maybe now things will finally settle down for them. For all of us. At least," she said, getting up to resume her apple-peeling, "it will be once the insurance money comes in and Darryl gets his cast off. And won't that be a relief? Land, I've hardly been able to sleep for worrying. And my appetite's just shot—my wedding ring's so loose it nearly flew right off my finger yesterday when I was scrubbing out the sink. Oh… I'm sorry, honey…" She twisted around, peeler in one hand, apple in the other. "You need something to drink with that?"

It was then she noticed L.B. was wearing that clouded, careful expression he got when he had bad news he felt she needed protecting from. And generally speaking, he was right—it didn't take much to get her down in the dumps, which was why it was beginning to occur to her that those books she'd been reading for her book club were depressing her so much. This last one, especially. In fact, if it weren't completely against her nature not to finish something she started, she was sorely tempted to donate it to the library only half read. And my goodness, what was with her mind wandering so badly these days?

Renee put down her peeler and said, as she always did, "L.B.? Is something wrong?"

And he said, "No, of course not, what makes you think there's something wrong?" as *he* always did, even though they both knew he'd once again tucked the truth behind his back like a little boy with a stolen cookie. But that was the way it had always been between them, for nearly thirty-five years.

Only this time, instead of feeling relieved that her husband had seen fit to shield her from whatever this was, she found herself sharply annoyed. A reaction that surprised her nearly as much as it must have L.B. when she said, "Because I know you're hidin' something from me, so you may as well tell me now and get it over with since we both know I'm going to find out eventually, anyway," after which she had to press a hand to her heart to steady herself. Mercy.

But a habit built up over nearly four decades wasn't eradicated in an instant. Meaning that L.B. only said, "I'm not hidin' anything from you, sweet pea. Nothing you need to worry yourself about, at least." He stood, wiping his mouth on a napkin, then leaving it neatly folded on his plate—say what you will about his background, he had displayed good table manners right from the start. "Your car need gassing up?" he asked, and she tried to shake off the annoyance clinging to her like so many burrs.

"I think I've still got half a tank, at least."

"I'll run it over, top it off, then." He crossed to the back door to get her car keys off the hook, apparently spying Jenna Logan's book lying on the counter next to the bill folder. "Since when did you start reading mysteries?"

"I haven't yet. But I thought I should buy it, at least. Since she's Dawn's sister-in-law and all."

L.B. picked it up and turned to the first page, scanning it. "Looks good," he said with a chuckle, then returned to give her a peck on the lips. "I'll be back in a minute. And wipe that worried look off your face," he said in a manner clearly meant to soothe. "Everything's gonna be okay, I promise."

Only after he left and Renee went back to her peeling—at this rate, she'd be lucky to get the pie in the oven in time for next Christmas—she found herself wondering how it was that the very traits that made her fall in love with L.B. to begin with now irritated the very life out of her.

And what, exactly, she intended to do about it.

Chapter Twelve

The sound dragged Faith awake, sucking her out of a postholiday sleep so deep she half thought she was still dreaming. For several seconds she lay there, heavy-limbed and slightly dizzy, cocooned in her own body heat under the comforter, dreading the "Mama!" that had in all likelihood invaded her dream. George Clooney had been in it, she remembered, snuggling back into the pillow with a half smile—

"I can't feel…no…*no!*"

She flipped over, her heart threatening to beat right out of her chest, her palm landing on Darryl's damp arm as George Clooney's cockeyed grin vaporized.

"Darryl!" she whispered, shaking him. "Darryl! Wake up! You're havin' another bad dream!"

With a soft cry, he jerked awake, sitting bolt upright, a trembling hand streaking through his hair. He twisted to look at her in the dark. "Hell, Faith... I didn't clobber you or anything, did I?"

"No, I'm fine," she said, smushing the pillow under her cheek. "Although now I'll never know what George Clooney wanted with me."

Looking toward the foot of the bed now, Darryl grunted, his scent radiating from him, prodding other parts of Faith's anatomy awake. Honestly—after all the sex they'd had in the past week, she'd have thought her body would've said, *Enough, already.* Just goes to show.

"Sorry," he said, yanking her brain back on track.

"It's okay," she said gently, reaching over to rub his forearm, her yawn doing nothing to dispel her sense of unease. Oh, sure, on the surface everything seemed fine: the holidays had gone off without a hitch, she and Darryl were sharing a bed again, she was having orgasms like they were about to be taken off the market. And with every day that passed, the cavern inside her seemed to close a little more—or so she willed herself to believe. But now she was being awakened regularly by her husband's night terrors, which only went to prove that pretending, or even believing, everything was back on track didn't make it so—a realization that pervaded her thoughts like an annoying hum you can't identify. "What were you dreaming?"

He stilled for a second, then shook his head. "I don't remember."

She tamped down the impulse to call him on the lie, saying instead, "You should try. So you don't have the same dream when you fall back to sleep." When he shook his head this time, she said, very quietly, "This is the third nightmare you've had in as many nights. So unless you want me to start sleeping in the living room again, I suggest you tell me what's going on."

A light sleet began ticking softly against the window; outside, a car with a souped-up engine passed, tires hissing against the wet street. "Did I...say anything?" he finally said.

Faith's heart jammed at the base of her throat. "Sort of. Something like 'I can't feel...', then 'No!' a couple of times. You remember now?" she asked, the nighttime chill flash-freezing her skin underneath her nightgown as she pulled herself to a sitting position behind him, digging her fingers into his bare shoulders. "Lord, your muscles are like rocks. Honey, it's okay…you can tell me what's wrong."

After a moment, he reached up to cover her hand with his. "I don't want to worry you."

"Oh, for pity's sake, Darryl!" she said, smacking his shoulder. "We've been married for more than a decade! I've given birth five times! I'm in the PTA, for crying out loud! I think I can handle it, whatever it is—!"

"I might not ever regain full use of my left hand."

"What?" she said with a strangled breath.

She heard him swallow, saw his right fist clench on his bent knee. "There's nerve damage in the broken arm. They can't tell if it's permanent or not. Or how long it'll last if it isn't. If it is…" He pushed out a breath. "I can't work on cars with one hand, Faith."

"No," she said, her head spinning. "No, I don't suppose you can." They sat in silence for several seconds before she asked, "Have you given any thought to what you might do if—"

"I'm working on it," he said, in the manner of a man who doesn't have a clue. Her heart twisted for him, only to straighten right out again and say *Hey!*

"How long have you known about this?"

He paused. "Since just about the beginning."

She shifted to sit beside him, facing his profile. "You've kept this to yourself for more than a month?"

"I told you. I didn't want you to worry."

"No, you figured it was better to let me *wonder* what the heck was going on than tell me straight out."

In the darkness she could sense his eyes boring into hers. "I was only thinking of you. And the kids."

"I'm not one of the kids, Darryl," she said in a low voice.

"I didn't mean it like that. But you can't be mad at me for wanting to protect you."

"The heck I can't. For heaven's sake, Darryl—what kind of marriage do we have if we keep hidin' things from each other?"

"The kind that's worked for us for twelve years?" he said softly, just as the whole pot-and-kettle aspect of the conversation hit her. Brother—could she dig herself into a hole or what?

The bed creaked softly when Darryl got

up and walked over to the window, adjusting the miniblinds to look outside. "You know what they call a couple where both parties are completely honest with each other?" His gaze shifted to hers. "Divorced."

"I'm not saying we should be giving voice to every thought that passes through our brains," she said, "but how are we supposed to fix a problem if we never discuss it?"

"That works two ways, you know."

"This isn't about me."

That got a dry laugh. "Oh, baby, it's always been about you. From the moment you gave me reason to believe I had a shot at winnin' your heart, it's been about you. And the thought of losin' you…"

"That's not gonna happen, Darryl."

"You don't know that."

"Excuse me, but I'd appreciate you not presuming to know what's in my head."

He laughed out loud this time. "You must be kidding! Your body, I know my way around," he said, sending a flush over her skin she was just as glad he couldn't see. "Inside your head? No damn way. What I do know, however, is that you can't count on anything goin' the way you thought it would. You can hope, you can even work toward a goal, but no way in hell can you predict the curveballs life's gonna throw you along the way."

She uncurled herself from the bed, the carpet tickling her bare feet as she padded over to him and slipped her arms around his waist from behind, laying her cheek against his smooth, rock-solid back.

"You are not going to lose me," she whispered. "Whether you ever get the use back of your arm, whether you ever earn another penny, you are not going to lose me. And I am not going to think any less of you for being scared."

For once, he had the good sense not to contradict her.

"I told Faith," Darryl said, knowing full well he was about to blow the Sunday afternoon serenity all to hell. But if ever a situation called for asserting his own prerogative about his own marriage, this was it. He knocked back the last of the Bud, the empty can clattering into the recycle bin in the corner of his father's garage. "About my arm."

L.B. jerked his head out from underneath the hood of his wife's car, a trio of creases gouged between his brows. And not because he was having a problem changing the spark-plugs, Darryl didn't imagine.

"What did you go and do a fool thing like that for?"

"Because she'd already figured out something was wrong, for one thing. And for another, I finally realized I had no business keeping something that big from her."

Not to mention if he didn't start owning up to the truth, he had no business expecting her to. Oh, sure, she was back in their bed. On that score, everything was just fine. Better than fine—how long had it been since he'd feared for his heart? But it was almost like she was trying too hard. *They* were trying too hard. And if Faith didn't think he could see the emptiness still lurking behind her eyes, she was sorely mistaken.

"Why?" L.B. said, shaking him out of his thoughts. "For crying out loud, you said yourself this could all blow over anyway, the damage probably isn't permanent—"

"No, what I said was the damage *might not* be permanent. But I can't count on *maybe*, can I? And the longer I put off facing the very real possibility that I might not recover, at least not enough to go on the way I have been, the worse it's gonna be for everybody."

"So you dumped it all in Faith's lap."

"No, I finally got it through my thick head that sharing the burden might actually help me figure out what to do next."

"It's your duty—"

"For crying out loud, L.B.—don't you think I've figured out what my duty is by now? Only maybe trying to use *your* definition in *my* situation doesn't work. Like trying to install sparks for a Mustang into an Explorer—one size does not fit all. I'm not you, and Faith's not Mama, and maybe part of the reason Faith and me have been having problems is because I'd missed that point. Well, now I get it. I'm not going to keep her by treating *her* like a child."

The garage reverberated with the slam of the hood as L.B. finished. His face all screwed up, he ripped a paper towel off a nearby roll to wipe his hands. "I do not treat your mother like a child, Darryl."

"You don't exactly treat her like an adult."

His father's face reddened. "Now you listen here—I worship the ground that woman walks on, I always have. I treat her the way a woman should be treated, with respect and consideration for her feelings—"

"Unlike the way your fathers treated your

mothers. I get it, L.B.," Darryl said gently. "I do. And nobody's saying that's not admirable. But maybe there's such a thing as going overboard, you know?"

"And maybe you've got no idea what you're talking about. What your mother and I have has worked for more than thirty years. A husband and wife…they each have their roles, don't they? And once you get those roles figured out, why on earth would you want to go messin' around with 'em?"

Their gazes clashed for several seconds before Darryl walked over to a folding metal chair in one corner of the garage and sank into it, rubbing his useless fingers with his other hand. "Because maybe sometimes a couple gets caught up in what they think those roles should be, instead of stopping for a minute to ask themselves what it is they really want from each other. You rescued Mama from something she didn't want. But with Faith… I'm beginning to think I rescued her from something she *did*."

"And what on earth would that be?"

"Opportunity, maybe? The chance to be something more than the wife of a mechanic in her one-stoplight hometown?"

L.B.'s brows crashed together. "She ever come out and tell you this?"

"No. That doesn't mean that's not what she's feeling."

"And maybe you're makin' things more complicated than they are," his father said with an irritable edge to his voice. "Seeing ghosts where there aren't any—"

"Then again," Darryl said, equally irritated, "maybe I'm not."

L.B. tossed the towel into a plastic garbage can. "You know what they say about being careful what you ask for."

"Don't think I haven't thought of that a time or six in the last little while. Believe me, L.B., this isn't a path I'm exactly chomping at the bit to explore. But it's either that or lose her. And yes, I'm sure, so don't even bother asking."

His father's features softened some, then. "So what do you think Faith really wants from you?"

"When I figure that out," Darryl said, "I'll let you know."

Faith finished wrapping the last string of lights around the plastic frame, tucking it into the battered cardboard box they'd been keeping the lights in ever since they got married, the corners thick with at least five years' worth of duct tape. First Sunday afternoon she'd had off since she started working, and she'd spent the entire time doing all the stuff Darryl—who'd taken Jake and Sierra with him when he went over to his parents'—either hadn't been able to do or simply hadn't done over the past several weeks. In between that, she'd been shuttling Crystal and Heather to separate friends' houses and visiting with Dawn before she plumb forgot what it was like to talk to another female her own age.

"Looks like somebody could use some new boxes," the brunette now said from a few feet away, where she was sitting cross-legged on the floor endeavoring to teach their babies how to play with each other. Good luck with that was all Faith had to say.

"I know." Faith taped the lights box closed. "Every year I swear I'm gonna get us some of those nice red-and-green plastic bins from the Home Depot, but somehow I never get around to it. You got all your stuff put away?"

"Ethel did it a couple days ago...no, no, Max, that's Nicky's toy. See, you've got the doggy? No, the horsie's Nicky's...oh, for Pete's sake!"

It was downright ridiculous, feeling covetous of Dawn and Cal's housekeeper. The old woman had been with Cal's family since long before he was born; at this point, their keeping her on was far more for Ethel's benefit than theirs. But honestly, Faith was getting real tired of feeling like she was trapped in permanent PMS.

She stacked a couple of the smaller boxes and carted them out to the kitchen to set them on the floor by the garage door, returning to the living room just as Max—three months younger and a good deal heavier than Nicky, with a set of lungs on him like one of those opera singers Cal's brother Hank liked to listen to—gave voice to his displeasure about not getting the horsie. Faith squelched a laugh, though, as Nicky first frowned at his "playmate," then turned his face up to Faith with this "What the heck's *his* problem?" look.

Dawn pulled her distraught son onto her lap and also looked at Faith, although her expression wasn't quite as mellow. "How on earth did you get through *five* of these?" she asked, rocking her wailing, bald-as-a-cue-ball baby.

"Mass quantities of Wild Turkey," Faith said, deadpan, adding, "Just kidding," at

Dawn's horrified expression. "Aw, somebody's real sleepy," she said of the baby. "Keep rocking and he'll pass out in a few minutes."

"How can you tell?"

"Because his crying's got that funny hollow sound. For heaven's sake, the kid's nearly ten months old, you should have figured that out by now."

Her friend sighed. "What with my caseload these days, and what with Cal being so busy with the horses, Ethel takes care of him more than I do."

Suddenly irritated, Faith stood, hauling Nicky into her arms to cart him to the kitchen so she could give him a snack before his nap.

"What's with you?" Dawn said, following. Max's cries had already lost steam; Faith gave him thirty seconds, a minute, tops, before he was out. She also gave herself a few seconds for all the garbage in her head to play through. Cal and Dawn both had heavy-duty workloads, so it was petty and stupid to let herself think that Dawn had it easier or better than she did.

"Nothin'." Faith plunked Nicky into his high chair and handed him a sippy cup with milk and a graham cracker, which he promptly tried to stuff into his mouth like a debit card into an ATM. "It's…it's the weather, that's all." She grimaced in the direction of the kitchen window, her cheerful yellow curtains framing a dead, gray sky that had been intermittently spewing sleet and ice-cold rain for weeks. "I hate it, the kids hate it, the dog *really* hates it. I'm here to tell you, if the sun doesn't come out soon, I'm going to be a prime candidate for the booby hatch."

"I know what you mean." Dawn hooked her foot around a chair leg and tugged it out from the table, then sat, her now-sacked-out baby slumped against her chest, snoring softly. "But that's not all that's going on, is it?"

Faith turned to clear away the dishes she'd left on the table from lunch. "Why would you think that?" she said over Nicky banging his cup on the plastic high-chair tray, emitting a throaty chuckle each time milk geysered from the spout. Dot was right on the case, handily licking the drips suspended from the bottom edge of the tray. As well as Nicky's crumb-crusted fingers. "Oh, for pity's sake, Dawn," Faith said, "you can wipe the disgusted look off your face. A little dog spit never hurt anybody. And I hope to heck you're not one of those obsessive mothers who goes around disinfecting everything in sight, or who freaks out every time the baby gets a runny nose!"

After the dust died down, Dawn said, very calmly, "Not that you're on edge or anything."

Faith collapsed on another of the kitchen chairs, feeling like a popped balloon. "I'm sorry, I don't know what that was all about." Her mouth pulled up on one side. "Especially since I think you're a great mother. Especially for a first-timer. Believe me, you don't want to know some of the lamebrained things I did when Heather was a baby. Sometimes I wonder how I kept her alive."

Dawn laughed. "It's okay, honey, I totally understand. And for what it's worth, I don't do any of that obsessive stuff. Although I do draw the line at letting my child ingest dog saliva."

"Well, get over it, 'cause he's gonna ingest a lot worse than that before he graduates from high school..." With a groan, Faith let her head drop back. "Oh, God, just shoot me now."

She felt Dawn's hand on her arm. "Honey, you've been through hell the past few months. I think you've more than earned the right to be cranky."

Faith's eyes burned. Dawn should only

know. Though Faith really was glad Darryl had come clean with her about his condition, the thought of being stuck cashiering for the rest of her life was not sitting well. At all. She felt like a little kid being punished for something she didn't even do.

But she wasn't about to share this with her friend. Or anybody else. She wasn't a little girl, she was a grown woman. One fully capable of playing the hand that had been dealt her. So she just said, "I guess I'm just…really tired."

"I should imagine so," Dawn murmured, concern brimming in her rich brown eyes. "You haven't stopped moving since I got here. Do you ever just…relax?"

"You're kidding, right?"

"Yeah, that's what I thought. And I bet you can't remember the last time you did something just for you."

Faith gawked at her like she was speaking in another language. "For me?"

"You know. Like go for a walk alone. Spend a whole half hour in the tub. With candles. Take off for Claremore, or hell, even Tulsa and toodle around the mall all by yourself."

"I'm by myself when I go to work. Does that count?"

"No."

"I didn't think so," Faith said with a sigh, then leaned her temple against her knuckles. "Man, am I pathetic or what?"

"Hey—you know what we need?" Dawn said, smacking her hand on the table, which Nicky imitated. "A girls' night out. You, me, anybody else we can strong arm into going with us. Go out to Edna's, knock back a few beers, dance with cute guys we're not married to."

In spite of herself, Faith let out a hoot of laughter. "When's the last time you were up there?"

"Legally? Never. Why?"

"Uh-huh. And just how drunk were you?"

"Oh, come on—there's plenty of hotties around these parts."

"I know. We married 'em. And the leavin's ain't pretty."

"So we'll dance with each other, what the heck. And shoot some pool."

"Lord," Faith said wistfully, "it's been years since I played pool."

"And you remember Jimmy Calhoun?"

Faith's brows shot up. "Badass Jimmy? I thought he moved to Bushyhead some time ago."

"He did. But Mama tells me he's still got

his band, they play Edna's every Friday and Saturday night. He wasn't half-bad, as I recall."

"No," Faith said, memories flash-flooding her brain. "No, he wasn't."

"Neither were you," Dawn said gently, and Faith's eyes shot to hers...just as Jake and Sierra burst through the back door, both talking a mile a minute, eyes bright, faces splotched from cold and excitement.

"Nanny let us bake cookies!" Jake said, slamming a Tupperware container onto the table and ripping off his coat, which he let drop to the floor. Sierra followed suit, then climbed up onto Faith's lap, leaving a trail of elbow and knee-inflicted bruises in her wake.

"Let me guess..." Frowning, Faith grabbed Jake's arm and yanked him close enough to take a napkin to the kid's chocolate-smeared mouth. "Chocolate chip?"

"Uh-huh. Sierra an' me—ow, Mama, that hurts!—got to eat all the broken ones. How come you don't bake cookies?"

"Because I suck at it. Now go wash your hands. And take your sister with you."

"Aww..."

"Don't argue with your mother." Darryl's deep voice came from the doorway as he entered the kitchen, a pucker momentarily crossing his brow when he caught sight of Dawn. Not that he didn't like her, Faith didn't think, but she often wondered if Darryl felt a little out of her friend's league. But his face softened into a grin as he peeled off the baseball jacket. "Good Lord, Dawn—you got a linebacker there or what?"

"Don't I know it." She shifted the baby, then said, "Faith and I were just discussing getting a bunch of us gals together, goin' up to Edna's for a girls' night out one of these days."

Faith sucked in a breath—not that she needed Darryl's permission to go out if she wanted, but she would've at least liked to have been the one to broach the subject. Darryl had single handedly sprung a squealing Nicky from his high chair and was now bouncing the baby on his hip when Dawn's words apparently penetrated. His gaze bounced off Dawn's, then swung back to Faith.

"Edna's?"

"Uh-huh," Dawn said. "For nostalgia's sake, if nothing else. Did you know about Jimmy Calhoun playing up there these days?"

"Yeah," Darryl said, his eyes never leaving Faith's. "I knew."

Talk about your pregnant pauses.

"My, my," Dawn said, struggling to her feet with the sacked-out baby draped over her chest. "Would you look at the *time*…?"

"I know you're a grown woman, Faith! It was a knee-jerk reaction, okay? Dawn caught me by surprise, is all."

Faith closed the door to the boys' room, where she'd just put Nicky down for his nap, and glared at her husband. "But you'd be a lot happier if I didn't go."

"I'll admit the idea of you goin' out there on your own gives me pause," he said, following her down the hall. "I've got nothing against Edna's, but you gotta admit there were more than a few bottom feeders there, last time we went."

"Meaning Jimmy Calhoun, I presume."

"So sue me for not trusting the guy. Especially since he made no bones about having a thing for you."

"Yeah, a million years ago. Last I heard, he'd moved on."

"Several times, apparently."

"So the man has trouble with the concept of settling down. What's that got to do with me? Even back then, I never reciprocated his interest. Which you darn well know."

"That didn't stop you from singing with him."

Faith stopped by all the boxes stacked in front of the door to the garage, parking her hands on her hips. "*Singing* with him, Darryl. Period. For heaven's sake, I haven't even seen Jimmy since high school. So if that's your primary objection to this—"

"I just don't think Edna's is someplace you gals should go unescorted, that's all."

Faith blinked at him, then yanked opened the door from kitchen to the garage. "Seems to me," she said, hefting one of the decoration boxes, "the regular patrons would have a lot more to fear from us than we ever would from them. Besides," she added, wending her way through a decade's worth of accumulated junk, "women do go there alone. And actually live to tell about it."

Behind her, Darryl sighed. "It's not that I don't think you deserve a night out. I'm just not sure Edna's is the best choice."

She shoved the box into its appointed spot on the industrial shelving, then started back toward the kitchen. "But you're not going to stand in my way."

After a moment's silence, he said, "And risk further injury? No way. Just promise me—"

"You even think about telling me to stay away from Jimmy and you are a dead man."

He held up his hand, all conciliatory and whatnot. Only to floor her by saying, "By the way... I told L.B. that I came clean with you about my arm."

Halfway across the garage with the second box, she turned and looked at him. "Wait a minute...your father knew, but I didn't?" At Darryl's *Oh, crap* expression, Faith shook her head. Rome wasn't built in a day, either. "Never mind," she said with a grunt as she wrestled the next box into place, then wiped her hands on her butt. "So what'd he say?"

"Other than I'm a fool for telling you?"

Now it was Faith's turn to sigh. "You think there's any chance of dragging your father into this century anytime before the next one?"

"I'm working on it." He paused. "But I gotta get myself there, first." She'd no sooner gotten the third and last box put away when he said, "What would you say if I told you I was thinking about selling up?"

Her eyes flew to his. "You mean, the garage?"

"Yeah. Once all the repairs are done, I mean. It was a going concern, before the tornado hit. No reason why somebody wouldn't want it, I don't imagine."

"Oh." She would have sat down, if there'd been any place to sit. "You'd really give it up?"

"I may not have any choice, Faith," he said, and the deadness in his voice tore her up inside. Enough that she was almost ready to promise him she wouldn't talk to Jimmy if she saw him. "Least this way," he said, "we'd have something to tide us over while I figured out what to do next. Maybe even enough so you could quit working."

"Don't worry about that—"

"Would you hush?" he said quietly. "If you were doing something you loved, that would be one thing. But this…" He shook his head. "You deserve better, that's all. Better for *you*," he added, stifling her objection. And bringing tears to her eyes.

When she could speak again, she asked, "What's L.B. think about it?"

"He doesn't know. You're the first person I've mentioned it to." At her spiked eyebrows, he said, "Guess I can be taught, after all," with the same shy half grin that had turned her insides to oatmeal all those years ago, that drew her to him like iron filings to a magnet. She walked over to thread her arms around his waist and lay her head on his chest, where she might have stayed for the rest of the day, easy, had not all hell broken loose in the house.

"You want me to see to that?" Darryl said into her hair.

"Won't fight you for the privilege."

He'd no sooner left, however, than Faith heard all manner of commotion and voices outside, including one that sounded a lot like her mother's. Seconds later, she jumped when the garage door groaned open. Sure enough, there stood her mother, in jeans and several sweaters, her face dirt-smudged, her arms wrapped around—heaven help her—a box.

"Mama, what on earth are you doing here? And is that a cobweb in your hair?"

"Probably," Didi said, wasting no time in shuffling inside, only to stop, making a face at the debris stacked everywhere. "Your garage doesn't look any better than ours."

"Well, shoot, Mama, I could've told you that and saved you a trip." Faith took the box from her, only because she figured she should. "What's this?"

"I got to putting away the Christmas stuff and thought, you know, half this junk doesn't even belong to us, it's yours. So I figured it was high time it found its way back to its rightful owner. There's more in the truck."

The truck? Faith followed her mother, a sick feeling settling in the pit of her stomach. Sure enough, she counted at least six more boxes in the back of the pickup.

"And just where do you expect me to put this?"

"I don't know," her mother said, passing the nearest box to her, "and frankly, I don't care. Sell it, burn it, throw it away. Although I think your prom dress is in one of these."

"Like I'm ever gonna wear that again."

"You never know, one of the girls might like to play dress up with it."

Faith just sighed.

Ten minutes later, one corner of the detached garage out back was filled with the remnants of her childhood. Remnants she'd just as soon have left at her parents', thank you—

"One more thing," Didi said in a funny voice. Frowning, Faith twisted around, her breath leaving her lungs in a little gasp when she saw what was in her mother's hands.

"Oh, my word… I thought we'd sold that."

"You sold the electric guitar, not this one," Didi said, dusting off the banged up case with her sleeve. "Have no idea if it's even playable anymore, being subjected to all those extreme temperatures for so long. But again, the kids might get a kick out of it. Well, go on and take it," she said, jarring Faith out of her paralysis. "I've gotta get back, your father's already fretting about next Sunday's sermon. You'd think, after forty years, he'd have the hang of it by now."

The instant her mother was gone, though, Faith quickly set down the case and stepped back, like it might catch on fire or explode or something. Or, more to the point, like it was Aladdin's lamp and one little rub the wrong way might unleash the dreams and wishes and hopes of what seemed like a lifetime ago.

And wasn't that nuts? It was a guitar, for heaven's sake. Nothing more than wood and strings and varnish, incapable of being anything more than it was.

So she walked right back over to it, squatting down to release the abandoned instrument from its dark, airless prison. She flipped

up one latch, then the other, the sound seem-
ing to hover in the nearly empty space for a
moment like an indecisive, newly freed bird
as she pushed back the top. Lying there in its
threadbare, blue felt casket, the poor thing
was even more worn and scratched up than
she remembered. She'd been Faith's first, at
thirteen, rescued from a pawn shop that no
longer existed and treasured it every bit as
much as if it'd been a Stradivarius violin. And
if the old gal hadn't been much to look at,
she'd had a voice that could make you weep.

With a soft, damned-if-I-do, damned-if-I-
don't sigh, Faith plopped her butt down on the
icy cement floor and gathered the instrument
into her lap, soothing her with her words, her
hands. Apologizing. Tentatively, she plucked
the woefully out-of-tune G string, the mourn-
ful sound echoing deep inside her.

Behind her, Darryl's boots scuffed against
the floor. She twisted around, the guitar pro-
tectively clasped to her chest. He stood in
the doorway, his free arm braced against the
opening, his expression unreadable. But then,
he probably couldn't read hers, either—after
all, how could her face give a true idea of
her feelings before her head knew what those
feelings were?

"I take it Didi brought that over?" he asked.

She nodded, skimming her fingers over the smooth wood. Birch, she thought it was. "Yeah. Just this minute."

"Looks like you two have some catching up to do," he said softly, and walked off, leaving her with all those dreams and wishes and hopes scattered around her like so many dead leaves.

Chapter Thirteen

Why seeing Faith with the guitar had knocked him for a loop, Darryl had no idea. But for the rest of that day and well into the following week, he couldn't shake that fist-around-the-heart feeling that always comes with bad news. Like the way he'd felt the day he'd gone to see Ryan and had found out about his arm, in fact.

Even now, some six weeks later, even though there'd been no indication on Faith's part that getting her guitar back meant anything more than just that, anxiety still assaulted him from time to time. Apparently it was one thing to want Faith to come to terms with her reasons for taking up with him when she did, and the way she did, another thing entirely to face what that might mean.

Or more to the point, to face himself. Because from where he stood, it would seem his discombobulation stemmed from one of three things—selfishness, jealousy or (his personal favorite) insecurity. And wasn't that a kick in the butt? All that grief he'd given Faith about Jimmy…where the hell had that come from?

Darryl wasn't sure he wanted to know.

And in any case, he had plenty else to keep both mind and body more than occupied these days. For one thing, now that his cast was finally off, he had to traipse over to Claremore several times a week for physical therapy, which often left him more in pain than before he went, not to mention so wiped out he could barely think afterward. On top of that, the first major chunk of the insurance money had finally come in, so he and L.B.—who had apparently rethought the whole retirement idea—were finally, after weeks of bad weather, up to their asses with building codes and contracting bids and construction crews. One of whom was directly overhead, pounding a new roof onto the office.

Every day, practically, Faith asked Darryl

if he'd told L.B. yet about wanting to sell. And every day, Darryl found a reason why it wasn't time yet.

This being forthright business was a lot harder than it looked, was all he had to say.

A familiar looking truck pulled up to one of the pumps; Darryl grinned in recognition when Red Jenkins, the guy who'd bought the Bird off of him, got out of the cab and headed toward the office.

"Kind of a long way to come for a fill-up," Darryl said, yelling over the racket as he clasped the tall redhead's hand. The older man chuckled, pushing around a whole mess of freckled wrinkles.

"I happened to be passing through on my way to Tulsa, figured I may as well stop here as anywhere else. You take credit cards?"

"Sure do. Right at the pump."

"Great. But truth be told… I didn't stop in just for gas."

"Oh?"

He shook his head. "When I got the Bird back home, I had to show it off, you know. Little car show we had there awhile back. Anyway, some kid comes up to me, starts asking me questions about the car, who restored it, that sort of thing. Which is where you come in." He grinned. "We're talking a '41 Willys. You interested?"

Frustration flared in Darryl's gut. It was like standing next to a lake teeming with trout without a damn thing to catch 'em with. "Damn, Red, I would be but… I'm not doing any work these days. The garage is still not operational, obviously." He paused. "Neither is my arm."

"But I see the cast's off."

"There's more to it than that, unfortunately." He noticed another truck pull up to the second pump, watched as his father-in-law hopped out like a man half his age, adjusting his glasses as he read the price, shaking his head before fitting the nozzle into his tank. Darryl returned his attention to Red. "I'm sorry. Much as I'd kill to get my hands on an old Willys, I can't."

"That's too bad," Red said. "I'd think a project like that would be right up your alley. Well, I've got your pump blocked, so I'd best be going. Let me know how it goes, though," he said as Chuck pushed open the door. "It seems a damn shame to let all that know-how go to waste for the sake of one limb, you know what I mean?"

The two men nodded to each other in passing, then Chuck approached the counter, pulling a twenty, then—with a sigh—a ten out of his wallet. "He's right, you know."

"About what?" Darryl rang up Chuck's purchase and handed him his change. All fifty-seven cents of it.

"About your talent being more in your head than in your arm."

Darryl banged shut the register. "Faith told you?"

"We're family, son," Chuck said. "We're all in this together."

Suddenly feeling scraped raw inside, Darryl said, "Still. Can't see where one's much good without the other."

"Well, the arm without the brain might be a problem, true," Chuck said with a grin. "But the other way 'round—"

"Look, if you're worried about me being able to take care of your daughter—"

"No," Chuck said, firmly. "I'm not. And I never have been."

After a sharp nod, he said, "It's just…" Only that's as far as he got, because it was like pushing the words through broken glass.

"You thought you had everything figured out," his father-in-law said gently, "until life yanked it all out from under you."

Overhead, a loud thunk shook the ceiling, followed by some full-bodied cussing. The two men exchanged knowing glances, then Darryl said, "I keep getting so damn frustrated, thinking I should be *doing* something. Only I can't for the life of me figure out what that would be."

Chuck folded his arms over his chest. "Did you know I didn't start out to be a pastor?"

"You didn't?" Darryl said, wondering where on earth this was going.

"Nope. Until I was, oh, in my mid-twenties, I had no idea what I wanted to do. Didn't much care, either, frankly. Until I woke up one morning and it hit me I was about as close to becoming a bum as I wished to get, thank you. I panicked is the only word for it. Kept flitting from job to job, hoping something would stick. Until one day it occurred to me to stop flailing about so much and just shut up and listen, see what came to me." A grin stretched across his face. "Believe me, the last thing I expected was a call to go into the ministry. But once I stopped fighting it—which probably took another two years—I realized what a good fit it was. Forty years later, I can't imagine bein' anything else, *doin'* anything else."

He paused, like it was Darryl's turn. Only

Darryl shook his head slightly and said, "I'm sorry, I don't…"

"Just because the answer hasn't come to you yet doesn't mean there isn't one. And when we're up against a wall, we sometimes get so balled up thinking we need to be *doing* something, we often miss the opportunities that are right in front of us."

Darryl smiled, even though the tight feeling in his chest didn't ease up any. "That your way of telling me I need to chill?"

"Or at least roll with the punches, maybe." Chuck's expression softened. "And I have no doubt that you'll continue to be there for Faith. Even if not in the same way as before. Anyway…" He slapped the counter, then edged toward the door. "I need to get going. Say hello to L.B. for me…"

"Crew's gonna knock off for lunch soon," L.B. said, coming in through the back. "You wanna go up to Ruby's? My stomach's been rumbling for an hour already… That Faith's daddy out there, getting into his truck?"

"Yep. He sends his greetings, by the way… holy crap!" Darryl said, ducking when the roof shuddered again. "No, you stay, this one's on me," he said to L.B., then stormed outside, fully prepared to light into the numbskulls…just in time to see his mother headed his way as if marching into battle.

Armed with tuna and ham sandwiches, homemade coleslaw and half a peach pie (while Renee had to admit Maddie Logan's wasn't at all bad, she still maintained that her crust was a tiny bit flakier) and wearing the only pair of low-heeled shoes she owned outside of her bedroom slippers, Renee made tracks toward her son, who seemed to be looking at her as if not quite sure what to think. Of course, she was on foot, which was an anomaly in and of itself. Nor was it like her to show up out of the blue when the boys were working. But with the weather being so awful the past several weeks, and her normal postholiday letdown, she'd finally realized if she didn't get out of the house…well, there was no telling what she might do.

And she had to admit, now that she'd forced herself outside, she felt much better. The sky was a clear blue, the sun was warm on her head and back and there was hardly any wind to speak of. She'd even noticed some daffodil shoots coming up along her front fence, which definitely bolstered her spirits. So by the time she reached her destination, she was feeling much more like somebody she'd want to be around.

But my goodness, it was noisy. "Hey, Mama!" Darryl called out over a regular symphony of hammering and clattering, the deafening whirr of a power saw. "What brings you over here?"

"Thought you and L.B. might like some lunch," she said, holding up the bulging tote bag.

"Oh, yeah?" Darryl said with a smile that was still too strained for Renee's taste, despite his cast being off and the progress being made on the garage and the resumption, as far as Renee knew, of his and Faith's intimate relations. Clearly, something was still not right. But do you think any of the men in her life would think to confide in her, let her in on what was really going on?

Darryl had taken the tote bag out of her hands and was now looking inside, nodding in approval. It was still a shock to realize that her babies had all grown into men, men with babies of their own, a thought that didn't make her feel old as much as *dis*missed. *"Why don't you take it into the office?"* Darryl yelled over the noise. *"L.B. was just bellyaching about how hungry he was."*

Renee nodded, since she couldn't be heard anyway, then turned around and started across what was left of the blacktop. Oh, my—that construction worker wasn't *really* giving her the eye, was he? Yes, she took great pains to keep herself up, but in the stark daylight she seriously doubted she looked a day younger than her fifty-four years. She sometimes wondered who exactly the cosmetics companies thought they were fooling with all those wrinkle-reducing creams, only to find herself caught up short at how bad off she might be if she *didn't* use them.

L.B. was busy filling a new display with assorted doodads a person was likely to keep handy in the car, like ice scrapers and small flashlights and the like, Renee really didn't pay that close attention. He looked up when she came in, clearly surprised to see her there but without nearly the sparkle in his eyes she might have hoped. Still, she walked over and gave him a peck on the lips, just because. Over the past few weeks, even though she could not complain about the frequency of their sexual encounters, she had begun to feel that L.B. cataloged them right up there with changing the furnace filters or mowing the lawn—chores you tended to in order to keep everything running smoothly.

This was not an uplifting thought.

"What are you doing here?" he asked, and she told him about the lunch, and how she'd walked over. "In this cold?" he said, even though it was a perfectly fine day, just a little chilly, was all. Only then somebody popped his head in the door with a question, and she felt in the way, like she used to when she was a little girl and her mama had "company," so she simply left the bag of food in the office and went back outside, telling herself it was silly to feel hurt when she'd known L.B. would probably be busy.

However, the last thing she wanted to do was go back home and sit and stare at her four walls. Or her spotless carpet, or the neatly stacked magazines on her coffee table, or another damn soap opera.

She stood on the corner for a minute, her heart fluttering in her chest, the chilly spring breeze teasing her face, before turning east.

Faith was tempted to pretend she hadn't heard the doorbell—most likely it was only somebody trying to sell her something she didn't need. The light rapping on her front window, however, was harder to ignore.

Honestly. Was one hour all to herself too much to ask?

With an irritated sigh, she unfolded herself from the sofa and stomped over to the door, only to flinch when she opened it to find Renee standing there, looking oddly determined and a little lost at the same time.

"I'm sorry, honey, I know this is unexpected, but I saw the Suburban out front and I know Darryl's got the truck. I just came from there…"

Oh, boy. "Um…" Faith stood aside, trying to smile. "Come on in?"

"Oh, now, I don't want to put you out if you're in the middle of something," the older woman said, stepping around Faith and slipping off her heavy sweater, which she laid over the arm of a nearby chair. Her eyes lit on the guitar, lying on its side on the coffee table, and Faith felt her face warm.

"Why, Faith…when did you start playing again?"

Faith closed the door, then couldn't seem to figure out what to do with her hands. "Since after Christmas. Mama brought the guitar over, it'd been in their garage since…for a long time. I was just foolin' around with it, you know, for fun? Ohmigosh, I'm sorry! It's been so long since I've had company other than Dawn or Maddie..." She shook her head, as if to dispel at least some of the weirdness. "Would you like something to drink? I could put on coffee—oh! Have you had lunch yet?"

"Oh, now, I'm not expecting you to entertain me! Coffee would be nice, though. Although why don't you let me make it?"

Instead of demurring, as she'd done for the past twelve years, Faith heard herself say, "Renee? Bad enough you show up unannounced without also making it perfectly obvious you think your coffee's better than mine."

"But, honey, my coffee *is* better than yours," Renee said, and Faith had to laugh in spite of herself.

"Tell you what...how about a soft drink instead? They had a half-price sale at the store, I went a little crazy. Coke, Dr. Pepper, ginger ale, root beer..."

"Ginger ale," Renee said. "Diet, if you have it."

What else?

Like a bewildered puppy, Darryl's mother trailed Faith into the kitchen—which she'd cleaned not an hour ago, thank God—settling cautiously at the table.

"Where are the babies?"

"At day care," Faith said, still trying to puzzle out why Renee was there as she pulled a can of ginger ale out of the refrigerator. "Today's my day off, but they're used to being with the other kids now. I didn't want to disrupt their routine." The soft drink sparkled and fizzed as she poured it into two glasses, plopped ice cubes into each. She handed Renee hers, then leaned against the sink, listening to the bubbles pinging inside her glass.

"Renee, don't take this the wrong way… but what's this all about? I mean, in all the time Darryl and I have been married, you've never once dropped in on me."

To Faith's shock, tears filmed Renee's eyes. "I don't know," she said in a small voice. "Only it seems like everything's changed, when nothing's changed at all. Like I don't know where I fit in anymore. Or who I'm supposed to be. And I thought if I didn't say it out loud, to somebody, I was going to lose my mind." And before Faith could gather her wits enough to come up with an appropriate response, Renee added, "And it's all your fault, you know."

"*My* fault?"

Her mother-in-law yanked a paper napkin out of the holder on the table and dabbed at her eyes, then pushed out a sigh. "Actually, I suppose it started with your sister-in-law. Brenda. Oh, she never said anything outright, but it was clear she thought I was some sort of throwback, never wanting to work outside the home, when she never took off more than the six weeks after she had the two boys. And even SueEllen, with her website business and all. And then there's Maddie and Dawn and, well, practically every other woman in town seems to have some kind of life outside of the house. Except you," she said. "You seemed perfectly happy takin' care of the kids and Darryl, even if…" She clamped shut her mouth. Faith smirked.

"Even if I'm not the most domestic person in the world."

"That's not a criticism, honey, just a fact. My point is, as long as I thought you were happy being the kind of wife and mother I'd been, I felt—oh, what's the word, I read it just the other day in one of my books—vindicated, that's it. If I was feelin' out of sorts, I just chalked it up to the Change."

She grimaced. "Only then you had to go

feeling unsettled and what-all and I thought, well, damn, that shoots the menopause theory all to hell. In any case, it got me to lookin' more carefully at my own life, which is when it hit me that somewhere along the line, I got lost. The kids are gone, L.B. is like to suffocate me with his damn protectiveness—no mean feat considering he doesn't half see me anymore, I don't think—and what have I got to show for any of it? And you know what the worst thing is?" she went on, since clearly she was more interested in venting than listening to advice, thank God. "I have no idea what I'm supposed to do about this, or where to start looking for myself. All I know is I feel all used up. Sucked out dry. And let me tell you, honey, it's a real bitch."

To hear her mother-in-law—a woman Faith would have sworn she had virtually nothing in common with—voice many of the same thoughts that had plagued Faith herself over the last several months was unnerving, to say the least. But liberating, as well, in an odd sort of way.

Faith sat at the table, where she started fiddling with the edge of a place mat. "And here I was feeling badly because *you* seemed to have it so together."

Renee looked at her for a good long moment, then said, with a little laugh, "Well, aren't we a pair?"

They sat for a while after that, sipping their drinks and thinking their own thoughts, until Faith said, "You know, if we want our men to stop hovering all the time, I guess we have to prove to them we don't need them to hover."

"Ohmigod…they'd die."

"Yeah, well, it's either them or us. And right now, I vote for us."

Renee's carefully penciled brows drew together as she clearly considered this. Then she said, "I know it's none of my business… but are you and Darryl…?" She made a *You know* gesture with her hand.

"What?" Faith said. "Is Heather falling down on the job?"

Renee blushed and stammered for a second or two before Faith took pity on the poor woman.

"Yes," she said, her eyes falling on her nails. She really needed to do them, one of these days. "On that score," she admitted, returning her gaze to Renee's, "everything's back to normal."

Renee smiled sadly. "Does it…help?"

"Not as much as I'd like, unfortunately."

"So it's not just me, then," she said, obviously relieved.

"Not hardly. Not that I'm advocating banning it," Faith said.

That drew a wide-eyed, "Oh, no, me, neither," from her mother-in-law and they raised their glasses to each other.

Then Faith said, "This isn't about loving them, is it?"

"Apparently not," Renee said without hesitation. "But I'm beginning to think if I don't fix whatever this is inside me that needs fixing, the marriage won't be worth the paper the license is printed on. Does that make any sense?"

Oh, did it ever. More than Faith wanted to admit. Especially since she was finally beginning to grasp the concept of really *fixing* something instead of only covering it up. But rather than go down that road, she heard herself say, "You know… Dawn and I have been talking about a field trip out to Edna's sometime. A whole bunch of us. Nothing's set yet—everybody's either been dealing with sick kids or too busy or whatever—but… would you like to go with us?"

Twin dots of color bloomed in Renee's cheeks. "Oh, now, you gals hardly want a grandmother hangin' out with you. I'd cramp your style."

"You're assuming there's a style to cramp," Faith said, then wrapped her hand around Renee's. "Come on, it'll be fun. And crazy. When was the last time you were crazy?"

"About ten minutes ago," Renee deadpanned. Then her eyes popped wide open. "Ohmigosh...you will keep our conversation confidential, won't you?"

"Of course. Except..."

"What?"

"Not that our talking together isn't important, because it is. As a first step. But at some point, I think you need to tell L.B. how you're feeling."

"Oh, honey," Renee said, looking slightly alarmed, "I couldn't bear to hurt him. After everything's he done for me?"

"I'm not sure you have much choice. Unless you want your head to explode."

Renee finally agreed to think about it, but she wasn't promising anything.

An hour or so later, when Renee's visit had already begun taking on the surreal quality of a bizarre dream, Dawn called.

"Edna's, Friday, seven-thirty. Be there," she said, and Faith had a very strong feeling the dream was about to get a whole lot more bizarre.

Chapter Fourteen

By the end of the week, winter decided it wasn't quite done, after all, the temperature sliding right back down to freezing at night and not getting a whole lot warmer during the day. Unfortunately, the weather wasn't the only thing backsliding in Darryl's world. Despite his physical therapist's incessant cheerleading, he sure as hell couldn't see any noticeable improvement. So, seated in the back booth at Ruby's after returning from his latest session, nursing both a cup of coffee and the mother of all foul moods, he hardly noticed the scrawny boy of about twenty or so in jeans and a hooded sweatshirt conversing with Ruby. Until Ruby directed the kid in Darryl's direction, that is.

Damn.

The kid stopped in front of his booth, his hands stuffed in the pockets of a worn black hoodie with the name of some band or other across it. "You Darryl Andrews?"

Ah, hell…he bet this was the kid Red had mentioned. Still, no sense in being impolite. "That's me. What can I do for you?"

Without Darry's bidding, the kid slipped into the booth opposite him, which was when Darryl realized the boy wasn't a boy at all, but a young woman with the biggest green eyes he'd ever seen, her dark hair cut short and spiked up like his brother Danny sometimes wore his.

"I've just spent the better part of two hours trying to track you down," she said, like this was somehow Darryl's fault. Then she thrust out a banged-up, short-nailed hand. "Ronnie Lee," she said, giving his hand a fast, hard squeeze before jerking hers back, folding it with her other one to lean forward on the table, the very picture of earnestness. Several people were blatantly staring, but a well-aimed glare or two—from both Ronnie and Darryl—called a halt to that.

"I need your help," she said in a it's-a-matter-of-life-and-death voice.

"This wouldn't be about a '41 Willys, would it?"

Dark, unplucked brows slid up. "How'd you know that?"

"Red Jenkins. But, look, Ronnie—"

But she'd already bounced back to her feet, her hands jammed into the hoodie's front pockets. "I've got it with me. Parked down the street. It won't take but a second to take a look at her. Please?"

Their gazes duked it out for a couple of seconds before, with a heavy sigh, Darryl pushed himself out the booth and followed her. Before they got all the way outside, though, he could see a fair-size crowd had gathered around a flatbed hitched to a mud-spattered pickup the size of Nebraska.

"I couldn't believe my luck when I found her," Ronnie said, her bold manner as she strode through the crowd easily dispersing them. "But she needs a lot of help." Stopping beside the trailer, she fixed those big grass-colored eyes on Darryl, her hand on the car's dinged fender, her expression pleading, as though he were her last hope on earth. "Only I don't know near enough to do her justice.

Red said if anybody could save her, it would be you."

Whatever the car's original color had been, it was nearly impossible to tell now. Darryl guessed she'd been somebody's souped-up hot rod in the fifties, but now the rusted, listing Willys crouched on the trailer like a hurt, neglected pup trusting him to make it all better. In spite of himself, Darryl skimmed a hand along her cool, pockmarked fender, as if reassuring her.

"Does she run?"

"When the mood strikes," the young woman said, passion vibrating underneath her words. "I've fixed up older cars before, but nothing this old or in this bad a shape. That's why I came to you."

Suppressing a harsh sigh, Darryl removed his hand. "I was in an accident a few months back. Broke my left arm, badly." He finally looked at the gal. "I don't have full use of it. Certainly not enough to do the kind of work she'd need."

Ronnie gawked at him like he'd gone nuts. "Who said anything about *you* to fixing it? It's your expertise I'm after, not your hands. And don't think I'm expecting you to teach me for free, either. Whatever you charge, I figure I'll more than make it back when I sell her."

"There's schools for that. Good schools."

She blew a very unfeminine, dismissive sound through her lips. "Not for this," she said. "Besides, plenty of folks want to own old cars, but precious few of 'em want to be bothered with fixin' 'em up. So whaddya say? We got a deal?"

Just because the answer hasn't come to us yet, that doesn't mean there isn't one....

Faith's father's words exploded in his brain so hard, Darryl actually flinched. An explosion that suddenly jarred loose a whole host of possibilities, possibilities that went way beyond Ronnie Lee's single request, or this particular car. For sure, he needed to sit down and work out the details, but...

Damn. *Damn.* Why he hadn't thought of it on his own, he had no idea. But Ronnie was right, there was money in restoration. Lots of it. And he bet, too, that people would be willing to pay him to teach them how to do it. They had schools for damn near everything else...why not this?

And the sooner he got going, the sooner Faith could quit her job, and the sooner things would finally get back to normal. Not the same normal as before, but close enough.

He let out a laugh loud enough to startle more than one person standing nearby. "Yes, ma'am…we've got a deal."

Ronnie Lee's skinny face just about split in two.

"Faith! Faithie!"

Along with everybody else in the Homeland, Faith jerked around at the sound of Darryl's voice, just in time to see him roaring across the front of the store toward her register, beaming like the sun in July.

"Darryl! What on earth—?"

"I've got to talk to you, baby, right now— oh, hey, Hazel, I didn't see you standin' there…" He reached right across the scanner and grabbed Faith's hand, making her fumble for Hazel's box of saltines before they went flying. "This idea just came to me, about how I might be able to save the business? But I need to run it by you, see what you think…"

Tears burned behind her eyes at the fire in his, his unbridled exuberance igniting a reciprocal reaction deep inside her. He was one big smile, vibrating with excitement and something like wonder, like he'd just been yanked back from the brink of death, and all she wanted to do was fling herself into his arms and soak up his happiness, even if she had no idea yet what it was all about. However...

"Darryl," she whispered, "I'm right in the middle of ringing up Hazel's order?"

"What?" He turned back to Hazel, who was looking at him with some fascination. "Oh! I'm sorry, I just... Okay, then—when's your break?"

She glanced at her watch. "Ten minutes."

"Meet me in the parking lot," he said, and strode off, shouting "Hey!" to everybody he passed.

Goodness.

By the time Faith got out to the lot, Darryl had calmed down enough for her to at least make sense of what he was saying, but not so much that she didn't get caught up in his enthusiasm all over again. And no wonder—she couldn't have thought of anything more perfect for him than to start up a school. But more than that, to see him so happy, so *alive* after all those months of near depression.... She suddenly realized how devastating it must have been for him, to feel as though he'd lost his purpose in the world.

And how relieved he must feel now, to have found it again.

"So…what do you think?" he said, the earnestness in his expression making her melt inside, making her realize there was no sweeter joy that the one you share with somebody else.

Feeling almost giddy, she wrapped her arms around her husband, right there in the parking lot, giving him a kiss that would be the talk of the town for the next week, at least.

"It's about damn time!" Dawn yelled to Faith when she, Maddie and Renee pulled up between Dawn's Explorer and Carly's puny little Saturn the next night. "We were beginning to think y'all had chickened out!"

"Give us a break!" Maddie squawked back as she shoved open the passenger door. "We've got nine kids between us, we were doing well to get out alive, let alone on time!"

They'd agreed beforehand to meet up in Edna's parking lot, mainly to pool their courage before going in, although nobody had actually said that out loud. While a few of the abandoned husbands had gotten together at Ryan's to play poker and herd kids, Faith had left Darryl and L.B. in her kitchen, hunkered down over plans for Darryl's new venture, a subject that now so completely occupied his thoughts he'd barely even reacted when she'd told him she was leaving. Frankly, it was almost a letdown.

But here she was, goose bumps boogying over her skin at the twang of electric *gee*-tar, the throb of bass, spilling from the squat, neon-hazed building on the other side of the lot. She breathed in deeply, inhaling the beat as well as the damp, chilled, cusp-of-spring air, feeling her pulse align itself with the music, and thought, simply, *Okay*, just as Renee, in a tiered denim skirt and spike-heeled boots, threaded her arm through Faith's.

"Isn't this nuts?" her mother-in-law whispered. "I feel like a kid."

"Yeah," Faith whispered back. "Me, too."

"Hey, y'all," Dawn said, poured into a pair of designer jeans and a deeply V'd, wet-dream-inducing, red sweater. "We gonna stand out here all night or what?"

They made quite a group, from the tall and voluptuous Dawn, to waiflike, cowboy-booted Maddie in her customary baggy overalls over a long-sleeved Henley tee, to wild-haired Carly, her earlobes sparkling with an assortment of earrings, in her doll-size miniskirt, dark tights and a pair of stilettos that could double as kabob skewers. Jenna Logan, in her trendy pale green sweater set and white linen pants, a ribbon holding back her blond pageboy, moaned about how out of place she was going to look (an observation that nobody contradicted), while her "date" for the evening, Taylor McIntyre Salazar, Joe's new wife and Jake's kindergarten teacher last year, had taken the safe route by dressing all in black—sweater, jeans, pumps—her vibrant red hair piled on top of her head.

And rounding out the group—literally— was Faith, who'd been lucky to find a pair of jeans that weren't frayed at the hems, let alone a sweater that still looked even remotely in fashion. However, the occasion had provided the perfect opportunity to finally wear that pair of killer ankle boots she'd bought on impulse at Payless a couple years before, which had sat in her closet ever since. Truth be told, they hurt like holy hell, but if Darryl's considering stare in the vicinity of her butt had been any indication, they definitely gave a nice sway to her walk.

"Whoa," Taylor said, when they all tumbled inside, giggling like a bunch of fools. "Dark."

"And loud," added Jenna, recoiling slightly from the blast of amplified music and overly enthusiastic vocals from the band—and yep, there was Jimmy—giving it their all from the stage. Not to mention the almost deafening roar of conversation, the occasional explosion of boozed-up laughter from this or that booth or table, the pulsing thunder of boots against a wooden floor in time to a line dance. But Faith only had eyes for the bright stage lights, smoke-hazed though they were, as nostalgia trembled through her.

"Loud is good," Dawn yelled over the din. "Loud doesn't let you think."

More than a few heads turned as they plodded through air choked with the scents of beer, hot grease and eye-wateringly strong cologne (and not just from the women, unfortunately) in search of a table large enough to accommodate them all, when suddenly, as if by magic, there was an empty corner booth.

"See?" Dawn said, plopping onto the worn vinyl and skootching toward the middle. Her hair had grown out some, her dark bangs tangling with her lashes. She leaned forward, a series of gold chains glittering against her impressive cleavage. "Were we supposed to be here tonight or what? It's fate."

"Fate, hell." With feathers of honey-colored hair gleaming dully in the faint light given off from the wall sconce over the booth, Maddie Logan reached over to snatch up the hand-printed Reserved—Logan Party sign. "I called earlier," she said with a shrug when all eyes glommed on to her.

"Since when does Edna's take reservations?" Faith asked.

Maddie let out one of her sandpapery chuckles. "Ever since Ryan decked Hootch Atkins when he made a play for me in here, before we were married. Apparently Edna thought that was about the most romantic thing she'd ever seen—"

"Wait, wait, wait..." Dawn interrupted, eyes wide. "Ryan *decked* somebody? Ryan-Logan-who-wouldn't-squish-a-mosquito-if-it-was-biting-him?"

Maddie grinned. "Still waters run deep, what can I tell you?"

The waitress—blond, stacked, her spring-chicken days long behind her—materialized out of the smoke to take their order, prompting a discussion of who would act as designated driver and who wouldn't, depending on who was still nursing (Maddie) and who wasn't (Dawn and, at long last, Faith).

Then Taylor, fingering a tendril of red hair that had escaped from her up-do, announced that, um, she couldn't drink, either…and all hell broke loose, leading Faith to wonder at the ability of human beings to get so excited about something so basic. And around here, so frequent.

"You're *pregnant*?" Jenna said with a squeal completely out of keeping with her conservative appearance.

"Uh-huh." The redhead was grinning so broadly she looked like her face would crack for sure. "Two months."

"And you're not puking your guts out?" Dawn asked.

"Not so far," Taylor said, at which Faith could feel a silent, if loving, consensus that this was someone just askin' to be hated. In any case, the waitress eventually left with their orders (four beers, three lemonades, and nachos all around, although Faith wondered if the nachos might present more of a potential hazard to Taylor's unborn child than the beer), and Faith eventually began to feel less and less like a sixteen-year-old who'd sneaked into the place with a fake ID.

As did her mother-in-law, apparently, who'd struck up a conversation with Jenna about how much she'd loved her book and that what she couldn't find at Jacqui's, she'd ordered online, just this morning in fact. Then she looked over at Faith and wrinkled her nose, smiling, lifting her glass of beer in a salute, which Faith returned.

"O*kay*," Carly shouted. The dance teacher was already twitching to the music, sending her longest pairs of earrings into a jittery blur. "Somebody's gotta join me on the dance floor before I expire."

"Not me, I'm pregnant," Taylor said, her Texan drawl more pronounced than usual, causing Jenna to wonder aloud if she was going to use that excuse a lot over the next several months. "Okay, so I'm a disaster on the dance floor," Taylor admitted. "Elaine from *Seinfeld* has nothing on me."

"I hear ya there," Maddie rasped. "Now, pool, on the other hand…"

"Are you even tall enough to reach the table?" Dawn teased her sister-in-law.

That prompted an indignant eye roll from Maddie and a simultaneous, "Hey. No short jokes!" from Carly and Faith as their drinks and munchies arrived. Right after, Carly dragged Jenna and Renee out on the floor, while Maddie convinced Taylor she could, too, teach her how to play pool. The band started up another number, prodding awake more of that nostalgia, even as Faith vaguely registered a reedy female voice, barely strong enough to slice through the smoke in the place, let alone hold its own against the backup. Pitiful.

"Hey," Dawn called softly across the table. She took a swig of her beer, her long gold earrings trembling through her dark hair. "You okay?"

"Sure. Why wouldn't I be?"

Her bottle in tow, Dawn slid around to sit next to her. "You need tonight, petunia." One slender hand snagged a dripping, cheese-slathered chip out of the paper basket in front of her. "Hell, we all need tonight."

"I know, but…"

"No buts. Except for maybe that fine pair over there," she said, nodding toward a swaggering duo checking out the prospects at the bar. "Which makes you wrong, by the way. Because in anybody's book, those are cute guys."

Faith chuckled. "It's dark. And they're, like, Heather's age. And aren't you taking this a little too far?"

Dawn eyed her curiously, then selected another nacho. "Okay, if one of them came over here and tried to hit on me, I'd give him a look that would fast-freeze his cojones. Admiring the view is something else again. Especially since it only reminds me how good I've got it at home. Speaking of admiring the view," she said, gesturing toward the stage with a cheese-soaked chip, "Jimmy's certainly aged a lot better than I would've expected. I'm not much into facial hair, but on him, the beard seriously works."

Licking canned cheese off her fingers, Faith twisted around in her seat. "Yeah, I guess. Same good-for-nothing grin, though."

"That's called charm, honey," Dawn said, and Faith laughed. Long-legged and smooth-tongued, Jimmy had been the bad boy all the good girls knew better than to get involved with, while secretly wanting to do exactly that. What Darryl didn't know was that Faith had even entertained a fantasy or three about him, when she'd been thirteen or so and Jimmy'd been seventeen. Then Jimmy had graduated and gone into the army, and Darryl's slow, sweet, deadly grins had pretty much annihilated those adolescent fantasies, replacing them with a reality that was far more precious. Even so, in those tight black jeans and white cowboy shirt, Faith's old fantasy still had some mighty fine moves. Not to mention a voice that could curl toes at a thousand paces. Now *he* was good—

She jumped at Dawn's laugh.

"Admiring the view, are we?"

Faith humphed as the others returned, piling back into the booth, guzzling their drinks and attacking the nachos like they hadn't eaten since Christmas. The conversation became a tangle of kid stories (they really were all hopeless), musings about what would happen next on this or that TV show, Carly's and Sam's upcoming wedding in September, and whether Ivy would marry Carly's father or just live with him (which she had been doing for several weeks now), which was frosting more than one person in town. Then the female vocalist started butchering one of Faith's favorite ballads, and it was everything she could do not to march up on stage and stuff something in the woman's mouth.

"Faith?" Maddie asked. "Are you all right?"

"I will be soon as that sorry excuse for a vocalist finds her true calling."

"Oh," Jenna said, her blue eyes trained on

the stage. "So it's not supposed to sound like that."

"Of course it's not supposed to sound like that! Country singin's more than just gettin' up on stage and warbling, it's about…"

"Soul," Dawn put in, pinning Faith with a pointed look.

"Yeah. And I'm here to tell you, that gal's more than a little short in that department."

"Now Faith had soul," Dawn said.

The other ladies all turned to her. "You sing?" Maddie asked.

Blood rushed to her cheeks. "Sang. Past tense. Another life."

"And oh, my," Renee said, laying her hand on Faith's wrist. "She was something to hear, let me tell you. Used to send shivers up my spine—"

The mic squawked, effectively silencing the crowd. "Okay, folks," Jimmy announced from the stage, his hot-fudge baritone reverberating through the large room. "Since by this point everybody's probably too drunk to hear all that good anyway—"

He grinned, his smile as bright and deadly as it ever was.

"—anybody who wants to strut their stuff, now's your chance. If we know it, we'll play it. If we don't, we'll play it anyway. So come on now, don't be shy." He leaned over and growled into the mike. "You know you want to."

Faith was chuckling along with everybody else when suddenly a voice shouted out, right over her head, "Over here, Jimmy!"

She spun around to see Dawn jabbing her hands in Faith's direction. "What do you think you're doing?" she squeaked, but Jimmy had already shaded his eyes with his hand, saying, "Faith Meyerhauser? Well, I'll be…get yourself up here, girl!"

Faith waved her hands in front of her face, frantically shaking her head, but it was no good, somebody'd already aimed one of the spotlights at the booth, and Dawn was laughing and shoving her out of her seat. Everybody else was shouting and clapping and whistling and yelling, and she felt her face flame even as her heart started doing this funny little bump-skip thing in her chest.

Still, she hissed, "I'm gonna git you for this," at Dawn as she backed away on watery legs, tugging her sweater down over her hips and running a shaky hand through her hair. Dawn lifted her beer toward her, grinning, giving Faith the distinct impression she wasn't terribly intimidated by the threat.

Well. Guess there was nothing left for it except to pray she didn't make too big a fool of herself. So, with as much dignity as she could muster, Faith turned, head held high, heart pounding, and started toward the stage, impaled by the searing spotlight beam like she was an escaped prisoner. By this time, having a victim in their sights, the crowd was making so much noise she half feared she'd be deaf by the time she reached the stage and wouldn't be able to hear herself. Which, considering how long it had been since she'd actually sung for anybody other than the dog or Nicky, might not be such a bad thing.

Somehow, she got up the three steps to the stage, her boot heels cracking like pistol shots as she walked across the worn plank floor toward Jimmy and the mike. Dear Lord, it took everything she had not to wipe her sweaty palms down her jeans. To her surprise, Jimmy's trademark badass smirk softened at her approach. He covered the mic with one long-fingered hand; when he leaned toward her, his cologne nearly made her gag.

"It's been too long since the world's heard your angel voice, sweetheart," he said with a sincerity that surprised her. "So what'll it be? And you want to go solo or let us back you up? Your call."

She knew an up-tempo song would be far more forgiving of her still-rusty voice, but it was a ballad that came to her, so it was a ballad she decided to sing.

"C'n I borrow your guitar?" she asked, and with another grin, Jimmy handed his over, then got her a stool, too, when she asked for one. Once settled into place, the heel of one boot hooked over the stool's lower rung, she thrummed the strings for a second or two, then looked out into the darkness. Mercifully, the blinding lights of the stage obliterated the audience, so she could pretend she was still at home, singing in her living room.

"It's been awhile since I've done this," she said into the mic, a tremor racing along her skin at the sound of her own voice carrying out into the room. "So be kind, okay?"

And for sure, those first few notes weren't exactly the prettiest things in the world, and her diaphragm quaked from disuse and nerves something terrible. But by the time she reached the first chorus, she'd begun to get her footing, the words welling up from someplace so deep inside her she'd forgotten its existence. Oh, she flubbed the lyrics once or twice, but the soft ripple of laughter from her audience was sympathetic, bolstering, buoying her up and over the glitches and into a place she hadn't visited in far too long.

The final chord floated out into the darkness, hanging like a raindrop on the end of a branch for several seconds before it faded away completely. Two, three seconds later, the applause started, clapping and shouting, several people yelling her name, loud "Whoo-hoos!" from Dawn, sounds that winnowed through her, wrapping themselves around her heart like her childrens' hugs. Faith sat there, soaking it up, her grin getting bigger and bigger, as the hole inside her finally, for the first time in what seemed like forever, finally got plugged up.

Plugged up so tight, in fact, that she could hardly feel the fear.

Chapter Fifteen

It was after midnight by the time she dropped off Maddie, then Renee, who thanked Faith over and over for including her, saying she couldn't remember when she'd had so much fun. One hand on the door handle, her mother-in-law smiled at her in the darkness. "And hearin' you sing again...oh, my. A shame you only did the one song, though."

"That was the only one I remembered all the words to," Faith lied, not sure herself why, when Jimmy had practically begged her to do another number, the panic had gripped her so bad she'd hardly been able to breathe. Luckily, though, Renee let it go at that.

When she got home, however, Darryl and L.B. were still huddled over the table, papers and heaven knew what spread out between them.

"Ohmigosh—you're still at it?" she said, hanging up her jacket.

Darryl blinked up at her, his forehead wrinkled. "You're back? What time is it…?" as L.B. shot up from the table, muttering something about getting home before Renee freaked, she didn't like being in the house by herself at night. Before her father-in-law was out the back door, though, a noise behind Faith caught her attention. She turned to see a tall, skinny kid with spiked hair at the kitchen door, bouncing a fussy Nicky on a bony hip swallowed up inside baggy jeans.

"Hell, Ronnie," Darryl said, pushing himself to his feet as well and scrubbing the heel of his hand into his eye. "Ruby'll have my hide for keeping you here so late. You better get goin', too…"

"No, it's okay, she gave me a key so I can let myself in. You must be Faith," the kid said with a big smile, handing Nicky over, which was when Faith realized that Ronnie was, in fact, a striking young woman with model cheekbones, huge green eyes and a Julia Rob-

erts mouth. "Hope you don't mind me gettin' the baby up, he was fussy, like maybe
he's teething or something? I'm the oldest of
seven, so I've got all the cries down. Ohmigod, he's so cute I could just eat 'im up, *yes,
I could*," she said to Nicky, who was clearly
the one doing the eating up at the moment.
"Okay… I'll see you tomorrow, Darryl? No,
no, you stay put, I'll let myself out. Nice to
meet you," she said with a nod to Faith, and
was gone.

"*That's* Ronnie?" Faith said.

"Uh-huh," Darryl said with a yawn, draping one arm around her shoulders to steer
her toward the hall. "Since this whole school
thing was her idea, L.B. and I thought it
wouldn't hurt to get her input—" another
yawn "—about how to set things up, what
to charge, stuff like that." He tugged Faith
close enough to plant a kiss on her temple.
"You have a good time?" he asked when they
reached the door to their bedroom.

"Uh, yeah…let me get the baby back to bed
and I'll be right in."

A few minutes later, Faith returned to their
bedroom to find Darryl already in bed, on
his side, eyes closed. She hurried through her
bedtime routine, then got under the covers,

only to sit up with her arms wrapped around her knees, her bedside lamp still on. "So how old's Ronnie, anyway?"

"No idea," Darryl mumbled. "Mid-twenties, maybe. Why?"

"Oh, no reason." Faith pause. "She's very pretty."

After a moment, he rolled over, a let-me-guess smile playing around his mouth. "Baby, the only thing I've got the hots for is her car, okay?"

"Did I say anything?" she said, and he made a deep, chuckling sound in his chest, and she heard herself blurt out, "I sang tonight."

His expression shifted to wary. "What do you mean, you sang?"

"It was all Dawn's fault. In the middle of one of the sets, Jimmy extended a blanket invitation to anybody who wanted to get up on stage, and Dawn kinda pushed me up there."

"I see." He scrunched his pillow up under his cheek, scrutinizing her like he was trying to read her mind. More power to him, was all she had to say. At this point, she'd pay somebody to decipher the scrambled mess inside her head.

"So how was it?" he said at last.

"Strange. Like I'd been time-warped."

"Was it fun?" he asked softly.

"Terrifying is more like it."

"Terrifying like being on the wrong side of a fence with a charging bull, or terrifying like goin' down a roller coaster?"

"Both."

He reached under the covers to skim his hand up her shin, making her very glad she'd shaved this morning. "I seem to recall you love roller coasters."

"I know," she said. "Charging bulls, however, are another thing entirely."

"It's safe over here," he said, patting the mattress. A grin slid across his mouth. "No bull."

"Oh, yeah?"

"Yeah. Lose the nightgown."

"And how, exactly, is that *safe*?"

"Get yourself over here and I'll show you," he said.

Goodness. It was nearly 1:00 a.m., and Renee felt as if she was plugged into one of those amplifiers at Edna's, she was so wired. Listening to Faith sing, finally setting free everything she'd kept bottled up inside her for so long, had had a profound and disturbing effect on Renee. To the point where, when she heard L.B. come in through the back door, she wasn't sure she could hold in her thoughts anymore.

This could be interesting.

Still dressed and sitting on the sofa with her legs tucked up under her, Renee listened to the familiar swoosh and clunks and clinks of his hanging up his jacket, hooking his keys on the peg rack beside the refrigerator.

"I got home as soon as could," he said upon entering the living room, "since I know how you hate bein' alone at night."

And just like that, something gave way within her, setting her insides to churning so furiously she half expected to froth at the mouth when she spoke. "For heaven's sake, L.B., it was for all of ten minutes. I'm not exactly quaking in my boots. Besides, since we haven't spent a night apart since we got married, how do you know whether I mind being alone at night or not? And yes, I had a good time tonight, thanks for asking."

He gave her a funny look. Not that she blamed him. "You didn't exactly give me a chance to ask, did you?" When she sort of humphed, he crossed his arms and said, "Did I miss something?"

"Well, one of us sure did," Renee said, lifting her chin, feeling like that Stella Moon character in Jenna's book, ready to take on anything life tossed in her path. What was odd, though, was that while she definitely saw bewilderment in L.B.'s expression, she didn't see any particular surprise. As if he'd somehow seen this coming. "I'm just not sure what, yet."

L.B.'s shoulders slumped a little at that, before, with a sigh, he sank into the love seat across from the couch. He watched her for some time, then said, "Do you think I treat you like a child?"

And there it was, the key to the whole blamed mess, sitting right there in front of her. Only it fit into a slightly different lock than she might have expected.

"Yes," she said. "Only I think the problem's more that…that I've *let* you treat me like one. So it's not entirely your fault. But now I want you to stop."

He looked…lost. And as big and strong and protective as that twenty-year-old boy who'd rescued her from hell all those years ago. "Just like that?"

Renee felt the pull of tears behind her eyes. "Well…maybe we could ease into it," she said. "Take it on a case-by-case basis. Like letting me put gas in my own car, for instance. And trust me to figure a few things out on my own now and then instead of coming to my rescue over every little thing."

"I only meant—"

"To take care of me, I know," she said gentv ly. "And I will always love you for that. Always. But it's like when the boys were learning to ride their bikes—you had to let go, and they had to fall over a few times, before they figured out how to find their balance. L.B.— we don't know which of us is going to go first, but if it should be you—"

"Then the boys'd take care of you," he said, but she shook her head.

"No, L.B. That's not their job. And the idea of being a helpless widow gives me the willies. Besides, I guess if I raised three boys to maturity, I can probably handle getting myself there, too. Even if I am about thirty years past due." She took a breath. "This isn't about me loving you less, L.B., believe me. It's about me loving myself more. About… about me finally seeking some outlet for my creative energies that doesn't involve you, our sons or this house."

His brows lifted. "You mean…like a job?"

"Like *something*. I just don't know what yet. It might even mean you havin' to get supper for yourself, every now and then."

Well, he just gawked at her like she was a talking fish for what seemed like a full minute, only to burst out laughing, which was the last thing she expected.

"You'd actually trust me in your kitchen?"

Oh, dear Lord—she hadn't thought of that. Even so, she swallowed down the panic and said, "Desperate times call for desperate measures," deciding that was renewed respect, rather than alarm, she saw in her husband's eyes. Then she added, "Faithie sang tonight, at Edna's," and L.B.'s brows popped up again.

"What do you think that means?" he asked.

She shrugged. "Guess it depends."

L.B. only nodded, not needing to ask her what she meant by that.

To be truthful, when Faith had confessed to her impromptu performance up at Edna's that night, Darryl had had to fight with everything he had in him not to make a bigger deal out of the issue than it was. But the fact was, his reaction had stunned him, despite his having seen this coming weeks ago—right about the time her mother brought back the guitar.

He'd made love to her that night—and at every opportunity since—like it was the last time.

And over the past couple of weeks, between his being so involved in moving forward with the next phase of his life, and Faith's not bringing up the subject even once, the near panic finally subsided. Far as he could tell, it had been a one-shot deal. She'd gotten something out of her system, and that was that.

Or so he'd convinced himself, until his mother took it upon herself to get up another expedition to the honky-tonk, and he saw the little spark of excitement in Faith's eyes after she hung up the phone. And no male with half a brain dismissed sparks of excitement in his woman's eyes, especially those that had nothing to do with him.

"You sure you don't want me to go with you?" he'd said, since the group this time would only be Faith and Dawn and his mother.

"We're wearing our creep repellent, I promise," she'd said, giving him a highly unsatisfactory kiss before heading out. But he noticed she was wearing a shiny turquoise blouse he hadn't seen before, tucked into a pair of new black jeans. And her fanciest earrings, a long, dangly pair that sparkled every time she moved.

Which was why, after asking L.B. to come over and keep an eye on the kids, Darryl was now standing inside Edna's, scanning the smoke-hazed crowd for the three Bustkateers, as Dawn had dubbed them, only to realize Faith was up on the stage.

So much for it being a one-time thing.

Pride, then something else, tumbled through his gut at how right at home she looked up there, the stage lights kissing her blond curls, sliding over the turquoise satin of her blouse right where it strained across her breasts. She smiled as she sang, brazenly flirting with the audience, the tune some old thing Darryl dimly remembered from his youth, something sassy and sexy and guaranteed to make a person feel pretty damn good just to be alive. And the audience was eating it up, clapping and tapping along, clearly under her spell.

As Faith was under theirs, he saw. Even from way back here, he could see a passion in her eyes he hadn't seen since forever, could feel his own skin tingle from the glow that radiated from her as she sat there, the sounds coming from her throat like liquid gold.

"I wondered if you'd show up," Dawn said at his shoulder. When he didn't—couldn't—

speak, she added, "She's somethin' else, isn't she?"

He finally found enough of his voice to say, "I hear this was your idea?"

"Now, does that appear to you like somebody who had to be coerced? She looks like the weight of the world's been lifted from her shoulders, doesn't she?"

His chest suddenly too tight for his lungs, Darryl whipped around and shoved his way back outside, the cool night air slapping him in the face as he marched back over to his truck.

"Darryl!" Dawn called behind him. "Darryl, for God's sake—" Her hand landed on his arm, tugging him back around. "Where are you going?"

"Home," he said, digging his keys out of his pants pocket, only to have them smacked out of his hand before he could get them into the door lock.

"Hey—!"

"Hey, yourself! What's the big idea, slinking off into the night instead of, I don't know, standing up on a table or something and letting the world know how proud you are of your wife? She's freaking *fantastic,* you moron!"

"I know she is! And I'm not slinking!" He snatched his keys off the ground, feeling like about a hundred horses were stampeding inside his brain. He knew his reaction didn't make a lick of sense, but he couldn't help it. Once upright again, he slung one fist toward the building. "Did you *see* her up there?"

Dawn's chin lowered as her hands landed on her hips. "Yeah. I did. But the question is…did *you?* All she was doing was *singing,* Darryl. Using talent she's kept buried for her entire married life. Please don't tell me you resent that."

"Of course not, it's just…"

"It's just what, for God's sake?"

"*Dammit,* Dawn…" He took a deep breath, then another, vainly trying to tamp down the brutal emotions ripping him apart inside. "You have any idea what it's like to stand there, and see that look on her face, and realize she's never, ever worn that look for *you?*"

He yanked open the truck door and climbed inside, Dawn not even trying to stop him when he peeled out of the lot.

"Hey, Faith…got a sec?"

Still getting her breath back after that last number, Faith smiled up at Jimmy from her table. Renee had gone off to the ladies', but where Dawn had gotten to, she couldn't begin to imagine. "I already told you I can't stick around for the last set, Jimmy, I've got to get back home—"

"This isn't about tonight. You mind if I sit?"

She shook her head, about a thousand questions going off in her brain as Jimmy dropped into the chair across from her. He gave a little wave toward the waitress to get her attention, then leaned back, studying Faith intently.

"You know," she said, "I really hate it when you do that."

A smile flashed underneath his mustache. "Sorry. I can't help it, though. I mean, you were cute and all back in school, but now... mmm, mmm! That husband of yours is one lucky man, that's all I have to say."

Faith took a sip of her Coke, barely noticing Renee deep in conversation with Edna, over by the bar. "You came all the way over here to tell me that?"

"No, I came all the way over here to make you a proposition." When she stopped with the Coke halfway to her lips, Jimmy laughed. "Not that kind of proposition. I don't mess around with married women. Least not with those whose husbands are likely to care. No, this is strictly business. Suzanne—our vocalist—gave notice tonight, did you know?"

"No, I didn't."

"Yeah, she's taken up with some guy out of Dallas. He wants her to move down there. And the boys and me decided we'd like you to take her place."

Faith's drink thunked down onto the table. "You can't be serious."

"Why wouldn't I be? The crowd obviously loves you. And you obviously love the spotlight, darlin'. Sure looks like a no-brainer to me."

Faith glanced over at Dawn, who'd just returned to the table and looked as shell-shocked as Faith felt. "Oh, man, Jimmy... I cannot tell you how flattered I am. But a couple songs every once in a while on a Friday night is one thing, performing every Friday and Saturday... I can't do that."

"Why not? I'm not saying it'll make you rich, but we get half the cover. Even split four ways, the way I guarantee you're gonna pull 'em in? Could be a couple hundred bucks a night, for starters. And we've got plans, already got a couple of gigs booked in Tulsa, one in Oklahoma City in June…like they say, this could be the start of something big."

The shaking started somewhere around the soles of her feet, taking over her whole body so fast she had to grip the edge of the table to keep her voice steady enough to talk. "I've already got something big. It's c-called my family. It wouldn't be fair to them, leaving 'em every weekend. I'm sorry, Jimmy…" She dragged in a breath, letting it out on "…but the answer's no."

He stared at her for several more seconds, before, with a nod, he got up, snagging his beer off the waitress's tray before she got all the way to the table. But instead of walking away, he turned back.

"Tell you what…" He tugged his wallet out of his back pocket, flipping it open to extract a slightly worn business card, which he handed to Faith. "You think it over. Better yet, why don't you give it a shot as a star attraction, instead of this just-so-happens thing we've been doing these past couple of weeks? I mean it," he said when she laughed. "Word's already gotten out how good you are. With a little advertising… I'm talking sellout crowd, no sweat. Because I dare you to sit up there in front of a packed house, a packed house because of *you*, and tell me you can walk away a second time."

This time, when his eyes met hers, her face heated. "I don't know what you're talking about," she said quietly, and he laughed.

"The hell you don't." Frowning, he slipped his wallet back in his pocket, taking a pull of his beer before saying, "I never did understand why you got cold feet back then, why you didn't go for the brass ring that was dangling right there in front of your nose."

"Cold feet had nothing to do with it," Faith said, rubbing the back of her neck with a trembling hand. "My life just took a different turn, is all. And besides...brass ring? Please. I was just another kid with big dreams. That kid doesn't exist anymore, Jimmy."

Jimmy regarded her steadily for several seconds, then said, "No, she sure doesn't. And thank God for it, is all I have to say, because the woman who took her place looks, moves and sounds ten times better than that kid could have even dreamed of. That skinny little teenage kid had promise, no doubt about it. But you..." He hissed in a breath. "You, darlin', are the real thing. So like I said, you think about it, let me know. The offer stands for...let's say, a month? If I don't hear from you by then, I'll take that as a firm no and won't bother you about it again. Deal?"

Oh, Lordy, Lordy, *Lordy*. If this wasn't deer-in-the-headlights time, she didn't know what was. "If I say yes—and I'm not sayin' I am, I'm only asking—it would just be for the one time? And I'd get a quarter of the take?"

A slow smile stretched across Jimmy's face. "Yes, ma'am. On both counts."

"Okay, then. I'll think about it. And…" She held up the card. "I'll be in touch."

"I'd appreciate it," Jimmy said, then touched the brim of his hat and strode away, no less than half a dozen sets of eyes glued to his fine backside. Faith shook her head, then finally looked back at Dawn, who was wearing the expression of someone who'd just swallowed an entire cow. Sideways.

"Dawn? What's the ma—"

"Darryl was here."

"What do you mean, Darryl was here?"

The brunette shoved her hair behind one ear. "I don't know if he was checking up on you or if he was just curious or what. But…" She pushed out a breath. "His reaction to seeing you up on stage wasn't exactly positive."

Nearly dizzy with anger, Faith practically knocked over her chair in her haste to stand, yanking her purse off the chair beside her. "This whole thing was your idea, you know. I never would have even gotten on that stage in the first place if it hadn't've been for you—"

"Oh, no you don't!" Dawn said, standing as well, just as Renee came click-clicking back to the table, her smile melting when she realized she was walking into a firestorm. "I am not taking the blame for your years of denial! And I sure as hell am not taking it for something that would have happened anyway, sooner or later!"

"Faith, honey...?"

"It's okay," she snapped at her mother-in-law, knowing there was no point in even trying to refute Dawn's words, only to immediately regret her sharpness in light of the distressed look on Renee's face. "Sorry," she said, putting a hand on the older woman's arm. "Dawn'll take you home."

She barely made it outside before the tears came.

Although more or less composed, Faith was still shaky by the time she got home to find Darryl sitting in the living room, watching TV with the lights off.

"Kids all asleep?" she asked. He nodded.

Dot shimmied up to her, nosing her fingers. She petted the dog for a moment, then lightly cleared her throat and said, "So how come you left Edna's without saying something?"

Darryl reached up to turn on the lamp by the sofa, then clicked off the TV. "How come you didn't you tell me you were going to sing tonight?"

"Because I wasn't sure I was going to."

"Faith. Please."

"Okay, so maybe I wasn't *ready* to tell you."

"Why not?"

The pain in his voice—that of a child who doesn't understand why he didn't get invited to the birthday party—twisted her up inside more than she already was. "I don't know," she said. "Maybe because it's been forever since I had something that was all mine, so I wanted five minutes to cherish it? But I swear I wasn't keeping you out of the loop on purpose. Okay," she said at his disbelieving laugh, "maybe I was, but not to hurt you or make you mad."

"Never mind that that's exactly what you did."

"I'm sorry," she said. "I really am. Although…maybe now you'll understand why

I flew off the handle when I found out about your arm."

His gaze swung to hers, his expression thunderous. "You did this to get back at me?"

"Of course not! But at least I didn't keep the truth from you because I didn't think you could handle it!"

"Which I did for good reason! For God's sake, Faith—every time I turn around, you're cryin' about something. You're a walking bundle of emotions, always have been. I didn't want to upset you, that's all. So how does that make me the bad guy?"

"It doesn't! But neither does feeling things deeply make me weak, or unable to rise to a challenge!"

"Doesn't it?"

"No!"

"Then I guess you've changed more than I thought."

The tone of his voice caught her up short. "What are you talking about?"

He watched her for a long moment, then said, "Did you think I didn't know why you took up with me when you did, why you didn't seem all that upset when you got pregnant and we 'had' to get married? You were usin' me, Faith. Using me and Heather to hide behind, because 'out there' was too damn scary, wasn't it? Getting pregnant, getting married…" He shook his head. "Real convenient how that happened, right when you were on the brink of maybe having a career."

Her lungs ached from trying to pull in a breath. "You knew?"

"Damn straight, I knew. But you know what? Back then, I didn't care. As long as you were mine, I didn't much give a rat's ass how that happened. You needed me to protect you, take care of you, that was fine by me. And I guess I figured, what the hell, you probably didn't want a singing career all that much anyway, if getting pregnant was all it took for you to give it up."

"It's true, I didn't—"

"Dammit, Faith…being afraid of something doesn't mean you don't want it! If anything, it's a sign of just how badly you do want it. And when I saw you up on that stage tonight…" His gaze held hers, one side of his mouth lifting. "You had the exact same look on your face I see on Heather's when she dances. It's like you finally let the bird out of the cage. And there's no putting it back in now, is there?"

"All I d-did was take the cover off the cage,

maybe," she said, quaking inside so badly she could hardly get the words out. "But believe me, I have no intention of letting the b-bird get away."

"Oh, Faithie…" He leaned forward, scrubbing a hand down his face before looking back up at her. "Don't you get it? Seeing you tonight was like watchin' you meet up with an old lover you'd never made a clean break with, who you still had feelings for."

"It's not like that—"

"Yes, it is," he said softly. "Your singing fills something inside you in a way I can't, and never will."

Pain vising her heart, she pushed herself out of the chair, walking over to the window. Moonlight drenched the backyard, silver-tipping the barely budded out tree branches. It had been a night much like this when she'd sneaked out of her house after her parents were asleep, practically running the three blocks to where Darryl had parked, waiting for her, a pair of sleeping bags zipped together, an air mattress already in the back of his pickup. They'd driven out to the woods behind the old Double Arrow and parked, scrambling into the back of the truck, not undressing until they were inside the sleeping bags because it was too cold.

As near as she could tell, they'd made Heather that night. The sounds of their fumbling and giggling, the groan and creak of the truck as they frantically mated—nuance not being something either one much cared about at the time—were the only noises to lance the deep, late winter silence. She remembered the thick, rich glaze of moonlight over Darryl's skin, the almost desperate look of triumph in his eyes when she opened to him, pleaded with him. That night was the first time he'd told her he loved her.

The condom had torn; he'd freaked. She'd told him it was okay, she'd just had her period...

Faith turned back into the room, her arms crossed over her ribs.

"You're right," she said quietly. "About me being scared. When that agent approached me...all I knew was, I was nowhere near ready for what he was offering. Although to tell you the truth, I don't know to this day whether I was more petrified of failing or succeeding." She waited a moment, then said, "You, on the other hand, were safe. *Here.* And most important, crazy about me."

"But you didn't love me."

"Oh, Darryl… I was such a mess back then, I have no idea what I was thinking about anything. But while I made more than my share of dumb decisions, picking you wasn't one of them. That's why I keep telling you that what's going on with me now has nothing to do with you. The same way fixing cars fills something inside you that has nothing to do with me, right?"

"Except fixing cars was never going to take me away from you," he said harshly. "If anything, it was just the opposite, since that was my means of taking care of you."

"Okay, so maybe that wasn't the best analogy. But I've made my life, haven't I? With you and the kids. My wanting to make use of whatever talent I might have now…it's not a threat, Darryl. To you or to our marriage. For heaven's sake, I'm hardly going to pack up and move off to Nashville!"

"Even though you might be tempted?"

She actually laughed. "I'm tempted to do a lot of things I have no intention of acting on. Everybody is. It's called being a grown up. Being responsible—"

"But the fact remains that you didn't pick me over your singing, you picked me because you were running *away* from your singing. So any way you look at it, that makes me second choice."

"Honestly, Darryl—have you heard a single word I've said? There is no way I'm walking out on this marriage!"

"Why?" he said, rocketing from the sofa, covering the space between them so quickly she backed up a step. "Because you're *responsible?* Because you made a promise you can't back out of? Or because you're still too scared to go for it?"

"And how on earth could I possibly do that? I've got five kids, for crying out loud!"

She sucked in a breath, as if she could retrieve the words. Words that didn't even make sense. Not that, judging from the ravaged expression on Darryl's face, she had the remotest hope of making him understand that.

"Darryl, I—"

"No more lies, Faithie," he said, his voice heavy as lead. "Please." He expelled a harsh breath. "If it's all the same to you, I think maybe I'll stay up at the shop tonight."

"There's no need to leave, Darryl—"

"Yes, there is," he said, then started to walk away, only to turn back when he reached the door. "This house is too damn small for all of us and your regrets, too, Faith. And it's high time at least one of us faces that fact."

"Mama?" Heather said behind her after Darryl had shut the door. "Mama, what's wrong…?"

Her throat way too clogged to speak, Faith simply folded her firstborn into her arms and held on for all she was worth.

Chapter Sixteen

How odd, Faith thought as she carted her cash drawer up to the office to check out after her shift, that you could go about your daily routine as though everything was perfectly normal, while inside you felt like a zombie.

Except as far as she knew, zombies didn't generally feel as though their insides had been gouged out with a grapefruit spoon.

It'd been well into the wee hours before she finally got Heather reassured enough to go back to bed, but only after making the child promise not to let on to the younger kids than anything was amiss, a lie she'd perpetuated this morning by telling them that Daddy'd left early for work. It being Saturday, she'd then distributed them to various grandparents, as usual, where they still were. But when she turned down the street leading to her childhood home, instead of stopping at her mother's to pick up her babies, she kept right on going until she found herself sitting in the church's parking lot.

Her hands clamped around the steering wheel, she sat for heaven knows how long, staring through a sheen of tears at the small, unpretentious white building. All she wanted—all she'd ever wanted—was to do the right thing, for everybody to be happy.

How could such a simple plan go so horribly wrong?

Darryl handed Coop Hastings his change and slammed shut the register drawer, provoking L.B. into giving him at least his fiftieth *What the hell's wrong with you?* look of the day. Only this time, as soon as Coop was out of earshot, L.B. finally gave voice to the question.

"Didn't sleep well," Darryl said. Growled, actually.

"Any particular reason?"

"No," he said, half because he was feeling

ornery and half because he didn't want to drag his father into it, and half (okay, that was too many halves, but ask him if he cared) because he was simply too damn pissed at having run into yet another impasse in his life.

Except then L.B. said, "Your mother nearly talked my ear off about Faith's performance last night," and before Darryl knew it, he'd poured all his misery and confusion and frustration out to his father in a way he never had before.

But then, he'd never been this confused and miserable and frustrated before, not even when he'd thought his injured hand had meant the end of his livelihood.

His expression impassive, L.B. listened to the whole sorry tale, interjecting nothing except an occasional "I see," or "What did she say, exactly?" from time to time. And when Darryl was spent, leaving him feel like a wrung-out washrag (only not nearly as intelligent), his father nodded for several seconds, then said, "Care to hear my take on the issue?"

And God help him, Darryl did.

"What in tarnation are you doin' in here?" A half smile tilted Faith's lips at the sound of her father's voice behind her, but she didn't move. Or open her eyes.

"I think it's called praying. You've heard of the concept?"

"Once or twice." Although she couldn't hear his footsteps on the worn gold carpet, the pew creaked slightly when her father leaned his weight on the back before settling in beside her. "You askin' or listening?"

"Both." She opened one eye. "Mama send you to check up on me?"

"You driving by instead of picking up the little ones right away was bound to set off an alarm or two."

Of course. "So...you here as my daddy or my pastor?"

"I'm flexible," he said with a shrug. "So what's going on?"

"How about my marriage is falling apart and I don't have a clue how to put it back together again?"

"I see." He paused. "Heather did mention, when I picked her up from dance class, that Darryl'd spent the night at the filling station."

Faith might have laughed if she hadn't been so miserable. No career in undercover work for that child, that was for sure. Then she sighed. "We had a fight. Sort of."

"What about?"

"My taking up my singing again. At least, I think that's what it was about. I keep trying to fit the pieces of the conversation together, but…" She turned to her father, a hard little knot lodged in the space between her brows, and tried as best she could to fill him in, but she doubted any of it made much sense.

"So… Darryl believes deep down you still want a real career? And you think he feels threatened by that?"

"Apparently. Although nothing could be further from the truth, on either count. Which I told him. Over and over. I might as well have been talking to a brick." She leaned her head back, once again closing her eyes. "I don't want my marriage to fall apart, I really don't. But from where I'm sitting, it looks like the only way I can do that is to forget about my singing entirely and go back to the way things were. Except…"

"What?"

She opened her eyes, letting them meet her father's again. "If I do sing, he's going to be jealous. But if I don't, he's going to be on my case about not being 'honest' and having 'regrets' and God knows what else. Talk about your no-win situations."

"Yeah, I see how that could be a problem," her father said, leaning one arm across the back of the bench. "Although, you know, maybe you're not giving that husband of yours near enough credit for one or two things."

"Such as?"

"Like being adaptable, for starters. No, don't laugh," he said when she did just that. "I don't think I'll ever forget the look on Darryl's face when the two of you came and told us you were pregnant. He was embarrassed, yes. But also determined to do the right thing. Not because he 'had' to, but because he was crazy about you. Sure doesn't sound as though anything's changed on that score. So my guess is if he could adjust to that earth-shattering event at eighteen, he can probably adjust now. If you give him that chance." Chuck paused. "But that's where the second thing comes in."

"For heaven's sake, Daddy," she exclaimed when he didn't say anything right away. "What?"

Her father reached over and gently tugged one of her curls, concern swimming in his eyes. "It seems to me," he said softly, "that maybe Darryl understands you a lot better than you understand yourself. And that what you're reading as stubbornness or paranoia is more likely sheer frustration. Honey," he said when she tried to interrupt, "even the most adaptable man on earth has to know what he's really working with. And from where I'm sitting, you're either incapable or unwilling to give that to him." He paused again. "And you never have been, not really.

"Because put yourself in his place, for a moment. For twelve years, you kept your real feelings about your music buried. Whether that was good, bad or indifferent, I can't say. But from his standpoint, your suddenly 'findin' yourself' or whatever you want to call it has come out of the blue. And now you're asking something different from him, and my guess is he hasn't the slightest idea how to go about being whoever you need him to be." Chuck paused. "Especially if you went into the marriage under false pretenses."

"What makes you think—?"

"When you didn't seem all that upset about the pregnancy, your mother and I kind of guessed it wasn't entirely an 'accident.' At least on your part. And funny how it happened right after that agent came to see you." Her father folded his hands together on top of the pew. "With the timing and all, it wasn't real hard to put two and two together, that you got pregnant and got married so you wouldn't have to face things you didn't want to face."

"But... Darryl wanted to marry me."

"I know. That doesn't make what you did right. That was a lot to saddle an eighteen-year-old boy with, honey. A helluva lot."

"Oh, Lord," she said, leaning forward to bury her face in her hands. "I'm a horrible, horrible person."

"No, just human," her father said, rubbing her back. "Shoot, honey, everybody screws up. Lord knows you're sittin' beside a prime example. But if we're lucky, we come to our senses, figure out where we went wrong, maybe even grow a little. It's called *grace*. Which is another way of saying that it's all good, in the end." When she gave a soft laugh, he said, "So what I'm saying is, you and Darryl need to go all the way back to the beginning, figure out what's worth salvaging. Start over, but from a solid foundation this time."

"Assuming that's even possible," she said tiredly.

Her father grew quiet for a moment, then said, "Let me share something with you. My grandmother was just about the best knitter you'd ever want to meet. In fact, she was so good she used to make up her own patterns. Sometimes, though, as good as she was, she'd get tripped up and make a mistake, have to rip the whole thing out. What used to amaze me, though, is how she never got particularly perturbed about it, even those times when she'd already put hours and hours into the project. When I finally asked her about it, she shrugged and said, 'Just 'cause I made a mistake don't mean the yarn's still not good. And now I know better than to make that mistake again, don't I?'"

Faith twisted around to look askance at him. "Yeah, well, that only works if you know where you went wrong the first time, doesn't it?"

"Don't you?"

She searched her father's eyes for several seconds, then sighed. "I take it you mean the honesty thing."

"That would be it," he said. "And right alongside that is the *fear* thing. No wonder Darryl wonders about your true feelings—nobody takes kindly to the idea of being thought better than the alternative, you know?"

At that, Faith pushed herself to her feet and out into the aisle, standing for a moment in the shaft of sunlight streaming through the frosted window before turning back to her father. "But it's not like that. Not now. Which I've told him. Yes, I'm willing to rip my marriage apart and start over, but what on earth good does that do if we can't agree on a new pattern—?"

The sound of the door opening at the back of the church made them both turn. Faith recognized Darryl's solid silhouette, haloed by the light in the foyer. The door swung shut, bringing him into focus as he made his sure, steady way toward them.

"If you don't mind, Chuck," he said, his gaze firmly on hers, "I'd like a few minutes alone with my wife."

"No, no...not at all," her father said, standing. Once out in the aisle, though, he faced her and said, "Seems to me I left you in this young man's care once before, not too far from this very spot. I'm thinking this is a good sign. How about you?"

All she could do was nod, what with her heart about to beat out of her chest and all. Her father squeezed her shoulder, then started up the aisle, the two men acknowledging each other with a slight incline of their heads as they passed. Then Darryl's eyes found hers again, and she saw in them a determination the likes of which she hadn't seen since she'd been the one walking down this aisle toward him, all those years ago.

And something like hope bloomed in her chest.

Darryl stopped just short of being close enough to touch her, facing the altar, his fingers slipped into his front pockets.

"Y'know, it was right here, on our wedding day, that I made a lot of promises to you," he said, hearing his voice reverberating in the empty space. "Seems fitting, somehow, to remember them here, too."

Without giving her a chance to respond, he took a seat in the front pew and leaned back, his legs stretched out in front of him. Faith seemed unsure whether to join him or not. Just as well. Considering what he had to say, a little distance between them right now probably wasn't such a bad idea.

"Dawn told me about Jimmy's offer," he said quietly, not looking at her.

"Oh, um… It's okay, I've already decided not to take him up on it."

"Oh, but I think you should."

"What?" At her flummoxed expression, Darryl squelched the grin that was dying to pop out. "Don't be ridiculous," she said. "I can't do that."

"Why not?"

His calmness was clearly freaking her out. "Because… I just can't. I already told Jimmy there's no way I can be away from the kids that much. Or…or you."

"I see," he said. "Except I've been think-ing…there had to be some reason why you stopped singing altogether, after Heather came. Why you kept shoving it down inside you. And my guess is, that was because it didn't take all that long for you to realize how badly you'd screwed up, not going after your dream."

Now he smiled the smile of a man who has nothing left to lose. And, just possibly, everything to gain. "So now I'm gonna ask you a question," he said, crossing his arms over his chest. "And if you love me, you'll answer it honestly, instead of telling me what you think I want to hear. What do *you* want, Faithie? If you didn't have kids, if you didn't have a husband, if there was nothing holding you back…?" Then, keeping her gaze locked in his, he waited.

Even from here, he could see a fine trem-bling overtake her body, a flush color her cheeks. And finally, after what seemed like forever, she whispered, "To see how far I could actually take this."

"By that I take it you don't mean in the grocery business?"

A shaky laugh bounced out of her mouth. "N-no."

"Bird's out of the cage?"

She nodded, her pulse pounding at the base of her throat. "But…oh, God, Darryl… I'm so, so *scared*."

Darryl sighed. *Finally.* He pushed himself to his feet, coming to stand in front of her, slipping his good hand into hers. "You know, at first I was tempted to believe that me and the kids had gotten in the way of you doing what you needed to do. That we'd, I don't know, trapped you or something. Until it hit me that it's not us that's holding you back. It never was. It's you. That you're still using the kids and me as an excuse to avoid facing whatever's keeping you from doing something you love." He lifted their linked hands, tucking hers against his chest. "Something that'll eventually kill you if you don't figure out a way to do it. So, darlin', I'm hereby givin' notice that I'm not letting you get away with that anymore."

She tried to pull her hand out from his, but he held fast. "Get away with that?"

"Using me to hide behind. I swore to take care of you, and protect you, and I'll do both to my dying day. But damned—" He glanced up. "Sorry." Then looked back at her. "—if I'm going to protect you from yourself. Oh, I'm not gonna lie, I was only too glad at the beginning to shield you from whatever it was that scared you so much. And not *just* then, either. I was petrified of losing you to something I couldn't understand. Still am. But, see, I was going at it bass-ackwards."

He lifted their hands, skimming his lips over her knuckles. "All I could think of after the accident was how to take care of my family the way I was supposed to. That's why I was so happy when the idea for the school came to me, that I could finally see my way back to 'normal.' That now I could be everything to you, the way I used to be. Except L.B. said something a little while ago that made a whole lot of sense, once I opened up my ears long enough to listen—which is that my duty is to be who *you* need me to be. Not who *I* think you need."

Her gaze swam in his for some time before, once again, she tugged her hand away.

This time, he let her go. Gave her the freedom to determine her own destiny, as it were. She walked over to the altar, her arms folded over her ribs.

"Just when I didn't think it was possible to love you any more than I already did…" Her curls, long again, swished over her shoulders when she shook her head. Then she turned to him, those big blue eyes all shiny. "I've always loved you, Darryl, even at the beginning, even when…even when I wasn't thinking as straight as I should have been. And somewhere along the line, I don't even know when, I fell in love with you so hard it took my breath."

"You're sure about that, now? You're not just—"

"No, I'm not," she said quickly, cutting him off. "Which means…which means I'm pretty darn scared of losing you, too. But oh dear Lord…could I have made more of a mess of things?"

"How so?"

Her sharp laugh bounced off the rafters. "For crying out loud, I tricked you into marrying me, Darryl. And then I wasn't honest about *why* I tricked you! How much worse could it have been? Could *I* have been?"

"Well…you might not have fallen in love with me at all," he said, moving toward her. "Or you might have decided you really had made a mistake."

"But I did," she said, looking up at him. "And I didn't."

"So there you are." He folded his arms, resisting the impulse to haul her against him and kiss the living daylights out of her. Time enough for that after they got this all sorted out. And damned if they were leaving here until it was. "As long we're finally on the same page, who gives a rat's butt how we got here?"

"But…all that you said, about me trying for a real career…"

"Performers have families, honey. Heck, the Dixie Chicks have, what? Seven or eight kids between them? If you really want to do this, we'll work it out. No, I mean it," he said when she shook her head. "If we have to move, we'll move—the kids are young enough still that most of 'em should adjust easily enough."

"But your business…? The school?"

"Nothing says it has to be here, you know. I'm not tryin' to pressure you, honey," he said when she stiffened. "Only thing that matters right now is making sure you understand there are options, okay? Hell, you might eventually decide this really *isn't* what you want. At least you'd be able to lay it to rest knowing you'd tried. But the last thing I want is for you to wake up twenty, thirty years from now and feel like you missed your opportunity. Or that I'm somehow to blame for it."

"I'd never think that, Darryl."

"Maybe not. But that's not a chance I'm willing to take. And while I'm on a roll, let me give you something else to chew on—if you don't take this shot at seeing how far *you* can go, what kind of message is that sendin' to Heather? How can you tell her she has the right to pursue her dreams when you don't have the gumption to go after your own?"

"Oh…" Faith said, her mouth twitching. "That was *low*."

"Only took me the better part of a day to come up with it, too," he said, grinning full-out now. "And then there's the way you prodded my mother into doin' something for herself, too—"

"Okay, okay—I get the message. You don't want to be married to a hypocrite."

"Not any more than I imagine you want to be married to a dinosaur."

"Oh, I don't know…" She slipped her arms around his waist, smiling up at him. "Depends on the dinosaur."

Ah, hell. Those lips, that close… What was a guy to do?

"Mmm," Faith murmured some time later, snuggled against him. "I could stay here forever."

"I know what you mean," he whispered back. "But you can't. 'Cause you've got things to do, girl. And I'll be right beside you watching, and waitin', and cheering you on while you do them. And that's a promise."

"Oh, shoot, now I'm gonna cry," she said.

"So what else is new?" he asked, and she laughed and kissed him again, over and over, right there in the church, although somehow Darryl didn't figure God would mind in the least.

Epilogue

His elbows propped on one of the few picnic tables not piled with food, his booted feet crossed at the ankles in front of him, Darryl deliberately set himself off from the festivities in the aftermath of Carly's and Sam's long-delayed wedding. Not because he didn't feel a part of things, but just so he could absorb it a little better. Not to mention that Faith's voice sounded better back here, anyway.

Smiling the smile of the truly content, he leaned his head back to take in the deepening evening sky, the first stars of the night sparkling against the soft, clear blue like the rhinestones on his wife's dress. A late August breeze,

laden with the scents of barbecue and the out-
doors, teased the surface of the lake, tickled the
cottonwood and ash and birch leaves sheltering
the cabins at the Arrow, the rustling competing
with the giggling and shrieks of everybody's
kids racing around in the woods behind him.
No doubt more than one mama, including the
one living under his roof, was gonna have
five fits when she got a load of the kids' fancy
clothes at the end of the party.

Darryl leaned forward, his hands dangling
between his knees. Five years ago, the idea of
having a wedding at the Double Arrow, at that
time nothing more than a has-been, two-bit
motel, would have been laughable. Now look
at it. Oh, yeah, Hank Logan and his partner
Joe—who was hovering around Taylor as if
the eight-months-pregnant woman was about
to explode—had worked wonders with the
place, that was for sure.

A slight shuddering of the bench underneath him shook him out of his musings. Still
smiling, he turned toward L.B., who looked
surprisingly comfortable in his sports jacket
and bolo tie. His father raised his longneck in
the direction of the makeshift stage where an
hour ago Sam and Carly, with all six of Sam's
kids in attendance, had taken their vows in

front of Faith's daddy. Now Jimmy and his band, with Faith front and center, glittering and flashing like a fireworks display in her beaded silver dress, were doing their bit to keep things lively and help folks work off the calories from all that barbecue, not to mention the potato salad and the homemade mac-and-cheese and smothered chicken and God knew what else weighing down at least three tables nearby.

"She sounds real good," L.B. said.

Darryl grinned, like to burst with pride. "Doesn't she, though?" He leaned back again. "Did I tell you, she and Jimmy got an agent?"

"You're kiddin'? When'd that happen?"

"Last week. The daughter of the guy who originally expressed interest, before we were married. They've already got a couple of bookings. Nothing huge, but it's a start."

Right about then, Jimmy—all swagger and charm, as usual—joined Faith in harmonizing the chorus of an old Willie Nelson song, leaning close so they could hear each other, and L.B. said, "You okay with that?"

"You mean, her being with Jimmy? Why shouldn't I be?" The chorus done, Faith's eyes sought Darryl's, her bright smile when he lifted his hand in acknowledgment warming him down to his toes. "Believe me, I've got nothing to worry about."

"No, I don't suppose you do at that." L.B. took a swallow of his beer, his eyes glued to the stage. "She looks happy," he said.

"She is." Especially since she'd decided to give up her job at the Homeland to someone who might appreciate it more. "We both are."

"She okay with the move?"

Turned out there was no need for Darryl to bring up the subject of selling, after all—when it became perfectly clear they'd never be able to take the business in new directions in tiny Haven, L.B. had brought the subject up himself. And found a buyer. And with Heather's rapidly reaching the point where she was going to need more intense dance instruction, it just made sense to relocate to Tulsa. Not an easy decision considering neither Faith nor Darryl had ever lived anyplace besides Haven. Now that all the plans were more or less in place, though, it all seemed perfectly natural. And right.

"Oh, she's gonna miss everybody, but like she said, it's only forty-five minutes away." He looked over. "How about Mama?"

L.B. chuckled, his gaze firmly fixed on his wife, who was looking twenty years younger in a floaty, light blue dress and high heels, doing a semblance of the two-step with her seven-year-old grandson. "You kidding? She's already scouted out three Tulsa bookstores to see if they'd be interested in her starting a book club. Said something about taking Kelly Ripa's place, whatever the heck that means."

Darryl smiled, then said cautiously, "Chuck came to me yesterday, said he and Didi would like to invest in the business."

He waited for the blowup, but instead L.B. released a long breath, then nodded. "That's mighty generous of them. I'll make sure to search Chuck out later and thank him. And now," he said, pushing himself up off the bench, "I'd better go dance with my wife before my grandson wears her out." With a wave, he lumbered off, a man who sure looked at peace about a whole lot of things.

And it only took thirteen years to get here, Darryl thought, then grinned at the sight of his own wife making her way toward him, looking like a damn goddess in that low-cut dress. Since Faith needed more breaks than the band, the music was still going strong.

"Get over here, woman," he told her, swinging an arm around her waist and pulling her onto his lap.

"Oh, my goodness, Darryl," she said, laughing, "I'll crush you!"

"Not hardly."

"The way I've been eating lately?" She looped one arm around his neck, her perfume taking him hostage. "I nearly had apoplexy when I put this dress on and saw how tight it was, but everything else was packed. And what's really aggravatin' is that I can't even use pregnancy as an excuse anymore!"

Darryl squeezed her around the waist, making her squeal. Then she skimmed one long-nailed finger over his left arm. "How're you doin' today?"

"Look." He let go long enough to make the closest thing to a fist he'd been able to make since before the accident, and she beamed. And kissed him, only to then frown as she wiped sparkly lipstick off his mouth with her thumb. Out of the corner of his eye, he saw Dawn give him a thumbs-up, right before she dashed across the clearing toward the main building.

"What's with Dawn?" he said. "Every time I see her she's either going to or coming out of the bathroom."

Faith gave him one of those boy-you-*are*-slow looks, and he said, "Oh. When?"

"February. She's thrilled, but she swears

two's her limit. Unless it's another boy. Speaking of kids…got any idea where ours are?"

"Around. Last time I noticed, your mom had Nicky, Sierra had hooked up with Ryan's and Maddie's batch, and Jake was putting a very unique spin on the two-step with my mother. The other two are big enough to fend for themselves."

She snuggled closer and sighed, taking in the scene. "Life's sure going to be different after next week."

"Sure is." He paused. "You ready for this?"

She hissed in a breath. "It's not easy to leave everything you know. Everything you've always thought of as safe."

"But at least we're in this together."

"Ain't that the truth," she said, laughing, and he slipped his hand underneath his wife's hair to once again join their mouths, not caring who noticed that there was nothing even remotely safe or sweet or G-rated about this kiss.

"Is that a promise?" she whispered, and even he got the double meaning behind her words.

"You better believe it, darling," he said, and kissed her again.

* * * * *

HOMETOWN HEARTS ♥

YES! Please send me **The Hometown Hearts Collection** in Larger Print. This collection begins with 3 FREE books and 2 FREE gifts in the first shipment. Along with my 3 free books, I'll also get the next 4 books from the Hometown Hearts Collection, in LARGER PRINT, which I may either return and owe nothing, or keep for the low price of $4.99 U.S./ $5.89 CDN each plus $2.99 for shipping and handling per shipment*. If I decide to continue, about once a month for 8 months I will get 6 or 7 more books, but will only need to pay for 4. That means 2 or 3 books in every shipment will be FREE! If I decide to keep the entire collection, I'll have paid for only 32 books because 19 books are FREE! I understand that accepting the 3 free books and gifts places me under no obligation to buy anything. I can always return a shipment and cancel at any time. My free books and gifts are mine to keep no matter what I decide.

262 HCN 3432 462 HCN 3432

Name	(PLEASE PRINT)	
Address		Apt. #
City	State/Prov.	Zip/Postal Code

Signature (if under 18, a parent or guardian must sign)

Mail to the **Reader Service:**

IN U.S.A.: P.O. Box 1867, Buffalo, NY. 14240-1867
IN CANADA: P.O. Box 609, Fort Erie, Ontario L2A 5X3

* Terms and prices subject to change without notice. Prices do not include applicable taxes. Sales tax applicable in NY. Canadian residents will be charged applicable taxes. This offer is limited to one order per household. All orders subject to approval. Credit or debit balances in a customer's account(s) may be offset by any other outstanding balance owed by or to the customer. Please allow 4 to 6 weeks for delivery. Offer available while quantities last. Offer not available to Quebec residents.

Your Privacy—The Reader Service is committed to protecting your privacy. Our Privacy Policy is available online at www.ReaderService.com or upon request from the Reader Service.

We make a portion of our mailing list available to reputable third parties that offer products we believe may interest you. If you prefer that we not exchange your name with third parties, or if you wish to clarify or modify your communication preferences, please visit us at www.ReaderService.com/consumerschoice or write to us at Reader Service Preference Service, P.O. Box 9062, Buffalo, NY. 14240-9062. Include your complete name and address.

HHBPA17

Get 2 Free Books,
Plus 2 Free Gifts—
just for trying the Reader Service!

Get 2 Free Books,
Plus 2 Free Gifts—
just for trying the Reader Service!

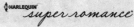

Get 2 Free Books,

Plus 2 Free Gifts—

just for trying the Reader Service!

HARLEQUIN

HEARTWARMING™

HWI7